DARKNESS LANE
The Second Geneva Chase Mystery

"... entertaining...Kies neatly balances breathless action with Geneva Chase's introspection and sleuthing savvy."

—Publishers Weekly

"Multiple murders and shocking twists are key components in Geneva's ultimate uncovering of the truth. The flawed but dedicated heroine anchors Kies' second mystery with a compassion that compels readers to root for both justice and redemption."

—Kirkus Reviews

RANDOM ROAD
The First Geneva Chase Mystery

"Kies' debut mystery introduces a reporter with a compelling voice, a damaged woman who recounts her own bittersweet story as she hunts down clues. This suspenseful story will appeal to readers who enjoy hard-nosed investigative reporters such as Brad Parks' Carter Ross."

—*Library Journal*, starred review/debut of the month

"Kies tells a taut, fastpaced tale, imbuing each character with memorable, compelling traits that help readers connect with them... those who enjoy J.A. Jance's Beaumont series or Sue Grafton's Kinsey Milhone will appreciate Geneva Chase."

—*Booklist*

"A hard-living newspaperwoman juggles multiple men and battles the bottle on her way to redemption via a high-profile murder story. ...Kies's fiction debut lays the groundwork for an entertaining series."

—*Kirkus Reviews*

"The bad choices made by Geneva "Genie" Chase, the narrator of Kies' arresting debut, have landed her back in her hometown of Sheffield, Conn., working for the local paper. When a multiple murder—the six victims were all members of a sex club, and the murder site was their clubhouse—is discovered in a Long Island Sound mansion, Geneva is the only reporter on the scene. ...Kies has created a likable if flawed heroine readers will want to see more of."

—*Publishers Weekly*

"It's a page turner, quick to draw the reader in as they search for answers alongside the dysfunctional, yet remarkably endearing, Geneva Chase."

—*Carolina Shore Magazine*

Darkness
Lane

Books by Thomas Kies

Geneva Chase Mysteries
Random Road
Darkness Lane

Darkness Lane

A Geneva Chase Mystery

Thomas Kies

Poisoned Pen Press

Poisoned Pen
PRESS

Copyright © 2018 by Thomas Kies

First Edition 2018

10 9 8 7 6 5 4 3 2 1

Library of Congress Control Number: 2017954236

ISBN: 9781464210013   Hardcover
ISBN: 9781464210037   Trade Paperback
ISBN: 9781464210044   Ebook

Poisoned Pen Press
4014 N. Goldwater Blvd., #201
Scottsdale, AZ 85251
www.poisonedpenpress.com
info@poisonedpenpress.com

Printed in the United States of America

For Jessica and Joshua, Alexander and Jessy,
Thomas and Gillian, Henry and Jake,
and Cindy and Lilly.

Acknowledgments

I'd like to thank my publisher, Barbara Peters and my editor, Annette Rogers, from Poisoned Pen Press, who were there to help me make this book a much stronger story. You ladies are terrific to work with. Your advice is always spot on.

I'd like to thank my fabulous agent, Kimberley Cameron, for pulling me out of the slush pile and matching me with a wonderful publisher. Through your incredible patience, grace, and friendship, you've changed my life. I'll always be grateful!

I'd like to thank Judie Szuets and Debra Hanson, two wonderful people I used to work with back in my newspaper days. Your voices are inside my head when I write dialogue for Geneva Chase.

I'd like to thank Dawn Brock from Coastal Press who, when I needed yet another hard copy of the book to work from, would drop everything and print a copy.

Thank you, Allie Miller, for the author's photo and making me look good.

I'd like to thank my incredible wife, Cindy Scherching, for her love, encouragement and patience. You give me the confidence to keep on writing.

And finally, I'd like to thank everyone who read *Random Road* and told me how much they enjoyed spending time with Geneva Chase. Writing can be a lonely, solitary endeavor. Hearing your compliments makes it all worthwhile.

"Sadness flies on the wings of morning,
and out of the heart of darkness comes the light."
—*Jean Giraudoux*

Chapter One

I was nearly done editing Darcie's piece on last night's particularly gruesome homicide over on the east side of Sheffield. A forty-three-year-old woman, claiming to have been routinely abused over the course of her twenty-year marriage, waited until her husband, Jim, had gotten blind-ass hammered and passed out in their bed. Then she calmly poured gasoline over his entire body while he snored away and lit a match.

By the time the fire department got there, the house was completely engulfed in flames, and he was long past screaming. The police found Betsy Caviness standing on the curb watching the fire department vainly attempt to extinguish the fire.

She was calmly drinking merlot out of a plastic cup. "I'm just toasting my husband," she told them sardonically.

That's my headline.

I pulled her mug shot up on my computer. Mrs. Caviness looked like someone had worked her face over with a meat tenderizer. One eye completely swollen shut, her skin mottled purple and black, her lips cracked open—it was a Halloween mask of pain and terror.

I know she had options other than roasting her husband alive and I'm all for due process, but I felt pity for that woman. Twenty years of physical and mental torment can make for a whole lot of crazy.

I also know, because I'd written a story about Jim Caviness

last year when I was still on the crime beat. He wasn't a nice guy. He'd been arrested in December for trafficking minors for sex. He beat the charge when the three girls he'd victimized disappeared, seemingly off the face of the earth.

I finished the edit on the Betsy Caviness piece and pushed the button to send it to the computer geeks in composing, when I saw my resident millennial, Darcie Miller, standing in the doorway of my cubicle, her emerald eyes wide, expression somber.

"Genie, better take a look. Got a missing fifteen-year-old." She pointed to the computer screen on my desk. "Isn't that how old your daughter is?"

Icy fingers brushed the back of my neck while the constant clattering din of the newsroom seemed to go preternaturally silent.

I turned, quickly found her entry in the queue, and brought it up on my screen.

POLICE ASK HELP IN LOCATING MISSING 15-YEAR-OLD GIRL

SHEFFIELD, CT-Authorities are actively seeking the whereabouts of Barbara Leigh Jarvis, last seen in the vicinity of West Sheffield High School on the morning of Monday, October 17.

According to the Sheffield Police Department, Miss Jarvis left her grandmother's home at 1217 Bedford St. to walk to school. School officials report that she never arrived and didn't attend any classes that day.

Barbara (Bobbi) Jarvis is 5 feet-6 inches tall, weighs 110 pounds, has brown hair, brown eyes and was dressed in a purple and white long-sleeved shirt, black windbreaker and blue jeans. She was carrying a black backpack.

Anyone with knowledge of her whereabouts should call the SPD at 1-800-555-6565.

Adrenaline hit my nervous system hard. Bobbi Jarvis was Caroline's best friend.

Instinctively, I reached into my oversized bag hanging from the back of my office chair. Taking out my cellphone, I brought up the family locater app. It allows me to track where Caroline is in real time. A tiny street map appeared with an electronic pushpin stuck firmly where the high school was located.

Caroline's in school, right where she's supposed to be.

I was still new at this mothering thing. I've never actually had kids of my own so raising a teenager was a fresh and exasperating experience. Worrying all the time was becoming the new normal for me.

I looked at the police press release again.

I've been writing stories for newspapers and magazines for eighteen years, mostly on the crime beat covering murders, assaults, rapes, arsons, robberies, sex scandals, and fraud. If it was ugly, I wrote about it.

I'm a professional so most of the time I stayed dispassionate.

But there were stories that left scars.

They were about kids who disappeared and either showed up dead or vanished altogether. And that was the worst, because the parents never got closure. It was an open wound that never healed.

I glanced back at my computer screen. The color photograph accompanying the story was a professionally done glamshot of Bobbi Jarvis smiling into the camera. Her brown eyes sparkled, artificially whitened teeth gleamed in her warm, generous smile, and her long, lustrous chestnut hair was brushed to perfectly frame her pretty face. The coy dimple in her chin added to her girlish charm.

It occurred to me that, in the photo, Bobbi was a teenager trying much too hard to look like an adult.

She didn't look like that the last time she had dinner with us.

My eyes involuntarily moved from my computer screen to the silver-framed photograph of Caroline Bell resting on my desk next to a stack of manila folders. No, Caroline's not my daughter as Darcie, my crime beat reporter, suggested. I'm the girl's guardian.

She's the fifteen-year-old daughter of Kevin Bell. Kevin had been my lover and my fiancé. The same night I proposed to him…yes, I proposed to *Kevin*…he asked me if I'd take care of Caroline should anything bad happen to him.

And then, tragically, it did.

Caroline is blond, has her dad's blue eyes, an infectious smile, freckles, and she's a bit of a tomboy. In that photo, she was wearing a sleeveless top, shorts, and a Red Sox cap but no makeup. She was gingerly holding a live lobster she'd chosen from a tank for dinner. I'd taken the picture last summer while we were vacationing on Cape Cod.

That had been the one-year anniversary of her father's death. I wanted us to be in a happy place on that unhappy occasion. But as much as we both loved Cape Cod, being there hadn't kept either of us from remembering him and feeling the awful loss. Kevin died before he should have, before we were ready. It was like ripping off a band-aid, quick and painful…and tearing out my heart at the same time.

Caroline Bell and Bobbi Jarvis were buds and sophomore classmates at West Sheffield High. They shared the same teachers for English and World History. They loved the same music and movies. They were both in the band and the Drama Club and were passionate about the theater.

They were both just discovering boys.

Or so I thought.

Bobbi was pretty and polite but rarely spoke about her family. I chalked that up to her parents being divorced. She lived with her grandmother. Caroline had told me it was something she wasn't proud of. Neither one of Bobbi's parents seemed to want her in their lives.

That's got to hurt.

Bobbi had been to our house a few times for dinner and to

study. She was serious about becoming an actress, taking pro-fessional acting classes outside of the Drama Club. One night, Bobbi surprised me by quoting lines from *Macbeth* and sing-ing a few bars of the song "Popular" from *Wicked*—a weird juxtaposition of witch theater. All while eating spaghetti and meatballs in our kitchen.

That was the night both Caroline and Bobbi were wearing their baseball caps on their heads turned around backwards. Caroline had on a Red Sox cap.... Bobbi was sporting the Yankees logo. In my house, that's an insult. But she was a guest, so I let it ride.

That was also the night the two of them attempted some-thing akin to rap that left me in stitches.

It was the evening, when Caroline was out of the kitchen, that Bobbi looked up at me and said, "Caroline's really lucky to have you, Genie."

I smiled back at her, grateful for the compliment. "She's been through a lot, losing both of her parents."

Bobbi stared off into the distance. "Yeah, but at least while they were alive, they loved her."

That broke my heart. She was certain that she'd been rejected by her mother and father and they didn't love her.

And now she's missing.

I picked up the cup of cold coffee sitting on my desk and took a sip. It was from this morning and tasted sour, like old caffeine and rancid lemons.

Back out in the newsroom, Darcie sat in front of her com-puter screen, delicately tapping away at the keyboard. I'm her editor. I've been the daytime news editor since last December.

I loved getting the pay raise that came with the promotion.

But I hated being harnessed to a desk. I missed seeing my name, Geneva Chase, on the byline of a good story.

When I got the promotion, I was the one who suggested that Darcie take my place on the crime beat. She was a waif with big, green eyes. When she was working, her shoulder length red hair was usually tied back in a ponytail. She wasn't particularly tall, about five-five, but she had long legs and, even at her tender age, she knew how much of them to show to get men to talk to her. Darcie had good instincts; she already knew how much concession her looks could buy with men.

Ben Sumner, owner and publisher of the *Sheffield Post*, had brought her onboard nearly a year ago, straight out of J-School.

Sure, she was inexperienced but she wrote well, got her facts straight, and worked on the cheap.

Initially Ben had put her on features, knocking out puff pieces for the "Living" section, covering the rubber chicken circuit and the grip-and-grins. When I became editor, I took a chance on Darcie and put her on the cop shop where there was real news.

If Bobbi's disappearance had been any other story, I would have let Darcie follow up with the detective on duty to see if there was any information not included in the release. But I had a personal stake in this. I picked up the phone and punched up Mike Dillon, the deputy chief of police.

"Genie?" He answered recognizing my number on his Caller ID.

I visualized Mike. Tall, lean, angular face, clean-shaven, he had the intense brown eyes of a wolf focused on the hunt. I thought he was handsome in a vaguely predatory way.

"Hey, Mike." I let my voice drop. We'd been seeing each other, casually, for the occasional dinner and movie. He was recently divorced and we were friends with infrequent benefits.

Over the last few months, Mike had been pushing hard for us to move our relationship to another level. He wanted us to be more of a couple.

I didn't.

"Genie, what a nice surprise. What happened, did you fire Darcie?" He genuinely sounded worried.

"No, she's still here."

"Good. She's adorable."

"Yeah, that's what I want on the crime beat, adorable."

He chuckled. "What's up?"

I stared at the girl's photo still up on my screen. "What's the deal on Barbara Jarvis?"

He hesitated and I knew he was consulting his ubiquitous notebook. "Let's see, we got a call from Theresa Pittman, her grandmother, yesterday at five-thirty-five p.m. Told us that the last time she saw her granddaughter was sometime around seven in the morning when she left to go to school. Mrs. Pittman grew alarmed when the girl didn't come home. She got really spooked when she found out her granddaughter never made it to any of her classes."

"No Amber Alert?"

"No sign of foul play."

I eyed my coffee cup and toyed with the idea of taking another swallow of the bitter swill that remained. "Have you talked with her parents?"

My voice must have betrayed me because he asked, "Do you know this girl?"

"She's one of Caroline's friends."

"Yeah, we talked with her parents. They don't seem very worried. Both of them think she got into an argument with grandma and she's hanging out at a friend's place. Have you checked under Caroline's bed?"

"I will when I get home tonight." My answer was only slightly sarcastic. Against my better judgment, I went ahead and took gulp of cold coffee. It was nasty. "Is that what you think? That she's chilling with a friend?"

"Ninety-nine percent of the time, when a fifteen-year-old goes missing, it's because they got pissed off at mom or dad or grandma and split. They hide out for a while. When they run out of money or run out of clean clothes or their friends get sick of them, they show back up again."

"What now?"

"This morning we talked with her teachers and some of

the girl's friends at school. We sent out a statewide alert to all the other PD's along with her photo and we e-mailed Darcie a press release. Did you see it?"

"I'm looking at it right now. We'll run it in the morning, but I'll post it on our website just as soon as I'm off the phone with you."

"Like I said, there's no sign of foul play. We've talked to everyone we can think of. We wait and keep our eyes open."

"I'd be about crazy if Caroline went missing."

"I know. I'd feel the same way if something happened to Davy." Mike was speaking about his son, also fifteen and a student at West Sheffield High School.

"Have you asked Davy if he knows Bobbi Jarvis?"

"I called him at his mom's house last night. He says he doesn't know anything more than she's a theater geek."

That's what all the members of the Drama Club called themselves.

As I said good-bye and hung up, I thought about Mike. When I first moved to Sheffield and became a beat reporter for the *Post*, he and I had a flirt-cute thing going on but never followed through on it.

Back then I was in the middle of an affair with a married man, and Mike and his wife were still together. No way was I going to date two married men at the same time.

A girl has to have standards.

Then everything changed when I fell in love with Kevin Bell.

But my time with Kevin had been all too short and I found myself tragically alone. About the same time Kevin died, Mike went through a divorce and we gravitated like a couple of lonely planets. Needing the company of each other but circling in distant, comfortable orbits.

Friends, but not much more. A few dates, a few movies, a few awkward nights in the sack. I liked Mike, but I didn't think I'd ever love him. The spark just wasn't there.

I enjoyed having him ask me out, though. A woman needs to feel attractive.

And I keep telling myself that I am. I'm tall, five-ten in flats. Shoulder-length blond hair that my hairdresser does her best to keep looking good. I haven't resorted to Botox but I'm noticing some wear and tear around the corners of my blue eyes and the corners of my mouth. Depending on what I'm wearing, I still get approving looks when I walk into a room.

I go running when I get the chance and work out at the City Center, mostly sweating on the elliptical. As far as long legs, mine put Darcie's to shame.

"Ben wants to see you in his office." I looked up from my computer screen. The advertising director, Dennis Marion, filled the open portal of my cube. In his fifties, he had a stomach that spilled out over his belt and wore clothes that never seemed to hang right. His tie was loosened and, judging from how bloodshot his eyes were, he was more hungover than usual. He affected a gray-and-brown goatee that I thought resembled a gerbil clinging to his chin.

Over the last year, our professional relationship was best described as strained. He and I had gone a couple of rounds in recent months, generally stemming from one of his advertisers getting arrested or sued for something newsworthy. Dennis would stamp his feet and argue that if I ran the story, they'd pull their advertising and I'd be costing the newspaper money.

Yeah, well, that's life.

"What's Ben want?" I asked.

His doughy face, usually ruddy in complexion, was beet red. The ad man wore the doomed expression of a chubby rabbit looking down the barrel of a shotgun. "Paper's got a problem." Without another word, he shuffled out of my cube.

I felt the coffee acid churn in my stomach.

The last time I heard Dennis mutter the words, "paper's got a problem," I had to lay off one of my reporters.

The building's original use was as a furniture store. The open layout of the *Sheffield Post* was one cavernous room on a single floor, chopped up by butt-ugly green, cloth-covered, movable partitions about five feet high used to define departments. The drab interior walls of the building itself were a chipped and discolored tan, and a quarter of the fluorescent lights either had bulbs blown or bad ballasts. The gray carpeting was coffee-stained, frayed, and threadbare. The office furniture was a well-worn collection of mismatched desks, chairs, and filing cabinets.

The gray lady was showing her age and nobody was willing to buy her any makeup.

All the reporters, ad salespeople, graphic artists, and IT guys have desks clustered together in their own departments like warring tribes of Bedouins forced to work together to survive. Company managers—the editors, ad director, classified ad director, and the graphic arts manager—all had glassed-in cubicles that we worked in. We sarcastically called them fishbowls.

Only one individual in the whole company had a real office to call home— Ben Sumner. When I walked in, he was seated at his massive, polished mahogany desk. Behind him was a large window, blinds raised, overlooking the company parking lot and beyond that, clusters of trees that lined the Merritt Parkway. The foliage caught my eye. It was mid-October and the leaves stubbornly clutched to branches, offering an eye-popping display of gold, burgundy, and vermilion.

He looked up from his laptop and gestured that I should sit in one of the two upholstered office chairs. As I did, I glanced up at the framed glossy photographs on the walls. Most of them were of Ben sailing on various oceans around the globe. When he wasn't running the newspaper, he was out on his forty-two-foot sailboat, *Press Time*.

Just because reporters and editors don't make a lot of money doesn't mean publishers can't enjoy an affluent lifestyle.

Ben is fifty, tall, attractive, and still has a thick, full head of dark brown hair. I suspected that he used over-the-counter chemicals to keep the gray away.

Hey, but who am I to judge? My hairdresser is my best friend.

He was lean and fit and, even in the winter, his face was tan. He'd only recently resorted to reading glasses behind which his hazel eyes studied me as I sat down.

Ben took them off, then folded and placed them carefully next to the photo of him, his long-suffering wife, Louise, and two boys, one in Yale and one in the Marines.

Ben wasn't smiling.

"What's up boss?" I tried sounding upbeat.

"Genie, I just finished meeting with Dennis."

"Oh?"

"He says Barrett's advertising is going all digital."

Barrett's was an upscale chain of department stores located exclusively in Fairfield County, Connecticut. It carried lines like Valentino, Michael Kors, Escada, Etro, and Brunello Cucinelli—slightly outside my newspaper pay-grade that was more accustomed to Walmart, Costco, and Target.

For the last ten years, Barrett's was our biggest advertiser.

"Are we keeping *any* of their advertising?"

He held up his hand and formed a zero with his finger and thumb. "Nope."

Barrett's pulling out was really bad news.

"We're going to have to do another round of layoffs."

The caffeine in my stomach felt like a bubbling lava pit trickling into my lower intestine.

Who's getting the ax this time? Me?

Ben answered my unasked question. "You're going to have to cut Darcie."

Last hired, first fired.

"How about laying off someone from advertising?"

"We are, one of our sales staff. And one from graphic arts and two from production. We're going to be down to the bone. I don't know how we're going to get a paper out."

I took a deep breath. "When?"

He glanced up at one of his photographs. It was the one where he was sailing on a choppy ocean off the coast of the Florida Keys. "Do it this Friday."

"Me?"

He looked me directly in the eye. "It's part of your job description."

I hated this part of the job with a white-hot passion. Ben was all too willing to be a part of the hiring process but when it came to cutting staff, he was always out of the building. I doubted if I'd even see him come in at all on Friday.

He stood up and turned around, gazing out of his window. "You know, I'm thinking about selling the Post. We don't have the economies of scale that a chain has."

Do you even know what that means? How about selling that damned sailboat instead?

"Seems a little extreme, Ben."

He faced me again and shoved his hands in his pockets. "I just said I was thinking about it. I've contracted with a designer to upgrade our website. Make it more user-friendly and interactive."

"Think that will help?"

He shrugged.

I've had bylines on hundreds of stories in four newspapers, three magazines, and a half dozen websites. The industry had changed to the point where working for my hometown newspaper felt like I was riding on the back of a slow, lumbering dinosaur wading into a tar pit.

"If I'm laying off Darcie, who's going to do the crime beat?"

His attention snapped back to me again. "Why, you are."

"And who's going to edit?"

For the first time that day, I saw him smile. "I am. C'mon, it'll be fun."

I was going to make a smart-ass remark, but honestly for the last six months, I've been bored as hell. Editing isn't nearly as much fun as running down a story out on the street.

I just wished I didn't have to let Darcie go.

I'd grown fond of that little millennial.

When I got back to my desk, I eyed my coffee cup and considered walking over to the pressroom to see if they had a fresh pot on.

The photo of Bobbi Jarvis was still up on my screen. I hadn't pulled the trigger on the story yet to send it to the IT guys. I studied her photograph one last time then hit the button to send the piece to another queue in another computer.

I glanced at the picture of Caroline again.

Don't you ever go missing on me.

Chapter Two

It was shortly before three when Darcie popped back into my cubicle. "The woman who torched her husband last night?"

"Yeah?"

"Judge Aiken set her bail at a million dollars."

"Of course, he did." I couldn't avoid snark in my voice. Judge Henry Aiken was a true sexist, hard-ass, son of a bitch. His muttered declarations during trials always made good ink. Two months ago, when he publicly growled that a rape victim "had it coming," he became a six-column headline, top of the front page. And the follow-up stories of demands from the public to remove Aiken from the bench made me giddy for weeks.

A member of the good old boys' network at the courthouse, the misogynist rat bastard was still wearing a robe and presiding over the court.

"She made bail."

What?

"Where did Betsy Caviness get that kind of money?"

From the piece I did last year, I recalled that Jim Caviness was a low-level thug who drank or snorted most of his ill-gotten profits just as quickly as he got it. The house in which he'd died was in a rundown neighborhood known for drug dealers and plywood-covered windows.

Even if it had been a nice neighborhood, Betsy Caviness

couldn't have used the house as security because now it was little more than a pile of smoldering charcoal.

"She didn't." Darcie referred to her reporter's notebook. "A group called FOL, Friends of Lydia, posted bail. Ever heard of them?"

I shook my head. "Who's Lydia?

The reporter shrugged.

"Got a phone number?"

"Got it from the courthouse. I can't find anything about them online." She wrote it down and ripped a page from her notebook, handing it to me. "Are you going to handle this or do you want me to?"

Does she sound testy?

Over the last month, Darcie was getting progressively moodier.

Keep that in mind when you're laying her off on Friday.

Thinking that I'd better get used to working the crime beat again, I answered, "I'll take care of it. You keep working on those smash-and-grabs from last night."

She went back to her desk, and I did an online search for Friends of Lydia.

Zilch.

Darcie hadn't lied. There was nothing there.

As hard as I tried, and I'm very good with online searches, I couldn't find where FOL was incorporated anywhere, either as a for-profit or a nonprofit. It was as if they didn't exist.

I punched the number Darcie had given me into the *Post's* landline and waited for an answer.

"Yes?" The low, smoky voice was female.

"I'm looking for Betsy Caviness."

"And you are…?" In a very slight Southern accent, she parsed her words slowly, as if she were savoring the taste of them.

"Geneva Chase with the *Sheffield Post*."

"This is regarding…?"

"Mrs. Caviness just posted a million-dollar bail. I'd like to know a little more about that."

Then a hand must have gone over the phone because there was only the faint sound of muffled conversation.

A few moments later, the woman came back on. "Would you like an exclusive interview?"

Damned straight.

"Absolutely, can you put her on the phone?" I looked at the clock on my computer screen. I knew that Caroline would be busy until about six, working on the Drama Club's annual fundraising project. I could easily do a phone interview, write it up, and be home by the time Caroline got there.

"Two conditions—one, it has to be face-to-face."

"Why?"

"We want you to see what that son of a bitch did to her."

"I saw her mug shot. It's not pretty."

"Face-to-face."

"Okay. What else?" I pushed papers around on my desk and wondered who I was talking to.

"You have to keep her location a secret."

"Is Mrs. Caviness in danger?"

There was silence on the other end of the line, as if the woman couldn't believe what she'd just heard.

Finally, she answered. "Yes. We'll explain."

"Mrs. Caviness' location won't be part of the story."

"Do you know the Metro Sheffield? Meet me in the lobby in fifteen minutes."

Oh, yeah. It's the most expensive hotel in this part of Fairfield County. I spent many a night there with Frank Mancini, the married attorney with whom I'd had a torrid two-year affair.

I had some hot, sweaty memories of the Metro Sheffield. I knew that hotel well.

I asked, "How will I know you?"

"When you come, carry a copy of your newspaper. That way I'll know *you.*"

I took the Dry Hill Road shortcut through an upscale residential neighborhood in the Brandywine section of town. I was surprised at how many houses were already decorated for Halloween. Pumpkins and cornstalks on porches, tombstones and plastic zombies atop leaf-covered front yards, orange lights in windows.

Not my favorite holiday, I've never decorated for Halloween. I love the candy, though.

Fifteen minutes later, I pulled into a space in the parking lot of the Metro Sheffield. I grabbed my bag and a copy of the newspaper and got out of the car. I was nestled amongst a herd of vehicles sporting logos like BMW, Mercedes, Cadillac, Volvo, and Lexus. Rooms that start at four hundred dollars a night attract people who can afford nice cars.

I walked into the familiar lobby. There was marble everywhere—in the fountain dead ahead of me, on the gleaming floor below, the walls. The furniture was all leather and brass. Silver vases filled with bright bouquets were scattered about on end tables.

The place screamed "money."

Next to the fountain, an African-American woman stood, arms crossed, feet spread, looking like she owned the hotel. She wore black designer jeans, a gold necklace, a white shirt, collar open, under a black sport coat.

She was somewhere in her thirties and tall, about my height, and trim. Perfectly manicured eyebrows framed her dark, piercing eyes. Her face was expressionless, lips pressed together. She owned high, granite cheekbones and flawless skin. Her relaxed jet-black hair fell in easy waves to her shoulders, framing and accenting her beautiful face.

The way she watched me enter the room, the woman reminded me of a predatory cat.

Her eyes bore in on the folded newspaper under my arm.

She stepped forward. "Geneva Chase?"

"Yes," I answered, holding out my hand. "And you are?"

She glanced at my hand but ignored it. The woman walked past me and stepped up to the plate-glass window, staring out at the parking lot.

A man stepped into her line of sight. He was Caucasian and dressed much like she was—black slacks, white shirt with an open collar, and a black sport coat. He had salt-and-pepper hair that was about two weeks overdue for a trim, was clean shaven, six feet tall, and also wore a serious expression.

Seeing him, she gave him a shrug, as if asking a silent question.

He gave her a nod and a thumbs-up.

The woman turned and faced me. "Okay. It looks like you weren't followed."

"Why would I be followed?"

She gave me a half-grin. "You can never be too paranoid."

"I don't think I caught your name."

She studied me for a moment. Then she said, "Here are the ground rules for this interview. When I say something is off the record, that means it never sees the light of day. Agreed?"

When she spoke, each word was its own distinct entity, as a thing of value.

I argued, "Too much goes off the record, I don't have a story and this is all a big waste of time."

"You'll get your story. Agreed?"

"Okay."

"Starting with my name, that's off the record."

"Agreed." I could feel tension growing in my voice.

"Shana Neese. Nice to meet you." She held out her hand.

When I shook it, the palm of her hand was calloused. She had hands familiar with hard work, like the hands of a farmer or a grave digger.

In the elevator on our way to the fifth floor, I asked her some questions. "Who are the Friends of Lydia? Are you a nonprofit? I couldn't find anything on the Internet."

She gave me a sideways glance. "We're more like a loose confederation of like-minded individuals."

"Are you an employee of the Friends?"

"No."

"How do you buy groceries?"

"Off the record?"

Oh, for crying out loud.

"Honestly? You want that off the record?"

Her expression became one of contempt. "I'm not part of this story."

I get the feeling that you are.

I demurred. "Okay."

"I'm a physical therapist." The hint of a smile played on her lips when she said it.

"Who's Lydia?"

Shana's face softened. "Lydia was a sixteen-year-old who was sold to a pimp by her drug-addicted father. One night, in a drunken rage, the pimp beat the girl to death with a broomstick. The Friends of Lydia are dedicated to helping women, particularly minors, who are enslaved by sex traffickers as well as women who are the victims of domestic violence. We consider that to be slavery as well."

"Can I put that in the story?"

After several heartbeats, Shana nodded. "Yes. The Friends have been in the shadows for way too long. Plus, we're on record as posting bail for Mrs. Caviness."

When she said it, I could tell she was uncomfortable that even the name of the organization should go public.

What is she afraid of?

Chapter Three

I didn't have any illusions about what this interview was all about. If Betsy Caviness couldn't get a favorable plea deal, she'd go to a jury trial. What better way to influence the jury pool than to get a story in the newspaper about how much of a violent, rat-bastard her husband had been?

I was fine with that. From what the arrest report had said, if I'd been there and watched what Jim Caviness had done to his wife that night when she poured the gasoline on him, I would have probably lit the match.

The hotel room we entered was one of Metro Sheffield's many suites—two beautifully appointed bedrooms with king-sized beds, complete with wide-screen televisions, computer station, couch, and two comfortable upholstered chairs.

We went straight to the sitting room.

Recognizable from her mug shot, Betsy Caviness was seated on the couch wearing one of the hotel's fluffy white bathrobes.

Back in the day, I loved wearing those, under which I'd have on nothing but an attitude.

A second woman was seated in one of the chairs. She wore a professional-looking outfit: dark brown ankle-length skirt, tan sweater, sensible shoes. The woman was in her forties, wore her hair fashionably short, and sported large gold hoop earrings. I thought she wore slightly too much eye makeup.

They both stood up when we came into the room.

The woman in the serious clothes eyed me with suspicion.

I introduced myself by stepping forward. "I'm Geneva Chase with the *Sheffield Post*."

"I'm Connie Taylor, Betsy's attorney." She spoke quickly, all business.

"I'm Betsy Caviness." She was slight, only about five-five and looked to be in her late fifties, but I knew from the arrest record, she was only forty-three. It was difficult to tell how much she weighed because of the robe, but I guessed she was just a tiny thing.

An easy target for that thug husband of hers.

I believed that once in her life, Betsy had been very pretty. But years of physical abuse had taken a toll. She'd smiled at me when she told me her name, allowing me to see that three of her front teeth had been knocked out.

Her mug shot hadn't done her justice. Her face was mottled with black and purple bruises, her left eye was swollen shut, and there were five long, dark red marks on her neck, where I guessed her husband had scratched her throat with his finger-nails while he was choking her.

Gesturing toward the couch, Connie said, "Please, Geneva, sit down."

I sat down and Betsy did the same. Connie sat in one chair while Shana stood across the room, staring out the window, studying the parking lot five floors below.

I started the ball rolling. "First of all, Mrs. Caviness, thank you for your time."

"Please, call me Betsy."

Turning on my recorder, I asked, "How old were you when you married Jim Caviness?"

"I was twenty-two."

"And you're forty-three now."

She nodded. I saw that in odd patches, her curly hair was scarce enough for me to see her scalp. Did her husband yank out handfuls of her hair, too?

"Did you ever have children?"

"No. One night he kicked me so hard that when I went to the hospital, pukin' up blood, the doctor told me I'd never have kids." She looked down at the carpeting. "It's probably a blessing."

This is going to be a rough interview.

"How are you going to plead at the arraignment?" The question was more to the attorney than to Betsy.

Connie spoke up. "We're going to plead not guilty. It's a clear case of justifiable homicide. Betsy feared both serious bodily harm and imminent peril of death."

"How soon after you were married did the abuse start?"

She thought for a moment.

I watched the one eye that wasn't swollen shut. It was a light blue, made lighter by the bruising around the socket and patches of red marring her sclera, the white part of her eye. She was looking at something behind Shana, perhaps she was remembering a better time in her life.

"Maybe a year or so after the wedding. That's when he got physically abusive, mostly when he was drinking. But he had a nasty mouth right from the get-go."

"Betsy, I'm going to ask you a hard question. It's a question that will come up in court. Why didn't you leave him?"

A tear welled up in her open eye. "He made me feel small, worthless, like no one else in the universe would love me. Plus, he told me that if I left him, he'd kill my parents and all the rest of my family, my aunts, uncles, and cousins. He'd bury my entire family and nobody would ever find their bodies."

I glanced up at the attorney who studied her client's battered face, watching how Betsy would handle tough questions.

Then I stole a quick look at Shana who was staring back at me, quietly nodding.

"Do you believe your husband was capable of killing someone?"

Her one good eye locked onto my own. "Oh, yeah, not only was he capable. He done it, done it lots a times."

Holy crap, what did I just stumble into?

I waited a couple of heartbeats to see if anyone was going to say that this was off the record.

When nobody spoke up, I said, "Tell me about that."

"When we were first together, he worked construction. He brought home enough to pay the bills, but we never had enough left over for anything nice. We never went out to eat and most of our things come from the Salvation Army.

"Then the recession hit and construction went all to hell. We went through long periods when Jim wasn't workin' at all. I did the best I could by cleaning people's houses and condos. For a while, I worked at this hotel cleaning rooms." She gestured around her. "I cleaned this room, I don't know how many times. God Almighty, the messes people leave behind in a hotel room. Like animals."

I needed to get her back on track. "Explain what you said about your husband killing people."

"It was about the same time that Obama got to be president. Lord, how Jim hated Obama. No offense, Miss Shana."

Shana gave the woman a shy grin. "None taken, Miss Betsy."

"Then, a few years ago, Jim got a job with a company called Wolfline Contracting. Started bringing home good money."

"I'm not sure I've heard of Wolfline Contracting." I took out my phone and started to do an Internet search.

Shana spoke up. "Don't waste your time, Geneva. It's legitimately incorporated in the state of Connecticut, but you won't find anything else—no website, no phone number, and they use a post office box for an address. There's an office in Greenwich, but it's empty. No employees, no furniture."

Then it was the attorney's turn. "It's a dummy company—a front."

"For what?"

Shana explained, "Moving dirty money from point A to point B."

"Do you have hard evidence of that?"

"If I did, I would have turned it over to the FBI a long time ago."

I focused back on Betsy. "What was your husband doing for Wolfline Contracting?"

"He didn't tell me much. But what little he said, it scared me. Usually it was after he'd been drinking, and then he wouldn't remember none of his words the next day. He said the men who run Wolfline had their hands in a lot of things."

"Like what?" I asked.

"Gambling, drugs, prostitution."

I glanced up at Shana.

She was staring out the window again.

I asked, "What else do they do?"

Betsy's single eye was wide with fear. "They buy and sell human beings. And when they're through with them, if they can't sell 'em for a profit, they kill 'em."

"Two years ago, your husband was arrested for prostituting three minor females. Do you remember that?"

"Oh, yes."

"Then the charges were dropped when the girls disappeared. Do you know what happened to those girls?"

"After Jim made bail, he stayed away from the house for three straight days. When he got back, he told me he wouldn't have to go to trial. There weren't any witnesses that could testify against him anymore."

"What did he do?"

"After finishing a bottle of Jack Daniels, he told me that the girls were buried upstate in the woods. Nobody would ever find them."

"Did he say that he killed them?"

"Just said that they were buried upstate. I didn't dare ask any questions."

"Did he tell you where upstate?"

She shook her head sadly. "I'm sorry."

"Who are we talking about here? Who's behind Wolfline Contracting?"

The attorney held up her hand. "This is where we have to go off the record."

Damn it to hell.

"Why? What are you afraid of? Who paid Betsy's bail? Who's paying for this room? Who *are* you people?"

Shana crossed her arms. "Off…the…record."

I turned off my recorder. "Okay, okay."

"Like I said in the elevator, the Friends are a loose confederation of freelancers. We're very secretive because what we do can be very dangerous."

"Who runs the Friends?"

"Right now, that's not relevant. You asked who posted bail and who's paying for the hotel room? Geneva, we have friends in low places and we have friends in very high places. The benefactor you're asking about cares deeply about what happens to women like Betsy."

Not getting a lot of straight answers here.

"Who's behind Wolfline?"

"It's a front for organized illegal endeavors."

"Columbian? Sicilian? Japanese? Korean? Skinheads?"

"Russians. But what makes this bunch so dangerous, is that they play well with others, they're not afraid to cross ethnic lines. It's all just business to them."

"Who's the boss?"

She quietly said, "We suspect that a man named Valentin Tolbonov is the brains. His brother Bogdan is the muscle."

"I don't know them."

"Not surprised. They stay pretty removed from the day-to-day operation."

Then suddenly the name rang a bell. "Wait a minute, is that Tolbonov Diamonds?"

"They have a exclusive shop in Greenwich. Make sure you take your checkbook."

I chuckled. "Not my checkbook."

Why the hell hadn't this guy been on my radar screen?

"And you're worried for Betsy's safety? Why? So far, what you've told me is hearsay. It's not admissible in court and I certainly can't use it for a story."

Shana answered. "Because of all the brain cells Jim Caviness burned up drinking and doing drugs, he had memory issues. So he kept a small notebook to keep track of where he was supposed to go and what he was supposed to do. That notebook has about six months' worth of Jim's activities written down, including meetings with men that are directly associated with the Tolbonovs."

I felt a strange thrill in the pit of my stomach. I always get it when I'm on the edge of a really good story. "That notebook didn't go up with the fire?"

Connie answered. "It's in a safe deposit box."

"You think that Wolfline knows that she has Jim's notebook?"

"Just this morning, while she was still in jail, she found a note in her cell that said for her not to tell anyone about the notebook or she'd be killed."

I glanced at Betsy. "Any idea how the note got there?"

She shook her head.

Connie answered. "It was someone on the inside, Geneva—someone who knew what cell Betsy would be in, even before she got there. So, you see, she's not safe if she's locked up."

"Why not just turn it over to the cops?"

The attorney gave a coy look. "We will, eventually. But it's good to have an extra card to play, just in case we need leverage with a judge or a district attorney during a plea negotiation."

I looked at each one of them in succession. "Seriously, these people are that dangerous?"

Shana's words were precise, her face expressionless. "Like Miss Betsy said—these people buy and sell human beings. And when they're done with them, they kill them. They have no regard for human life. None at all."

Chapter Four

I hustled back to the office and wrote up my interview with Betsy Caviness, leaving out the parts that were off the record. I also left out anything having to do with Wolfline Contracting and the Tolbonov brothers. Everything they'd told me needed to be confirmed. If it panned out, it would make a hell of a story entirely on its own.

The interview was tacked onto the piece that Darcie had written that morning about Mrs. Caviness' arrest.

I added my name to the byline. It felt good.

Disquieting to think what Mrs. Caviness had endured for two decades.

I wondered why so many people find themselves in self-destructive relationships?

You'd think after being married three times, I'd have the answer to that question.

Was that why I was holding Mike at arm's length? That at this time in my life, I didn't want a nice, normal relationship? That maybe I didn't deserve to be in one?

Is my self-esteem that bad?

I checked my watch. It was getting close to six. Jessica Oberon's mom had said that she would bring Caroline home from the community center where the Drama Club was setting up their fundraiser.

I really wanted to be home before she got there.

"She needs a sense of dependability, especially at home." That's what Dr. Tina Beaufort, Caroline's shrink, told me after Kevin died. I'd done my best to give her that. My job as editor helped. The position had regular hours versus being the cop shop reporter where you were on call all the damned time.

But sometime after we got back from Cape Cod, a year after her dad had passed away, I noticed that Caroline was putting distance between us. Then, in September, after she'd started her sophomore year in high school, I got a call from Rebecca Barton, the principal.

"I'm getting complaints from some of Caroline's teachers that she's not paying attention in class and, in some cases, been downright disruptive," Mrs. Barton told me. "The only thing she seems to be interested in is Drama Club."

Dr. Tina told me that the anniversary of Kevin's death may have triggered a defense response in Caroline. That the girl may be withdrawing from me because every other person she loved had died. It might be the reason she was zoning out in her classes.

Then Dr. Tina added, "Caroline's extreme interest in the Drama Club may be because on stage she's not Caroline. She's someone else. She's playing a role. She's outside of herself."

Caroline had become more distant, more argumentative, not only with me, but with many of her friends. She still remained tight with two of them—Jessica Oberon and Bobbi Jarvis.

And Bobbi was missing.

How is Caroline going to react to that? Or does she know where Bobbi is?

I got home, put out cardboard containers of sweet and sour chicken, fried rice, and egg rolls that I got from the Golden Panda, and let Tucker, my hyperactive yorkie, out the back door to run and do his business in the fenced-in backyard. Then I pulled a glass down from the shelf, opened the freezer, and dropped in two ice cubes.

I went upstairs, kicked off my shoes, and stripped off my clothes, including my bra. I threw on a pair of jeans and one of Kevin's old denim work shirts, way too big for me. I rolled up the sleeves. Then I opened my underwear drawer and pulled out a bottle of Absolut.

I know I have a problem. It's what had brought me back to Sheffield. I'd grown up here and this was the last place in the world I wanted to be.

I drank myself out of every good job I'd ever had.

I nearly did it here.

When Kevin died, and I became Caroline's guardian, it was the kick in the ass that got me sober. I needed to be straight for Caroline's sake.

For months I did AA meetings, had a sponsor, abided by the twelve-step process.

Then, when we were in Cape Cod, while Caroline was sleeping in our rented condo on the beach, I slipped out to the pub next door. When the kid who was tending the bar asked me what I wanted, I froze. I shouldn't be there.

It was wrong.

And I was weak.

I ordered a vodka tonic and that was all she wrote.

Now I'm a closet drinker.

A highly functioning alcoholic, no longer attending meetings, no longer speaking to my sponsor, no longer doing any steps other than getting upstairs to my bedroom where I hide the vodka.

I poured a generous serving into the tumbler and took a sip even before the ice could do its job. The familiar burn slid down my throat and I felt it spread through my body.

The ragged edges of my nerves were properly tended.

● ● ● ● ●

Drink finished, pleasantly buzzed, breath freshened with mouthwash, I went downstairs.

Caroline was there, playing with Tucker in the kitchen. "Look who I found in the backyard." She was down on her knees bouncing a tennis ball while Tucker jumped and barked and wagged his tail so hard his little butt shook. Tucker was nine pounds of adorable—a ball of animated fur, complete with lolling tongue and bright eyes.

I'd brought my empty glass back downstairs to rinse out in the sink. As I did, I noticed Caroline was eyeing me.

Does she know?

I asked her about her day. "How was school?"

She stood up and stretched. Caroline had grown over the last year—nearly five-foot-five. She was thin—not much more than a hundred pounds. I envied her metabolism, burning calories like a coked-up otter.

Her blond hair was down to the middle of her back, her eyes were as blue as her dad's, and she was girl-next-door pretty—pert nose, freckles, warm smile, perfect teeth. Boys were noticing her more now that she'd been developing into a young woman. She was wearing real bras now and we'd already had the talk about boys.

That had been surprisingly uncomfortable for me and I was amazed and dismayed at what she already knew.

Caroline had on a pair of ratty jeans and a gray UCONN sweatshirt. "It was crazy at school," she said. "But you must already know that."

Her voice carried an accusatory tone.

"Why, what happened?"

"We were all interrogated by the police. They were like freaking Nazis."

"Why?"

"You wrote the story. It's on your website."

Yup, there's attitude here.

"About Bobbi Jarvis?"

"Well, it wasn't about that woman who burned up her husband."

I forced myself not to get pissed off. Dr. Tina had said it was her way of keeping me at arm's length.

Rise above it.

"So, the police asked you questions about Bobbi Jarvis." It was a statement, not a question.

"They interrogated me." She sneered. "Because Bobbi and I used to be best friends. The cop got right in my face and he kept saying, 'you must know where she is, you're besties, right?'"

That took me aback. "Used to be best friends? No more?"

"Not since she got the part in that play."

"What play?"

She looked at me and frowned. "Jesus, Genie, I told you about it. I auditioned for it."

"Oh, yeah," I lied. I didn't remember it. She'd probably told me after I'd had a few tumblers of vodka. "Bobbi got the part? Is it a big deal?"

Her voice rose precipitously. "It's Peter freaking Cambridge. The guy who was in *Night Challenge?*"

Hell, yeah, it's a big deal.

Night Challenge was a mega-blockbuster a few years back. Peter Cambridge was the hunky lead.

That man is hotter than a book of lit matches.

"He's in the play?"

"Yeah."

"Wow. I didn't know he lived around here."

Fairfield County, Connecticut, is home to an amazing array of movie stars, Broadway actors and actresses, sports celebrities, bestselling authors, and Grammy-winning musicians. The region is a quick drive or train ride from Manhattan but far enough away to afford a modicum of privacy from the paparazzi.

Most of the population in the county had adopted an

attitude of "leave them the hell alone." So, if you see someone famous in a grocery store or having ice cream at Ben & Jerry's, you pretend to ignore them. I once sat right behind Tom Brokaw at a performance starring James Earl Jones at the Sheffield Playhouse, and it was everything I could do not to reach out and ruffle his hair.

But I didn't. It's not cool.

Caroline sat down at the kitchen table. "He and his wife, Angela Owens, live in Westport. From what Bobbi told me, Angela wrote the screenplay for *Night Challenge* and she wrote this play specifically for her husband as the lead. According to Bobbi, they're hoping to take it to Broadway."

"Bobbi's really got a part in that?"

"Yup."

"I remember that you told me you were going to audition for it." I lied again. "How come you didn't tell me how it went?"

She cocked her head and squinted her eyes. "Because I didn't get the part."

Get past this.

"Have they started rehearsals?"

Caroline picked Tucker up and held him on her lap. "I guess. Once Bobbi got the role, she was too important to be my friend anymore." The anger was hard to ignore.

"Maybe with getting the part along with her schoolwork, she just ran into a time crunch."

Caroline rolled her eyes. "Are you taking her side?"

This part of raising a teenager was a royal pain in my butt.

"Not taking sides." I reached up into the cupboard and pulled out two plates. "Want some Chinese?"

"You know, Bobbi even dropped out of Drama Club. She's not doing her bit at Death Mansion this year."

Ugh, I remembered Death Mansion from last year. It's the Drama Club's annual fundraiser. They take over the wide-open space at the community center at Hawke's Manor in Veteran's Park and turn it into a spook house with live characters, in costume, shrieking and jumping out at you.

Scary fun? I about peed my pants last year.

"What are you this year?"

It was the first time I saw her smile since she'd come home. "Rabid, ax-wielding killer clown."

"Super. Everybody loves killer clowns." Heavy on the sarcasm. She knew I didn't care for this event and I think she was enjoying my discomfort.

Caroline scratched behind the yorkie's ears. "So, because Bobbi's not interested, we're down a zombie."

"If I remember correctly, you had more than enough zombies last year."

Caroline shook her head and let Tucker gently chew on her fingers. "Can't have enough zombies."

I held up a hand. "I don't want to sound like a Nazi cop, but you don't have any idea where Bobbi might be hiding out?"

At first, she shot me a look. But then she softened a little and said, "If I had to take a guess, I'd say she was shacked up with her boyfriend, Tommy Willis."

• • ● • •

The nights are the hardest.

This was originally Kevin's house and this was his bedroom. Oh, sure, my framed posters and photographs are on the walls now and his *Sports Illustrated* swimsuit calendar is long gone. My books are on the bookshelves, my sheets and duvet are on the bed, and my television is sitting on the dresser.

But this is his bedroom.

I'd kept some of Kevin's clothes. They're hanging in the closet next to mine. Now and then, I open the closet door and hug his shirts and slacks to my face, wishing he were in them.

I kept his aftershave on the counter in the bathroom, next to where I keep my cosmetics. I open it and I can smell Kevin, almost as if he were standing behind me.

Where is the line between grief and fetishizing the dead?

I sat on the bed drinking vodka, feeling the loneliest I've been in a very long time. Things were going to hell at the newspaper, Kevin was gone, and Caroline was pulling away from me.

I felt utterly alone.

For a brief moment, I thought about calling Mike Dillon. He was a good guy. Reminded me a little of Kevin.

But he wasn't Kevin.

I downed a tumbler of Absolut and poured another.

And I thought about texting Frank Mancini.

Chapter Five

In my drinking days, it wasn't unusual to wake up to see a text or phone call I'd made but didn't recall. It was always shameful.

I sat on the side of my bed, naked, phone in one hand, the other hand covering my eyes in self-disgust.

What the hell am I thinking?

Frank was drop-dead gorgeous—six feet tall and fifty. He was a member at the most exclusive gym in town and he worked hard at keeping his body as fit as a twenty-year-old's. He dressed expensively, owned a rich Mediterranean complexion, dark chocolate eyes, closely cropped salt-and-pepper beard, and a brilliant smile. Frank is smart, witty, and he's a demon in the sack.

This is going to sound harsh, but when it came to sex, Frank was Dom Pérignon. Mike Dillon was Pabst Blue Ribbon in a can. Sure, you can catch a buzz with both, but who doesn't like the taste of champagne?

The problem with Frank?

He's married and he doesn't care.

For two years, I didn't care either. As a matter of fact, I liked it. It was taboo, it was forbidden. That only added to the spice.

Jesus, don't do this.

No, I didn't text him. I put the phone down on the headboard, finished my drink, and went to bed.

The next morning, while I made coffee, I wondered what the hell was wrong with me. Why couldn't I give up drinking? Why did I even think about Frank Mancini?

Am I that weak? Am I really that stupid?

A half pot of Folgers in my kitchen went a long way to mitigate the nest of bees buzzing in my noggin. On my way to the office, I stopped at Starbucks and bought a Venti Caramel Macchiato that cost me nearly as much as dinner last night.

As I sat in my cubicle, sipping high-rent caffeine, scrolling down through the e-mails, Ben Sumner walked in and dropped into one of my well-worn office chairs.

"Hey, Ben, what's up?"

Lord, my voice sounds like a mile of gravel road.

He appraised me with curious eyes. "You feel okay?"

I must look like warmed over crap.

"Yeah, didn't sleep well."

"We need to keep you healthy." His voice wasn't anywhere near the tone that would give me the warm fuzzies. "Darcie left a message at the front desk. She's calling in sick."

"Let me guess. I'm covering the beat today?"

"Looks like it, *amiga*. Guess you'd better saddle up. Hey, good job on the Betsy Caviness piece. How'd you score a face-to-face interview?"

"Right place, right time."

"Why are they making you keep their location a secret?"

"Her people think her life could be in danger."

"She has people?"

"Doesn't everyone? Okay, let me tie things up here and I'll stop by the station to pick up last night's incident reports."

"You know where I am." He got up without ceremony and headed back to his office.

With Darcie out sick today and her copping an attitude lately, it went a long way to ease my sense of guilt about laying her off.

Just as I was getting out of my beat-to-hell Sebring, Mike was exiting his new silver Jeep Grand Cherokee. I was happy that the insurance company had replaced his old one after the cat burglar had repeatedly rammed it with a HumVee last year—with me in it. By end of that rainy, summer afternoon, Mike's old Jeep looked like it had been pummeled by a tank.

"Morning, Mike." There was a bite in the air and I saw steam drifting from my lips as the words came out.

"Morning, Genie. What a nice surprise seeing you here at the station. Just like old times. Where's Darcie?" He opened the door for me.

"Sick."

"Hope it's nothing serious." We walked side by side through the waiting area. It was stark, with only two hard plastic chairs to sit in. Full color photos of retired officers hung on the wall. Commendations and awards sat in a wooden cabinet on shelves behind a locked glass showcase.

He punched in a code on a wall-mounted keypad and opened an interior door into a hallway.

"Stomach bug." As we walked, I asked, "Anything new on Bobbi Jarvis?"

"Nope. We still think she's hanging out at a friend's house."

"Did you talk to her boyfriend?"

Mike glanced at me. "Tommy Willis? That kid's a middle-class, white boy wannabe thug. All he told us was that he and Bobbi had broken up two weeks ago. Apparently, she got a part in some play."

"Caroline told me about that. Peter Cambridge is playing the lead."

Mike whistled. "How about that? I didn't know he lived around here."

The fluorescent lights in the ceiling raised hell with my headache as we walked down the hallway.

We got to his office where he opened the door, took off his jacket, and hung it on the coat tree next to his bookshelf.

Mike sat down at his desk and I sat in one of the plastic torture devices that pass as police office chairs. I asked, "Anything interesting happen last night?"

He opened the file on his desk and quickly thumbed through the incident reports. "Nothing as interesting as today's front page. Where is she, by the way?"

For a hangover befuddled moment, I thought he was still talking about Bobbi Jarvis. "Who?"

He frowned. "Betsy Caviness."

"I promised not to tell."

"Is she still in Fairfield County?"

It was my turn to frown. I cocked my head and changed the subject. "Have you ever heard of Wolfline Contracting?"

He gave me a suspicious look. "I've seen their trucks."

"Is it a dummy corporation to launder money?"

He glanced away from me, looking at something on his computer screen. "Not that I'm aware of. Did those Friends of Lydia you wrote about tell you that?"

I ignored him. "Heard of Valentin Tolbonov?"

Mike's eyebrows shot up and his attention snapped back to me again. "Was Jim Caviness mixed up with Tolbonov's crew?"

Answer a question with a question. "Is Tolbonov linked with Wolfline Contracting?"

"Stay away from Tolbonov, Geneva. Let the Feds handle him."

I felt a story orgasm coming. "What do you know?"

"Other than he sells diamonds? Nothing but rumors."

"What kind of rumors?"

He smiled. "This is uncorroborated, so I don't want to see in the *Post*. I heard that when he was just getting started in the diamond business, a dealer in New York cheated him out of a deal. He and his brother Bogdan kidnapped the dealer and his family and drove them upstate. Story says it was somewhere up around Albany. They tied the dealer to a tree and made him watch while one by one, Bogdan slit the throats of the wife and three kids. They buried the bodies and then, finally, buried the dealer…alive."

I felt a shiver of fear slide like an ice cube down the nape of my neck. "How true is that?"

Mike shrugged. "Personally, I think it's just an urban legend. But it goes a long way in keeping his crew members loyal. How is Betsy Caviness tied up with the Tolbonovs?"

I was tightlipped. "How about we go over the incident reports?"

He scowled at me but quickly listed last night's police calls—two DUIs, one bust for possession of a controlled substance, one college student who fatally OD'd on Fentanyl, and one B & E at the Inlet Motel coupled with the assault of the night clerk.

"Tell me about the assault."

Mike picked up the voluminous report, scanned it, and then handed it over to me. The arrest report was twelve pages long. New regulations were forcing beat cops to spend more and more of their time filing reports in absurd detail. It made a reporter's life easier, but cut short the time an officer was actually on the job.

Mike gave me the abridged version.

"Ken Appleton, age twenty-two, was working as the night clerk at the Inlet Motel when at about one in the morning, he heard a loud banging noise outside the office. He went out to see what was going on and spotted two men in hooded sweatshirts beating on the door of Room 103 with a sledgehammer."

The Inlet Motel is just off the East Sheffield I-95 Exit and sits on a piece of property that would be better served by a Trader Joe's. Built out of cinderblocks in the late sixties, it's a one-story building with twenty rooms that are reasonably clean and bedbug cheap.

When I was on the crime beat, there were many front-page stories that bubbled up at the Inlet Motel. Because of the proximity to I-95 and the inexpensive cost, it was a hotbed of adultery, prostitution, assaults, and drug deals.

"Instead of dialing 911 immediately, Mr. Appleton posted a video on Facebook Live so that the event unfolded in real time on the Internet."

"Why?"

Mike raised an eyebrow. "Nothing's real unless it's online. Isn't that the saying?"

"Did he ever get around to dialing 911?"

"He didn't, but several of the other guests did. Especially after the kid was spotted by the two men who took a break from beating down the door and spent their time kicking the crap out of Mr. Appleton. The kid's screaming was apparently enough to wake a few people up, whereupon they called us."

"I don't see where the two men were arrested."

Mike shook his head. "Nope, by the time my guys got there, the door was busted in, whoever was inside had left, and Mr. Appleton was a bloody mess."

I shuddered and recalled a murder that I'd covered at the Inlet Motel.

I visualized the inside of one of those rooms—queen-sized bed, dresser, ratty carpet, innocuous prints on the walls, faint smell of mold, cracked tile in the bathroom, mildew in the shower stall. I distinctly recall that, like many cinderblock motels that were built in the sixties, there was a small, opaque window in the bathroom to let in a little daylight.

A window that opened up into the alleyway behind the motel.

"So, whoever was inside, was he dragged out by the assailants?"

"Witnesses don't recall the men taking anyone out with them. But then again, they were all stoned, drunk, or didn't want to go on record."

"Who rented the room?"

Mike glanced down at the report. "Stephen Cogan, lives in Danbury. We contacted him and it turns out that someone had stolen his credit card information. He hasn't been anywhere near Sheffield in over two months."

"Thanks, Mike, guess that wraps it up."

He held up his hand. "Can I talk to you for a moment?"

Uh, oh. Nothing good starts out with that qualifier.

"Sure."

"Are you drinking again?"

"God, do I look that bad? I haven't slept well this week."

He didn't say a word. Mike just sat there, staring at me from across his desk.

I felt my face redden.

It's an old interrogation trick. Throw out an allegation and then let the perp squirm. Nature abhors a vacuum and conversation abhors silence. The first one to speak loses.

Three seconds, six seconds, ten, twenty.

I lost. "Look, Mike, I don't need this bullshit this morning. I got enough going on with Caroline giving me guff and crap happening at the office."

He held up his hand again. "It's none of my business. I'm your friend, is all."

That hurt. "Just my friend? I thought we were more than that."

Mike pursed his lips. "Really? I've asked you out three weekends in a row and you've found an excuse every single time."

"I'm just not in a good place right now for a relationship."

"I get it. That's why I'm going to give you the space you need to figure things out."

"So, we're breaking up?"

He chuckled and that pissed me off. Mike shook his head. "Genie, we've never really been together."

Chapter Six

Walking out of the police station to my car, I knew that Mike was right. Everything about him and me was a matter of convenience—my convenience.

When we went to a movie, it was because I wanted to. When we went out for dinner, it was because I wanted to. The few times we had sex, it was because I had an itch that needed scratching.

My needs, not his.

Just because Mike was right, I can't say that being kicked to the curb didn't sting.

I shook it off. Needing to get my mind onto work, I drove to 1217 Bedford Street, home of Theresa Pittman, Bobbi Jarvis' grandmother. It's a tree-lined avenue of upper-middle class homes, some ranch style, others split-level. The foliage in the half-light of the gray overcast sky was colorful but muted.

I noted that on every single tree, a small, white poster was attached.

Pulling to the curb and letting the car idle, I got out and took a closer look, bringing my camera. It was a legal-size sheet of paper inserted into a clear plastic sleeve and stapled to the tree bark. Bobbi Jarvis' face smiled at me while over her head was printed the word MISSING. Then below her photo it said, "Barbara 'Bobbi' Jarvis—missing since Monday, October 17. If you know her whereabouts, please call Theresa Ward."

Then it offered her phone number.

I took a picture. I might need the art for a follow up piece, depending on how the day went.

Getting back into the car, I drove to Bobbi's address.

I knew Theresa, but only slightly, since Bobbi and Caroline have both appeared in Drama Club productions, as well as having both worked on the club's 'haunted house' together. Theresa had confided in me that she didn't care for the Death Mansion fundraiser any more than I did.

I also knew that, thirty years ago, Theresa had been an aspiring actress-singer-dancer, appearing in a number of Broadway productions. Back then, her stage name was Terri McKay. She told me that even though she'd put her heart and soul into it, after several years she came to the sad realization that she'd always be in the chorus line, never the star.

So, Theresa moved to suburbia, got married, and had a daughter, Nina. Her husband, Harold, passed away when Nina was only ten. Theresa never remarried.

The split-level ranch at 1217 Bedford Street was tucked behind neatly trimmed shrubs fronted by a tiny, green smear of lawn. It was within walking distance of a Shop-Rite grocery store, a T.J. Maxx, and a few mid-range family restaurants.

It was also a short walk to West Sheffield High School.

I pulled my Sebring into the driveway and parked behind a maroon Chevy Tahoe. I climbed the concrete steps to the small porch and rang the bell.

When she opened the door, I was slightly surprised at how old Theresa Pitman looked. In the past, I was always struck by her youthful appearance, much younger than her sixty-plus years.

Theresa was nearly as tall as me, around five-eight, dressed in black slacks and a long-sleeved white blouse, accented by a dark blue silk scarf tied loosely around her slim, graceful neck. Her dark hair was layered, cut to the back of her neck, with a wisp of gray in her bangs. She was a beautiful woman with high cheekbones and perfect lips.

But that day, her face was pale, and her eyes were red and sunken. It was obvious that she'd been crying.

And for good reason. Her granddaughter had been missing for over two days.

"Geneva, please come in. It's always good to see you."

As I walked into the house and we climbed the carpeted steps to the living area, I said, "I wish I were here under different circumstances."

The tidy living room was simple enough—an off-white fabric-covered couch, oversized throw pillows, two recliners, end tables, bookshelves, flat-screen television mounted over a brick fireplace, oriental area rug covering a hardwood floor. Wine-colored mums in a ceramic vase rested on the glass surface of the coffee table.

A woman I didn't recognize was sitting on the sofa. She stood up as we entered the room.

Theresa introduced us. "Nina, this is Geneva Chase, from the newspaper." Gesturing toward the woman, she continued, "This is my daughter, Nina."

Nina wore skinny jeans, a black knit sleeveless top, and black sneakers. Her blond hair was short and swept stylishly to the side. Earrings were understated diamond chips. She had blue eyes, sculpted cheekbones, full lips, and the same dimple in her chin that Bobbi had. Even though she wore minimal makeup, the woman was stunning.

I saw where Bobbi's DNA had come from.

Theresa added, "Nina took the train in from New York last night to help look for Bobbi."

"Bobbi told me that you run an art gallery in SoHo?"

Without answering, Nina asked, "Have the police heard anything more about my daughter?"

"I'm afraid not. I just came from the station. Do you mind if I ask you a few questions?"

I could see the newspaper was face-up on the coffee table. The same photo on the posters outside was staring up at us from the *Sheffield Post*.

"Is this for another story?" Nina wasn't smiling.

"Mostly for me," I answered. "I don't know if Theresa told you, but Bobbi and my daughter are best friends."

It's sometimes easier to call Caroline my daughter than to try to explain to people that I'm her guardian. The terms "guardian" and "ward" sound Dickensian to me.

"Then maybe your daughter knows something." Nina's voice carried a hint of sarcasm.

I'm not sure I like this woman.

"Would anyone like some coffee?" Theresa asked.

Recalling the evil swill waiting for me at the office, I eagerly replied, "Oh, please."

The cream-colored kitchen wallpaper was tastefully simple, as was the Currier and Ives-style art on the walls. The cupboards were painted a rustic blue. An Early American-style table and chairs sat in the center of the cozy kitchen. In the middle of the table was a crystal vase filled with saffron-colored chrysanthemums.

Taking cups down out of the cupboard and placing them on the counter, Theresa asked, "How do you take it, Geneva?"

"Black, please."

Nina went to the refrigerator and took out a container of skim milk to pour into her own cup.

I hung my oversized bag on the back of a chair and did the same with my jacket. "Can I help you with anything?"

Theresa handed me the steaming mug. "I got it."

I toyed with the idea of taking out my recorder but decided against it. I could feel the tension in the room between Nina and me. I asked a question that was directed at both of them. "Any theories at all about where Bobbi might be?"

Holding her own cup of coffee, Theresa sat down. "You can start by talking with that young thug, Tommy Willis."

"Bobbi's boyfriend?"

"Up until a couple of weeks ago, that boy was calling my Bobbi at all hours of the day and night. No manners, that boy."

Nina sipped her coffee and spoke up. "I don't recall hearing Bobbi talk about a boyfriend."

Theresa snapped. "When's the last time you've spoken with your daughter?"

Nina bowed her head and remained silent.

"Do you mind my asking what might be a deeply personal question?" I directed it to Nina. "Why does Bobbi live here and not with you or her father?"

Nina cast a sideways glance at her mother.

Theresa glowered at her daughter.

Nina took a deep breath, let it out, and answered. "Bobbi's father and I got married way too young. We were nineteen, still in college, unsure what we wanted out of life."

"Unmarried," Theresa added. "At the time of pregnancy."

Nina pursed her lips. "We were married before Bobbi was born."

"What do you call it? A shotgun wedding?"

Nina turned angrily to her mother. "When are you going to let that go?"

Step in…diffuse.

"So, you were both young, nineteen, when Bobbi was born."

Nina's head bobbed slightly. "We didn't know anything about babies. Our marriage was on the rocks almost from day one. Anyone thinking that a baby will make it better has their head up their ass."

"Nina," Theresa hissed.

"Mother, I'm thirty-four years old. Think you can ease up just a bit?

"You and your husband are divorced?"

Nina took another sip of her coffee before she answered. "When Bobbi was five."

"That's when Bobbi came to live with me." Theresa put her hands on the table and folded them together, as if praying. "With me she's safe, life is stable, without drama."

Nina frowned. "I was having an awful time making ends meet."

I drummed the top of the table with my fingertips. "Tell me about your ex-husband."

"Adam is one of the best-looking men on the face of the planet, and he'll be the first one to tell you that." Nina stared off into space, remembering what he looked like. "Jet black hair, dark brown eyes, a killer smile, funny personality, always had a three-day stubble that women die for. He loved to party and so did I."

Theresa jumped in. "But when you have a baby, that party's over."

Nina gave the woman an angry glance. She went on. "But Adam had a dark side. He's a classic narcissist. Everything has to be about him. He has to be the center of attention. God help you if you point out a flaw or criticize him in any way. He considers that as a personal attack."

"Is that why you divorced?"

"Partly. I'm a bit of a narcissist myself. He wanted me to worship him, and I wasn't about to do that."

"Is that why you split up?"

"Oh, no, that was bad. I had a ton of reasons. But the last straw was when I caught him in bed, having sex with another man."

Chapter Seven

"Your ex-husband is gay?"

Nina's eyes glanced out the window for a moment and then locked back onto mine. "He's more bi than gay. He likes boys *and* girls."

"I recall that Bobbi said he's living here in Sheffield?"

Nina answered. "He used to live in a townhouse on the north side of the city."

Theresa looked surprised. "Used to?"

"He got behind in the rent. He's living in the back of his shop now."

I asked, "What shop is that?"

"He has a photography studio in the Harborview Plaza on Turner Avenue."

Theresa looked at Nina and asked, "Why did Adam get behind on his rent? I thought you said his business was good."

"It is," Nina stated. Then she turned to me. "Adam gambles on everything, horses, football, baseball, golf."

"He's bad at it," Theresa hissed.

Nina picked up her mug and held it pensively in front of her. "He called me last week asking for a loan. He said that he needed to give his bookie a few thousand dollars. If he didn't, they were threatening to break his legs."

Theresa pointed at her daughter. "You didn't give it to him, did you?"

Nina shook her head. "I've lost track of how much money he already owes me."

Changing the subject, I asked, "Tell me about this play that Bobbi's in with Peter Cambridge."

Theresa's face immediately brightened and she wiggled in her chair. "Oh, my God, this is Bobbi's big chance at being a star. It's called *Darkness Lane* and Peter Cambridge and Mona Fountain play the leads. In the play, they're a dysfunctional married couple and Bobbi plays their rebellious daughter."

When she said the words "rebellious daughter," Caroline flashed into my head.

Theresa continued, "The plan is to open the production here at the Sheffield Playhouse. The producer will invite reviewers from New York and he says he's certain it will garner raves. That'll give him the ammunition to rack up enough investors that they can open it on Broadway."

Nina sipped at her coffee. "Bobbi was so excited about getting the part she even called me." There was the hint of bitterness in her words.

"It wouldn't hurt you to pick up the phone and call *her* every once in a while." Theresa snapped.

I jumped in again. "Do you think you can get me a meeting with Peter Cambridge?"

Theresa studied me for a moment. "I can try."

"Tell me about Bobbi's temperament this past weekend. Was she angry about something? Is it possible the two of you had words?"

Theresa suddenly stood up and walked over to look out the window over the sink. "It was a quiet weekend. She'd gone to rehearsals both Saturday and Sunday. She didn't get home until nearly nine both nights, so I didn't see much of her."

Sensing that she was leaving something out, I asked, "Did anything unusual happen that might have made her want to run away?"

Theresa hesitated, weighing her words. "I got a phone call,

Sunday night, from Jake Addison, her drama coach from school. He told me that I should have Bobbi quit the production. He said that she was in over her head, that the stress she was under was affecting her grades."

"What did you say?"

She looked directly at me. "I told him in no uncertain terms that he should mind his own damned business. There was no way in hell that I would pull her from the play. This is Bobbi's big break. I told him that he was jealous because he auditioned for a part in the play and they didn't think he was good enough."

"Was that the end of the conversation?"

"He said that he was sorry I felt that way. He was only looking out for Bobbi. Then he hung up."

Theresa still had me fixed in her sight. I asked her, "Did you tell Bobbi about the phone call?"

She slowly shook her head. "I didn't have to. She was standing right next to me when I took the call."

"Can I see Bobbi's room?

The girl's room was much like the rest of the house, tidy and neat, everything in its place. Bobbi's clothes were pressed and hung in the closet. I saw that there were half a dozen empty hangers.

She'd taken clothes with her?

Framed posters of Broadway productions hung on the wall—*Chicago, Hamilton, Lion King*. The bed was made and stuffed animals were strategically placed near her pillows. Bookshelves were filled with framed photos, awards, ribbons, and citations from years of beauty pageants and talent shows. Books were stacked neatly on her desk.

But there was something missing, something glaringly not there.

There's no computer.

I looked at Theresa. "Does Bobbi own a laptop?"

"That's what the police asked when I showed them Bobbi's room. I bought it brand new last Christmas. All I can think of is she must have taken it with her. Bobbi had it stuffed into her backpack when she left for school."

"That's unusual?"

"Very."

"Does she have a cellphone?"

Theresa nodded. "I've been calling and calling. It goes straight to her voicemail."

I studied Bobbi's grandmother who had her back to me, staring out the bedroom window at the trees in the backyard. The woman was detail-oriented, almost to the point of being obsessive compulsive.

Nodding toward the window and the trees that line the street. "Did you put the posters up?"

Nina was right behind me. "We both did."

"You have some doubts that she's staying with a friend?"

Theresa took a long breath and turned to look at me. "I don't know where my granddaughter is, Geneva. You have a daughter." Tears filled her eyes. "You must have some idea what it's like to not know where your child is. Not knowing if she's safe or even alive." Her last words caught in her throat. "I know what the police are saying, that's she'll turn up in a day or so. But I don't want to leave any stone unturned."

I get it.

"Does Bobbi have a family tracking app on her phone?"

"Yes."

"And?"

"Useless. It doesn't work if the battery's not in the phone."

Kid doesn't want to be found.

I pulled my cellphone out of my bag. "I'm going to ask you for a huge favor. Can you add me as a user to your tracking app?"

"You mean so if she turns on her phone again, you can see where she is?"

"Yeah."

"Do you think that'll help?"

"Like you said, let's not leave any stone unturned."

Chapter Eight

The Jarvis Photography Studio is a small storefront in the Harborview Shopping Center. Anchored by a CVS pharmacy, the dingy strip center also hosts a Domino's Pizza, Sew-Much-For-You Fabric Store, Paws & Claws Pet Supply Outlet, and the Sheffield Beanery Coffee Shoppe.

I got out of my car and noticed that the lights were off inside the studio. I tried the front door and found it locked.

The sign on the door of the studio read, "Open Monday thru Friday - 8am to 6pm or by appointment." My watch told me it was a few minutes past ten. I took out my phone and punched in the number on the sign.

I got voicemail. *"You've reached the Jarvis Photography Studio. I can't answer your call right now, but if you'll leave a detailed message, I'll get back to you just as soon as I can."*

"Hi, Mr. Jarvis, this is Geneva Chase of the *Sheffield Post*. I'd like to talk to you if you can spare a few minutes." Then I left my phone number.

I cupped my hands and pressed my forehead against the glass door. The inside of the studio was open space. A counter, desk, couch, and chairs were grouped in the center of the room. The walls were covered with framed photographs. I could make out some of them—mostly wedding portraits.

I stepped back and glanced at the rest of the shops in the strip center. They were all open and doing business, including the coffee shop.

Always a good place for gossip.

The interior of the Sheffield Beanery Coffee Shoppe was typical in that it had the ubiquitous counter with a glass show-case offering scones, bagels, muffins, and cookies. Because of their faded colors and stressed appearance, the tables and chairs had an old-time feel to them. Black-and-white photos of his-toric Sheffield street scenes—old cars, horse-drawn carriages, churches, a passenger train down the middle of town—hung on the walls.

Around a dozen customers, some behind newspapers or books, were seated at tables scattered throughout the cozy room. The majority of the clientele, however, were attending laptops, tablets, or smartphones.

A man and a woman, somewhere in their forties, were behind the counter wearing green aprons with the shop's logo on them. She was smearing cream cheese on a specialty bagel while he greeted me with a broad smile. "What can we get for you?"

He wore a name badge that said "Rob." Rob was slightly shorter than me but made up for it in girth. His green apron strained against his mid-section.

Too many scones?

"Can I get a latte to go?"

"Absolutely."

The woman overheard us and offered, "I got it."

I noted that her name badge said "Kerri." Her hair was cut stylishly short and I couldn't tell if she'd let it go completely gray or she'd colored it silver. I thought it was very attractive.

I wouldn't have the guts to do that, though.

While the gleaming, fire-engine red machine gurgled and hissed, steaming the milk, Rob engaged me in small talk. "That will be four twenty-five. I don't think I've seen you in here before."

"I don't get to this part of town too often." I fished my wal-let out of my bag and handed the man my credit card. "What's the story with the photography studio next door?"

He shook his head. "I don't know, he didn't open this morning. I think he overslept again. He's living in the back. Showers at the city fitness center."

"Adam Jarvis is living in the back of the studio?"

Rob shot me a look of suspicion. "Who's asking?"

"Oh, I'm sorry. I'm Geneva Chase with the *Post*. I wanted to talk to him about his daughter."

He picked up a copy of the newspaper that had been sitting on the top of the counter. "Yeah, I read that she's missing. The cops were out here yesterday talking with Adam. Anyone have any idea where she might be?"

"Not yet. That's why I was hoping to talk with Mr. Jarvis."

Kerri handed me the paper cup with my coffee and said, "Better be quick about it. Adam told us he's thinking about selling his equipment and closing up shop."

"Business bad?"

The woman folded her arms in front of her bosom. "He owes some big money."

"To who?"

"His bookie. Adam has a bad gambling problem."

Rob got close to my ear. "Just last week, we saw two men get out of a Wolfline Contracting truck and walk into the shop with baseball bats."

Wolfline Contracting—second time in twenty-four hours that name has come up.

I frowned. "Did they hurt Mr. Jarvis?"

He whispered, "I think they just wanted to scare him."

Kerri shivered. "They scared me."

Rob offered, "I think they frightened off Adam's partner, though."

"Adam's partner?"

Kerri smiled. "Nice young man, not as good looking as Adam, but attractive. He has a nice face and a good sense of humor."

"So, Adam's gay?"

She thought for a moment. "He's told us about meeting women online but he said it never seemed to work out. We've seen this young man spend the night with him a couple of times now in the back of the studio. But we haven't seen him since Adam had the visit with the men with the Louisville Sluggers."

"He has a bed back there?" I motioned toward the studio.

"Blow up mattress, some chairs, a television. With all his digital equipment, it's pretty crowded."

"You've seen it."

"Oh, yeah. We like Adam. We bring him a sandwich now and then," Kerri responded. "I'd hate to see him move, but I know he's in a pretty tough spot."

"You think he's sleeping in this morning?"

Rob pointed past the plate glass window in the front of the shop, out toward the parking lot. "He must be. That Chevy Cruz out there? That's his."

My bag slung over my shoulder, latte in my hand, I went out to the parking lot and looked inside Adam's car. The backseat was packed to the rafters with clothing, books, towels, sheets, and blankets. There was a cardboard box in the passenger's seat up front that appeared to be filled with dishes and kitchen utensils.

I stared back at the studio, lights off—eerily quiet in the midst of this busy shopping center, cars coming and going, customers getting their prescriptions filled, buying treats for their pets, picking up coffee and muffins.

Adam Jarvis, are you hiding in there?

I walked around the side of the building until I got to the alleyway in the back. A dumpster sat at the far end, behind the pharmacy. Garbage cans rested next to closed doorways. Old pavement, pot holes, beer bottles tossed in the weeds—nothing pretty about this part of the strip center.

Still holding my coffee, I saw the rear of the coffee shop and then found the back door to the photography studio.

My heart leaped into my throat.

Fresh splinters of wood, bright against the weather-beaten exterior, protruded from the door jamb where a crowbar had ripped past the lock.

A robbery?

My first instinct was to call 911.

What if the bad guy was still in there?

At ten in the morning?

This had to have happened last night.

What if Adam Jarvis is injured and needs medical attention?

Mind made up, I slowly pulled open the door, the lock now useless, the broken hinges groaning in pain. Darkness lay ominously in front of me.

I stepped through the doorway, my hands scrabbled against the wall, looking for a light switch, not finding one.

I called out, "Adam? Adam Jarvis?"

I switched my coffee to my left hand and rooted around in my bag until I found my cellphone. I punched up the flashlight app. Its tiny, but powerfully focused beam of light illuminated the far wall.

Shining it around the room, I saw that Rob from the coffee shop had been right. The room was jam-packed. The air mattress took up most of the open space on the floor, a desk and chair sat off to my right. Digital equipment dominated nearly half of the area. Camera bags were hung from the walls, fighting for space with two metal filing cabinets.

There were cardboard boxes stacked on top of each other. I guessed they contained more clothing, dishes, and personal items.

I crept across the room to another doorway. Opening it, I found myself inside the studio, facing the plate-glass windows looking out at the parking lot. The lights were off, but with the gray daylight coming through the windows in the front of the building, it was much easier to see.

Turning off the flashlight app on my phone, I noted that I'd been right about the photos on the walls. With few exceptions, they were wedding portraits.

There was, however, a collection of both color and black-and-white photos of Bobbi Jarvis, hung together, prominently displayed on one of the walls.

Where are you, Adam?

Almost on cue, I spotted a photograph on the wall that had been taken of Adam. Nina had been right. With his sparkling, dark eyes, jet black hair, jaw stubble, and dazzling smile, he was devastatingly handsome. I saw what Nina fell in love with.

Looking around the rest of the room, I noticed the photography magazines on the coffee table and, in honor of Halloween, a crystal bowl of sample sized Hershey bars alongside a tiny, bejeweled skull on a plastic base. I pushed the button on the back of the base and the skull's eyes glowed red and it emitted an evil, disembodied laugh, *ha ha ha ha.*

I moved back to the doorway to Adam's office and found the light switch. The fluorescents overhead blinked to life. I took a sip of my latte and noticed one more closed door that had escaped me when I'd come in.

The bathroom?

I stepped over to the door, picking my way carefully around the air mattress and piles of Adam's dirty clothing.

No place to wash them, Adam?

Then I stepped on something sticky. Looking down, I saw that I was standing on a rust-colored stain.

What the hell?

Opened the door.

Jesus Christ Almighty.

It was awful

I jerked backwards, nearly losing my balance, dropping my coffee cup, splattering all over the floor.

My eyes and brain trying to make sense.

Adam Jarvis, in jeans and black tee shirt, seated on the floor next to the toilet, legs spread, his back against the wall, arms bent at impossible angles from his elbows, his fingers broken like grotesque claws, his face no longer human.

No longer pretty.

Skull crushed. Unseeing eyes, wide open with terror.

In a dark, sickening pool of drying blood, brain tissue, and skull fragments.

Chapter Nine

After dialing 911, I stepped back out into the alleyway and waited for the cops to arrive, fighting off nausea, trying to stop my hands from shaking.

Trying to forget what he looked like.

The first police cruiser showed up in seven minutes, blue and whites flashing, the next one seconds later. Ten minutes after my call, the alleyway had been closed off and tape was going up.

It took nearly a half hour to answer all of Officer Tony Ambrose's questions.

I waited another thirty minutes in the driver's seat of my Sebring as I watched more cruisers come and go, their blue and white's stuttering against the gray light of the overcast October morning.

Now and then a gust of wind would catch leaves in the air and whirl them around in circles until they finally fell, skidding across the parking lot. The same breeze would rustle the police tape and make it flutter, tugging against the portico columns to which it was tied.

Customers continued to come and go through the doors of the pharmacy, but, to a person, they stopped and stared at the proceedings.

I knew that I had a job to do, a story to write, but I was having a problem concentrating.

That poor man, what had they done to him?

In my head, I kept seeing him. The blood, the tissue, Adam's arms and legs at odd angles, like a rag doll thrown onto the floor. His fingers broken, bent backward.

My stomach roiled, I felt dizzy.

Knocking on my window.

I looked up and saw Mike standing outside my car.

Opening the door, I got out, my legs unsteadier than I would have thought.

"You okay?" he asked.

"Hell, yeah." But I leaned against the car for support. "Ready to make a statement?" I asked, rummaging in my bag until I found the recorder.

Mike patiently waited until I got ready. Then he started. "It appears that Adam Jarvis was murdered sometime last night by an unknown assailant. We have forensics inside now collecting evidence. His death was caused by blunt force trauma to the head."

His skull was caved in.

I waited but Mike didn't say anything more.

"That's it?" I asked.

"That's it."

"Off the record?" I turned off the recorder and dropped it back in my bag.

"Okay, off the record. Somebody took their time with Mr. Jarvis. I'll wait for the medical examiner's report, but it looks like someone broke his legs, his arms, and his fingers. Only after all of that, then he was killed."

"Why?"

"I don't know. Maybe to send a message. The owners of the coffee shop insist that he owed a bookie some money."

"They tell you a truck with the Wolfline Contracting logo paid Adam Jarvis a visit last week along with two guys with baseball bats?"

Mike nodded. He saw that I was shivering and reached out

and pulled me close. "I'm sorry you saw that." His voice was low and soothing.

His skull was caved in.

"I'm sorry about dropping the coffee."

He sighed. "It's not going to help us in the investigation." Still holding me. "Next time you see a probable crime scene, call 911, okay?"

"How do you do it?" I barely squeaked it out.

"It's part of the job. We do it because we have to do it."

"Think this has anything to do with his daughter's disappearance?"

He slowly shook his head. His way of saying that he didn't know.

I appreciated his hug. "Okay," I whispered, "I've got to write a story."

"In how much detail?"

"It's a family newspaper. I'll leave out most of the gore."

Five minutes later I pulled into the parking lot of Bev-Max. I went in and bought a bottle of Absolut. Then I got back in my car, my hands still shaking. I flipped the top off my Sheffield West High School Wildcats commuter cup, and filled it about halfway with vodka. The top went back on and the vodka bottle went into my bag.

I sat in that parking lot for another fifteen minutes, enjoying the warmth as it spread through my body and leveled out my fried synapses.

Then I drove to the office, sucking on a mouth full of Altoids, and banged out the story about Adam Jarvis' murder. Ben liked it so much, he immediately had it posted on our website.

I hope to hell someone has contacted Theresa and Nina Pittman already.

Wherever Bobbi Jarvis was, how was she going to handle the news of her father's death?

Once Ben had it online, he came out to my office and sat down. "Good job, Genie."

I gave him a halfhearted grin. "Thanks. You still thinking about selling the joint?" I waved my hands around the newsroom.

His answer gave me a jolt. "Someone's made me an offer."

"You're kidding. Since yesterday?"

"No, the offer's been on the table for over a month. They've been doing due diligence. Now it's up to me if I want to pull the trigger. Up until we lost Barrett's advertising, I hadn't taken it seriously."

"Who is it?"

"Can't say yet, but they'd be very good for all the employees."

"Bullshit."

"Seriously, they have the resources to offer better health insurance and a much better retirement plan."

"At what cost? C'mon, Ben, you'd miss this."

He stood up and glanced around the newsroom. It was a little after two and most of the desks had reporters at them working on tomorrow morning's copy. "Maybe. Hey, you look like hell. Tripping over that body must have been a bitch. Take the rest of the day off. Go home."

For whatever reason, I thought about the dried blood that must still be on the bottom of my shoe.

I knew that I had a commuter mug that still had vodka in it, but I wanted to be around people, somewhere warm and cozy. Just one drink in the company of others to muffle the nightmare of finding Adam Jarvis' body.

Chapter Ten

Sometimes, when I get into my car I'll have a song in my head and when I turn on the radio, that same tune will be playing. Occasionally, I'll be thinking of an old acquaintance, and out of the blue, they'll call me. Coincidences?

Synchronicity is the simultaneous occurrence of events which have no clear cause but seem meaningful. Which is another way of saying that weird shit happens.

When I walked through the door of Booker's Pub, I stopped for a moment to let my eyes adjust to the dim interior. The walls of the bar were bookshelves from ceiling to floor, filled with volumes of all kinds, fiction, nonfiction, classics, westerns, erotica, mysteries. There were even old encyclopedias—the kind families used to buy like subscriptions, getting a volume a month as they could afford them.

Then, of course, came the Internet. Encyclopedias became novelty items, historic relics on the shelves of pubs and museums.

Off to my right was a gas fireplace. I worked my way across the room, stepping around tables made of polished oak and leather chairs. People engaged in quiet conversation, soft jazz in the air—it was what I needed.

That's when I saw him.

Frank Mancini was seated on a bar stool, his back turned to me. He was gazing into the mirror behind the bar.

It had only been last night that I almost texted him.

For a brief moment, I considered turning around and leaving.

Does he see me in the reflection?

Everything in my life seemed to be shifting off its axis, rotating at a speed and angle different from mine.

I decided to stay.

I saw of a flash of recognition in his reflection in the mirror.

He got up off the bars tool and turned around. My heart skipped a beat.

The man is nothing if he's not beautiful. He flashed me a smile.

"Genie." He opened his arms to give me a hug.

Hold on, tiger.

I put the flat of my palm against his chest and shook my head. "I don't think so, Frank."

His face registered disappointment. "Okay, no worries." Then he glanced around the bar. "I'm a little surprised to see you here. I thought you quit drinking."

I sat down on a stool next to his. "I did." No further explanation.

He cocked his head in confusion.

"Look, a couple of hours ago, I found a man beaten to death. I thought I'd treat myself to a nice quiet drink. That okay?"

"I'm so sorry." He sat down and put his hand on mine.

I pulled it away. "Look, Frank, we can sit next to each other and I'd love to have someone to talk to. But no touching."

He held up his hands, then reached down to pick up his bourbon, taking a sip. "Okay, no touching."

The bartender appeared. I looked up at him. "How about a vodka tonic?"

He disappeared and I glanced up at the mirror, seeing Frank studying my face in the reflection.

"It must have been horrible. Finding that body."

His skull was caved in.

The young man swept by and placed the drink in front of

me. I hesitated before I picked it up, not wanting Frank to see my hands trembling.

"What can I do to help?"

I shook my head, picked up the glass and took a healthy swallow. The familiar warmth spread throughout my being almost immediately.

He asked, "Is this the first time in your life that you've found a body?"

"Once, I was the first one on a suicide scene. Man had hanged himself from a ceiling rafter."

"Sorry."

I took another healthy hit off my vodka. Then I asked, "How about you, ever find a body?"

He nodded. "When I was ten years old, I found my grandmother. She'd died of a heart attack while sitting in the toilet."

The scene of Adam Jarvis sitting on the floor next to the toilet flashed in front of my eyes again. I shuddered.

"It was a long time ago," he muttered, seeing me.

Typical Frank. It was always about him. He thought I'd shivered because of what he'd found when he was just a kid.

He turned and looked at me. "Other than finding dead bodies, are you doing okay?"

Red flag.

Frank was one of the best for feigning empathy.

"Peachy."

His eyebrows furrowed. "Want to know how *I'm* doing?"

I turned and looked into his face. "Still married to Evelyn?"

"Yes."

"Then, no, I'm not particularly interested in how you're doing."

"Ouch." He picked up his drink again.

I glanced at my watch. "How come you're in a bar in the middle of the afternoon?"

His face reddened. "I'm meeting a client."

I frowned. "What's her name?"

That's when my phone started chirping. "Damn it." I

reached into the bag hanging on the back of the bar stool and grabbed my cellphone.

The number was Mike Dillon's personal cell. I answered the call, curious. "Hi, Mike."

"Interesting development. I thought you'd like to know, being as you're so close to the case."

"What?"

"The owner of the Shell Station over on Wilkins Avenue recognized Bobbi Jarvis' photo from the front page of your paper. He remembered her getting into a car driven by a white male."

I felt a strange thrill in the pit of my stomach. "Yeah?"

"He has closed-circuit video. We caught the tag on the car. Monday morning, Bobbi Jarvis got into a car owned by Jacob Addison, the English teacher at West High."

And Drama Club coach. Son of a bitch.

"Can you e-mail me a copy of the video?"

"That's why I'm calling you. I've just issued an Amber Alert. I'm e-mailing the clip to all our press contacts. You'll have it by the time you get back to your office."

Oh, it'll come directly to my cellphone.

"We have a warrant to search Addison's apartment. I'm headed over there now."

Without asking Mike's permission. "I'll meet you there."

I hit the End Call button and looked at Frank, who was staring back at me with a bemused grin. "Let me guess, you've got something that's hot."

"Yeah." I was already grabbing my windbreaker and bag. I took a breath. "Look, Frank. Sorry if I sound rude. Nothing in my life is going well right now. But the last thing I need is to start up with you again."

He stood up. "Hug for old times' sake?"

I let him. I even put my arms around him and hugged him back.

Even though it felt pretty good, I knew going back to Frank would be a disaster.

Chapter Eleven

How well did I know Jake Addison?

I'd met him several times before and after Drama Club performances, during play rehearsals, and at last year's Death Mansion fundraiser. He was of average height, slightly below six feet, weighed in at about one hundred-seventy pounds, and had green eyes that I thought were pretty. The man had an easy smile, a thick head of wavy brown hair, and a resonant, pleasant voice.

Caroline had once described him as "retro." Jake enjoyed music from the forties and fifties as well as Broadway show tunes. She said he loved to talk about classic films and long-dead actors and actresses.

She'd said, laughing, "He even uses an old flip phone."

That was it. That was the extent of my knowledge of Jake Addison. It struck me how little I knew about a man with whom my Caroline had spent time.

Had she ever been alone with him?

The CCTV video hit my phone by the time I got out to my car. Even on my tiny screen, the resolution was remarkably crisp. On Monday morning, the sky was clear, the sun was shining, and the view of the eight pumps at the Shell Station was unimpeded.

Three cars were in view with their owners busily pumping gas into their tanks. A white Prius pulled into view and parked.

Jake Addison got out of the driver's side and walked across the lot and out of view.

To pay for his gas? Did he purchase anything else?

Moments later, he came back into range again, holding a plastic bag, which he tossed into the backseat of the car. Then he popped the gas cover and placed the pump nozzle into the side of his car.

He was casually dressed—jeans, sweatshirt, and deck shoes.

Not dressed like a teacher headed for school.

Jake finished pumping gasoline into the Prius, returned the nozzle, and replaced the gas cap. Then he stood next to the car, glanced around him and waved to someone, signaling that they should come to him.

Bobbi Jarvis dashed into view. Dressed in a black wind-breaker and jeans, she quickly opened the passenger's side door, took off her backpack, and slid inside.

At the same time, Jake got into the driver's seat.

And then they were gone.

Bobbi had gotten into his car willingly.

Since it was on the way to Jake's apartment, I decided to stop by the Shell station where Bobbi had gotten into the Prius two days ago. I noted that its location was an easy walk from Bobbi's grandmother's house, but it wouldn't have been on her usual route to school.

Gas stations have changed over the years. They don't smell like motor oil and old tires anymore. If you want that ambience, you go to an actual commercial garage or auto repair shop.

Now they're convenience stores selling everything—candy, chips, soda, beer, sandwiches, condoms, batteries, and dodgy looking fruit.

The man behind the counter was tall, heavyset, and balding. He had crimson-flushed cheeks, a gray walrus mustache, and tiny blue eyes. The nametag he wore said, "Hi, my name is Bill."

I stepped up to the counter. "How old is that coffee over there?"

He glanced over at the urn and squinted. "I just made it about an hour ago. I like to have a cup myself in the afternoon."

I checked the time. It was three-thirty. I had to keep track because it was my turn to pick up Caroline and her friend Jessica from the community center at six. I needed a little caffeine to counter the vodka buzz I had.

Pouring steaming coffee into a Styrofoam cup, I asked, "Are you the owner?"

He squinted again. "Who wants to know?"

I waved my hand. "Genie Chase. I'm with the newspaper. I saw the closed-circuit video you gave the cops. You have a good memory to recall that girl getting into the Prius from two days ago."

He smiled, showing me saffron-colored smoker's teeth. He reached behind him and pulled out a rolled-up copy of the *Post*. Bill laid it out flat on the counter in front of him and pointed to Bobbi's photo. "It jogged my memory when I saw her picture this morning. Monday, I was putting up this week's sale signs in the window, when that Prius guy came by to get gas. Then when he was done, this young girl comes out of no place and jumps into his car."

I put my coffee on the counter next to the newspaper and pulled my notebook out of my bag. "What's your name?"

"Am I going to be in the newspaper?"

"Maybe." I flashed him a sexy smile.

"Bill Fisher."

"Anything else you remember?"

He slowly shook his head. "No, that's just about it, I guess."

"In the video, it looked like the man was carrying a plastic bag. Did he purchase anything more than gas?"

Bill grinned again. "Oh, yeah. Cops asked me that question. I checked the credit card receipts. He bought ten dollars' worth of regular gasoline, two bags of barbeque potato chips, two bottles of water, and this." He pointed to a display that was behind the counter. Hanging on a series of hooks were packages of batteries, razor blades, and blister packs of pepper spray keychains.

"Pepper spray?"

He nodded.

"Can I see?"

He handed me a package. Easy to look at under the clear plastic, the hot pink container was about the size of my thumb and could be placed on a keychain. The package read—Police Strength, Finger Grip, 25 Bursts, 10 Foot-Range, only $8.98… Support National Breast Cancer Foundation.

Why would Jake Addison want one of these?

• • ● • •

Jake lived near the hospital in an old Victorian that had been chopped up into apartments. I knew the neighborhood. It was low- to low-middle-income and home to public servants, nurses, store clerks, struggling families, and teachers.

Police tape was already around the porch. One police cruiser was in the driveway and two more were parked on the street.

I texted Mike—*Can I come in?*

He texted back—*Are you kidding?*

Me—*I'm on deadline.*

Mike—*Keep your pants on, I'm working in here.*

A half hour later, Mike came out and stood on the old wooden wraparound porch. He spotted my car across the street, ducked under the yellow tape, and started down the front steps.

I got out of my Sebring, holding my coffee, and carrying my bag over my shoulder. A cold front had been moving in the entire day and the temperature had dropped. I put my coffee on the roof of my car and zipped up my jacket.

We met on the sidewalk. "What did you find?"

"It's not good."

"Tell me."

"Looks like some clothes might be missing. We found empty containers of hair coloring in the garbage."

"Like he wanted to alter their appearances?"

"Possibly."

"What else?"

He hesitated.

"Tell me."

"It appears that wherever Jake Addison went, he took his laptop computer with him."

"Like Bobbi did."

Mike took off his police hat and stared up the street. A school bus was stopped, red lights flashing. Children were getting off and running onto the sidewalk, laughing, catcalling.

I was mindful again that I had to watch the time to get to the community center to pick up Caroline and Jessica.

"We found a thumb drive. It looks like he might have tried to hide it."

"Did you see what's on it?"

His face clouded over. "Yeah."

"So?" Even as I said that, I could feel my nerves getting the better of me. It wasn't like Mike to be so reticent with information.

"It's a video."

"A video of what?"

I watched the muscles in his jaw as his teeth ground together. Then he said, "A male and female having sex. The man's face and body are mostly obscured. But the girl is definitely Bobbi Jarvis."

Chapter Twelve

Back at the office, I cranked out the piece on Bobbi Jarvis and Jake Addison, but left out the part about the sex video. Mike had asked me to embargo it, meaning I could use it in a story, but at a time that he chose—a time when the investigation was less sensitive.

I didn't mind. Once it got out that Bobbi had starred in a sex tape with her teacher, her life at West High would be over. Her classmates would be merciless. She'd have to move, change her name, live off the grid.

Simple as that.

But she'd have to do that anyway, wouldn't she?

She'd run off with her English teacher. She's shacking up with her drama coach.

Jesus, what a mess.

I glanced at the clock on my computer screen. It was five-twenty. I had to be done and out of the office and in my car in another fifteen minutes to be on time to pick up Caroline.

My office landline rang. "Geneva Chase," I snapped.

"Is it true?"

"I'm sorry, who's speaking?"

"Theresa Pittman, Bobbi's grandmother. The police were just here. Is it true?"

Oh, my God, the police have talked to Bobbi's mother and grandmother.

It must have been a particularly bad day for the two of them. Bobbi's father found dead, brutally murdered in the back of his shop this morning. Then evidence found that Bobbi and her teacher had left together for parts unknown.

"What did the police tell you, Theresa?"

"About Bobbi and Jacob Addison. Is it true? Does this have anything to do with Bobbi's dad being…?" Her voice trailed off.

"I can't imagine…I don't think…"

"I'm not sure I can take much more."

I heard a rustling noise and then a new voice came onto the phone. It was Nina, Bobbi's mother. "Geneva."

"Hi. I'm so sorry about all of this."

"Is this going to be in the newspaper?"

I sighed. "I'm sorry. When a school teacher kidnaps a student, it's not just going to be in the *Post*. It'll make national news, I'm afraid."

"Yeah, I know. The police didn't tell us much. They said they found evidence that Bobbi was with Mr. Addison. They didn't tell us what the evidence is. Do you know?"

I lied. "I don't know what they found at Jake Addison's apartment. I saw the video, though, of Bobbi getting into his car."

"They showed us that."

There was a long silence.

Nina started again. "When the police came here earlier in the day to tell us about Adam, they said you were the one who found him."

"Yes, ma'am."

"They told us that he died of blunt-force trauma. Do you think he died quickly? I'd hate to think he suffered."

Dear God, they tortured him before they killed him.

"I'm no doctor, but it looked to me like he didn't suffer," I lied again.

Another silence.

Nina said, "Peter Cambridge reached out to us after the news broke about Adam. He told us how sorry he was. Mom asked him if he could spare some time to talk with you. He said that they'd have some time around noon tomorrow. Would that work for you?"

On that hellish day, hearing that I'd get a chance to talk with one of my favorite actors gave me the first thing to smile about.

"Yes, that will work just fine. Nina, is there anything I can do to help you and your mother?"

"No, we're going to just take it one hour at a time."

Keeping my eye on the clock, I asked, "Do you think I can talk to your mother about Jake Addison?"

Without saying good-bye, I heard Nina pose the question to Theresa.

Then Theresa was back on the line. "What would you like to know?" Her voice was sharper now, angry.

"Is Mr. Addison married?"

"To my knowledge, Jake's never been married."

"Girlfriend?"

"We were never that close where he confided in me about his relationships." Then after a short silence, she added punctuation. "Obviously."

"Did Bobbi ever speak of him?"

I could feel the tension coming through the phone. "Yes, she thought highly of him. She thought he was very talented. She related well with him. That's really all I want to say."

"Thank you, Theresa. Once again, please let me know…"

She'd already hung up.

I hit the button on my keyboard to send my story to Laura Ostrowski, the night copy editor. Then I threw on my jacket, grabbed my bag, and headed for the door.

The parking lot for the employees of the newspaper was in the back of the building, leaving the few spots in the front open for visitors. I was moving fast when I shoved my way through the metal doorway, unto the concrete porch, and rushed down the steps,

Then I stopped dead in my tracks.

In the dimming twilight, I saw the indistinct outline of a low-slung, black Jaguar XJ sedan, idling behind my car, blocking my way.

In the far corner of the parking lot, sitting in the shadows, was a black Ford F-150 pickup truck. In the half-light, I saw it had an after-market addition, a front bumper guard that made the grill more intimidating, like a battering ram.

What the hell's this?

I dug my keys out of my bag, took note of where my can of mace was, and walked deliberately to my Sebring.

A man wearing a dark gray, ankle-length overcoat got out of the driver's side of the Jaguar and stepped toward me.

I froze. "Can I help you?" I tried to sound confident.

"Miss Chase?" The man stopped a few feet from me, sensing my unease. He was tall and thin. His hands were in the pockets of his coat. He was nearly bald and had a pronounced hawk-like, patrician nose. His wire-frame glasses sat tipped back on the top of his bulbous head. "I apologize for meeting you like this. It must seem like I'm ambushing you." He had a Long Island accent.

I glanced back at the dark shape of the pickup. The driver's door swung open and a man got out. Wearing a waist-length, black leather coat, jeans, and work boots, he was well over six feet with wide shoulders, muscular chest, and appeared to be chiseled out of a solid block of granite. The man was almost as intimidating as his vehicle.

He closed the door and, arms folded, stood motionless next to the truck.

I glanced back at the man in front of me. "Ambushed? Yeah, a little bit." I heard the sarcasm in my voice.

He attempted a smile. "My name is Eric Decker." Pulling a hand out of his pocket, he reached out toward me.

I saw he was holding a business card. I plucked it from his outstretched fingers. It contained his name and the words Attorney at Law. "Mr. Decker, I'm going to have to ask you to move your car. I'm late for an appointment."

He took a step closer and I stepped back. He said, "I represent Wolfline Contracting."

A name I kept hearing. "Good for you."

"The principals of the firm read this morning's news story with interest. They'd like to know how they can reach Mrs. Caviness."

"Can't help you."

He took another step. "It's urgent that we reach Mrs. Caviness."

"Principals? You mean Valentin Tolbonov?"

He remained motionless but when he answered, his voice was very low. "Miss Chase, these are men who are accustomed to having things done their way."

I nudged my chin in the direction of the ape and the truck. "Is Wolfline responsible for the death of Adam Jarvis?"

Decker's answer was to slowly shake his head, not in denial, but in sympathy. "They sent me hoping you'd be reasonable."

I pulled my phone out of my bag and motioned toward the Jaguar. "Look, if you don't get that shit-box out of my way, I'm calling 911."

Decker stepped back and glanced over at the man standing quietly in the shadows. Then he turned his attention back to me. "Miss Chase, my clients are insistent that you tell them the location of Mrs. Caviness."

"Are you threatening me?"

He looked nervously at the man in the shadows again. "Me?" He shook his head. "Not me. But I strongly urge you to comply."

Before I could hit speed dial for the cops, the back door to the building opened, the office lights spilled out into the night, and Matt Barnes, a pressman, stepped out for a cigarette break. Seeing what was going on, but not understanding, Matt stopped cold, still holding the door open. "Is everything okay, Genie?" he called.

I held up my phone, showing it to the attorney. "Should I call 911?"

Decker gave me a weak grin and nodded toward the business card I still held in my had. "No, ma'am. But if I were you, I'd strongly consider calling me with Mrs. Caviness' location."

Without another word, he got into the Jaguar. Almost at the same time, the other man got into the driver's seat of the pickup. The sedan pulled quietly away. The truck grumbled to life. The driver revved the engine, growling like a mythic beast before he put it in drive and slowly, arrogantly, rumbled out of the parking lot.

Matt fired up his lighter and lit his cigarette. "Friends of yours?" He gestured toward the alleyway that served as our driveway to the road.

"Nope." I hustled to my car, tossed in my bag and turned the ignition. I glanced at the clock on the dash.

Dammit, I'm going to be late.

While I drove, I punched in the phone number I had for the Friends of Lydia.

Shana Neese answered, seeing my name on caller ID. "Geneva. Good story in today's newspaper."

I watched the traffic as I talked. "Yeah, thanks. Hey, two guys from Wolfline came calling just a few minutes ago. They're hot on finding out where Mrs. Caviness is."

"Did they give names?"

"Eric Decker, attorney. I didn't get a good look at the second guy, he stood in the shadows and it was getting dark. But I can tell you that the guy was huge."

Shana's diction was perfect, her words measured. "Decker works exclusively for Wolfline. The second guy sounds like he might be Bogdan Tolbonov, Valentin's half brother."

"I wouldn't want to meet him in a dark alley."

"You don't want to meet him at all," she warned. "Did you tell them where you interviewed Miss Betsy?"

"No."

"Well, if they ask you again, tell them. We've already moved."

Chapter Thirteen

It was only a little after six when I powered the Sebring through the front wrought-iron gates of Veteran's Park. I was one of twenty other vehicles jockeying for space in the circular drive, queuing up in front of Hawke's Manor.

The Drama Club was still inside working on their spook house.

I found a spot, turned off the engine, and took a few minutes to study the Sheffield Community Center, also known as Hawkes Manor, a two-story, twenty-room, limestone Tudor revival, complete with stained-glass windows, walnut-paneled rooms, French doors, and a magnificent ballroom.

It was built during the Great Depression by Graham Hawkes, a wealthy industrialist untouched by the global economic calamity. He quietly bought up the property surrounding the mansion until he had acquired two-hundred-thirty acres of woodland—now a maze of hiking trails, barbeque pits, pavilions, two playgrounds, and dozens of picnic tables and known as Veteran's Park.

The only other building on the park's property was the Sheffield Playhouse, situated on the opposite side, half a mile away on the Post Road.

The Hawkes family had lived in the Manor building until 1971 when the last of the heirs sold it to the city for a dollar.

The city turned the space into a community center used for

meetings, parties, reunions, and nuptials. The massive stone terrace and beautiful garden made the perfect spot for outdoor wedding receptions.

Right at the moment, though, it sported scarecrows and winged gargoyles.

For the next two weekends, this would be Death Mansion, the annual fundraiser of the West High Drama Club. This would be the tenth year they had staged a haunted house-style attraction. The club had amassed an eye-popping collection of spooky trappings, decorations, coffins, smoke machines, and skeletons. By charging ten bucks a head, they made thousands of dollars to put toward their theatrical productions.

This was Caroline's second year as one of the theater geek worker-bees.

Friday night would be the dress rehearsal, and then Death Mansion would open to the public on Saturday afternoon, going every night until Halloween.

Drama Club parents were invited to the rehearsal on Friday. *Ugh.*

I hated this fundraiser. I don't like scary costumed characters jumping out from behind fake walls shrieking at me. I don't like scary movies, I don't like scary roller coasters, and I don't like scary books.

I don't like being scared. Period.

His head was caved in.

The vision of Adam Jarvis sitting in his tiny bathroom in his own blood, fingers and limbs at impossible angles, his skull crushed, made me shudder in the driver's seat of my car.

It doesn't get much more frightening than that.

Watching the front doors to the old house, I turned up the heat and willed the horrible vision away.

Blessedly, the kids started streaming out the front, double doorway. Caroline and Jessica were among the first. Caroline spotted me right away and they both walked briskly toward the car, chattering at each other, shaking their heads.

Back doors on both sides of the Sebring opened simultaneously.

Caroline nearly shouted, "Is it true?"

I hit the ignition, put it in gear and pulled away from the curb, hoping to get ahead of the other parents. Pulling out of the park's gates and into the heavy traffic of East Avenue was bad enough. Waiting in an interminable line of soccer moms in SUVs was a complete time-waster.

"Is what true?"

Jessica spoke up. "That Bobbi and Jake ran off together."

Jessica Oberon was one of Caroline's best friends. They've known each other nearly their entire lives. At some point over the past year, Jessica had gone Goth. Her black hair got spiky, she started wearing dark makeup and lip gloss, and she dressed in all black slacks, skirts, and tops. She even sported a dog collar.

Perfect for Death Mansion.

Caroline piped in. "It's all over the Internet."

Ben must have posted my story online the moment after he'd edited it.

Glancing at them in the rearview mirror. "Looks that way."

Jessica said, "I knew she was a slut."

"What are they thinking?" Caroline asked. "Their lives are over. He'll go to jail, and she'll never be able to show her face around here again."

Jessica's turn. "Ever since Bobbi got that part, she's been acting all better than everyone else."

Caroline growled, "And you could see the way Jake fawned over her, like she was the only one in Drama Club."

They were talking to each other at the speed of light—with no regard to me being in the car at all.

Jessica's voice got low. "Do you think they were fucking in school?"

A little decorum, ladies.

I took my eyes off the road for a second and stared at the

two of them in the rearview mirror. "Girls, I won't have that kind of talk in my car." My voice was louder and harsher than I had intended.

But it had been a really crappy day.

"Sorry."

"Sorry."

We rode in silence for a few blocks.

I tried conversation. "Did you get a lot done back at the community center?"

"Yeah."

"Yeah."

Different tack. "When did you find out about Bobbi and Mr. Addison?"

Suddenly, the two of them were animated again.

Caroline answered, "About fifteen minutes ago."

Yup, about the same time I sent it to Ben.

"How fast will the news spread at school?" I asked.

Jessica laughed. "Everyone already knows. Bobbi and Jake gave new meaning to the word viral."

I pulled up to the curb, dropped Jessica off at her house and waited for Caroline to get out of the backseat to sit up front with me. When she didn't move, I said, "C'mon, sit up here. When you're back there like that I feel like I'm working for Uber."

She gave a heavy sigh and got out, then slid into the passenger's seat.

"How about we go by Bella and pick up a pizza?"

"Okay."

I handed her my phone. "The number's in there. Want to call ahead?"

"Sure." She fingered the screen on my phone until she found the number. A moment later, "Yeah, we'd like to order a large pizza, please—pepperoni, sausage, half onion, half mushrooms. We'll pick it up."

Caroline dropped the phone into my bag that lay between us on the console.

It only took a few minutes for us to get to Bella, a tiny joint not far from our house that served pizza and subs. I liked it because it was convenient. And when I was picking up something and I was alone, I could wait at one of the tables and have a quiet glass of cheap wine.

When we walked into the shop, the smell of garlic was nearly overpowering. I told the woman in an apron behind the counter who we were and she let me know that it would be another ten minutes or so.

We sat at one of the tables, sliding in on orange, plastic benches. "You know who I feel bad for?" Caroline said.

"Who?"

"Bobbi's grandmother."

"It can't be easy for her."

Caroline had been animated when she'd been in the backseat of the car with her friend. There in the takeout joint, she was thoughtful and pensive, staring out the window into the night, watching the lights of the cars passing by. She said, "All the time and effort and money that her grandmother put into her career, then to get the break of a lifetime, a part in a play with Peter Cambridge—just to throw it all away."

"What do you think will happen to the play?"

She smiled slightly and raised her eyebrows. "The play goes on. Isn't that the saying?"

"Even without Bobbi?"

Caroline reached out and took a napkin out of a metal container. Absentmindedly, she rubbed at a smudge on the table in front of her. "I imagine they'll call for auditions again."

I offered her a grin. "Hey, I'm meeting Peter Cambridge tomorrow at noon. I can ask him. Would you audition again?"

"Hell, yeah."

I shifted gears. "Did Bobbi ever talk about Jake Addison in a romantic way?"

Her brows furrowed. "Before she got the part, she talked about him a lot. She said he was funny and cute. She told me she wished he was younger. Maybe she'd go out with him."

"Do you know if she spent any time with Mr. Addison alone?"

She balled up the napkin in her fist. "I know she'd gone to his apartment a couple of times."

"Why?"

"To run lines."

"For Drama Club productions?"

"Yes, and for *Darkness Lane*."

I looked up and saw our pizza being taken out of the oven by a guy wearing a sweat-stained tee-shirt with the Bella logo on the back. As I slid out of the seat, I asked, "Did Bobbi ever tell you that Mr. Addison said anything or did anything that she thought was inappropriate?"

I stood up and took my wallet out of my bag, then waited for Caroline to answer my question. When I glanced down at her, sitting there at the table, she was looking back up at me with a expression of disbelief.

"No," she said. "Bobbi never said anything to me about that. But the fact that she's shacked up with him somewhere, that speaks volumes, now doesn't it?'

● ● ● ● ●

I was lonely.

So much had happened that day, I wanted someone to share it with. To help me put it all in perspective.

Finding Adam Jarvis' body, Bobbi running off with Jake Addison, the threatening visit by the lawyer and the gorilla from Wolfline, Ben telling me he may be selling the paper, getting kicked to the curb by Mike Dillon.

And the unsettling coincidental drink with Frank at Booker's Pub.

All in one day.

I was in my bedroom, Kevin's bedroom. Sometimes it felt as if his ghost was there. I could almost feel him, touch him.

But not that night.

I was utterly alone.

I reached into my bag for the bottle of vodka I'd picked up earlier in the day. It was mostly full. I'd only had a little of it while I was in my car.

I didn't kill the whole bottle that night, but I put a serious dent in it.

Chapter Fourteen

"Genie."

What is it?

"Genie."

I opened my eyes.

"Caroline? What time is it, sweetie?"

"Someone just shot through our front window."

Holy shit.

I sat up, blinking, shaking the vodka cobwebs out of my head. "What?"

Caroline stood next to the bed. She was wearing an extra-large Red Sox tee-shirt and her hair was all bed-snarled. "I was asleep and I thought I heard a popping noise, like a loud firecracker. I got up and went into the living room. There's a bullet hole in the front window and in the wall behind the couch."

Her voice was weak, shaky—she was frightened.

So was I. I felt my heart slamming against my ribcage.

"Stay here." I grabbed my cellphone off the headboard.

I keep a two-foot weighted police baton under my bed. It looks like a tiny version of a baseball bat. I reached down and grabbed it.

I'm not sure a baton is any kind of match for a gun, but it made me feel better. I raced down the stairs, leaving the lights off in the living room. I crept over to the front window and pulled aside the curtain.

There, in the ghostly illumination of the streetlight, was a small hole in the glass, no bigger than a dime. I scanned the street. I didn't see any cars parked at the curb that were unfamiliar. There was no movement at all. Everything was as still as if it was a black-and-white photo.

I glanced at the crimson light of the digital clock on the cable box. It said it was three in the morning.

Staying low, I moved over to the wall behind my couch.

Yup, that's where it hit.

Placing the police baton on the couch, I held up my phone and punched in 911. Then I trotted back upstairs to the bedroom to where Caroline sat on my bed, holding Tucker on her lap.

"Did you call the police?"

"Sure did." I rifled through my bag, looking for a business card. When I found it, I told Caroline, "Stay here, sweetie, while I make a phone call."

In the distance, I could hear the faint wail of a police siren. Stepping out into the hallway, I punched in a number.

It was answered on the first ring, as if expecting my call—at three in the morning. "Eric Decker."

"You miserable piece of shit, you shot through my front window. You could have killed my daughter."

"I'm sorry, who am I speaking to?"

"You know goddamn well who this is. Tell your clients that I interviewed Betsy Caviness at the Metro Sheffield."

There was silence on the other end of the phone. Then, "Is she still there?"

"Of course not. They moved her."

"Where?"

"I didn't ask and they didn't tell me."

Another silence, longer this time. "We'd like a way to contact her. Do you have a phone number?"

It was my turn to stay quiet.

The voice on the phone broke the silence. "Geneva Chase,

find out where they're keeping her, please. She has something my clients want."

The phone went dead.

● ● ● ● ●

Less than ten minutes after I'd started talking with Officer Christina Fuller, Mike Dillon came into the house. He asked his officer, "Do you have everything you need?"

Holding her notebook, she answered, "I think so."

He looked at me. "I'm going to have Officer Fuller keep an eye on you in her squad car until sunrise. Is that okay with you?"

I nodded. "Yes, thank you."

She left and it was only the two of us in the living room. "Any idea who might have taken a shot at you?" he asked.

"Yeah, I've got an idea." Then I told him about my visit the afternoon before in the newspaper parking lot by representatives from Wolfline and the conversation I'd just had with Eric Decker over the phone.

He stared at the bullet hole in the window. "We'll have a talk with Mr. Decker in the morning. I'll bet he'll be able to prove he was nowhere near here tonight."

"Guaranteed."

"Hey, I've got someone who will replace your window. We can get it done tomorrow if you like." Then he studied the hole in the wall. "I know someone who can take care of this for you as well."

I managed a smile. "Maybe I'll keep it as a memento. When I have guests over, I can show it to them and they'll think I'm a total badass. As far as the window goes, I'll slap some duct tape over the hole. We'll get it replaced when I have time."

He glanced down at the baton I'd left on the couch. "What were you going to do with that?"

"I don't know. Think I should get a gun?"

"If you do, let me know. I'll help you pick one out. How's Caroline?"

I glanced up the stairs. "I gave her a Xanax. Last I looked, she was asleep. Scared her bad, though."

"I'll bet. How are *you* doing?"

"Oh, swell," I answered, then laughed, but when it came out, it sounded like a sob.

He reached out and took my hand. "Would you like me to stay here tonight? I could sleep on the couch."

I appreciated his touch. "Thanks, Mike. With Officer Fuller outside, I think we'll be fine." I reached out with my free hand and stroked his cheek. "I'm sorry it didn't work out between us."

He managed a grin. "Me, too. I always wanted to have a girlfriend who was a total badass."

Chapter Fifteen

Darcie slipped into my cube and sat down. "I've got the incident reports. One of them says that someone shot at your house?"

Last night, after Mike left, I had tried to get back to sleep. Even after a tumbler of Absolut, I could only manage a nervous, fitful slumber, awaking intermittently from dark dreams of hulking men in shadows and dead men sitting in the shadows on the floor.

The following morning, I didn't know which was worse, the hangover or being sleep-deprived.

I managed a contrived smile. "Yeah, bury that in the Police Log."

The Police Log was a daily column on page two that listed all the inconsequential crimes and incidents that happened the night before. These were the domestic disturbances, the DUIs, and noise complaints. Nothing that warranted valuable real estate on any of the pages of tomorrow's paper.

"Sure, random shot fired on Random Road." She smiled. "How's that?"

"Great. How are you feeling?" I asked, referring to her being out sick the day before.

She checked the screen on her smartphone before she answered. "I'm feeling better. Thank you for covering for me. Look, I'm sure there's not any good time to tell you, but I'm pregnant."

What?

I stood up, walked around the desk and hugged her. I wasn't sure what to say. She's not married. "So, congratulations?"

"Yes, it wasn't what John and I planned but we're both happy about it."

"John?"

"John O'Brien. We've been living together for almost a year. He's a software engineer."

I was at a loss for words. "Awesome news."

I wasn't an expert in human resources, so I wondered what the legal ramifications were for laying off a reporter who was preggers.

Darcie's face clouded over. "I hope Ben's cool with it."

Ben's going to have a cow.

"Why don't you let me tell him?"

"Thanks, Genie.

Rather than wait, I figured it was better to get bad news out of the way as early as possible. I grabbed the Starbucks coffee off my desk and carried it into Ben's office.

Without invitation, I walked in and sat down.

He glanced up from his computer. "Oh, come in, don't wait for an invitation." He wasn't smiling and his voice dripped sarcasm.

"I just found out the reason why Darcie was out sick yesterday. She has a bun in the oven."

He sat back in his chair. "This day just gets better and better." He glanced at his watch. "And look, it's not even nine o'clock yet."

"What?"

"Dowling Toyota/Mazda pulled their advertising."

"Why?"

"They got a new ad agency who believes in broadcast and social media. Tony Dowling and I went to high school together. He called me personally to tell me how difficult and painful the decision had been."

I sat silently with my hands folded in my lap.

Ben hissed his words. "Bullshit, Genie. Total and absolute bullshit. He's in love with seeing his own face on television."

"How bad is this?"

"On top of losing Barrett's? It's a frickin' disaster."

My stomach twisted like a spastic python.

He took his glasses off and placed them on his desk, taking a deep breath. "I'm postponing any layoffs."

I leaned forward. "What's that mean, Ben?"

"It means I don't want to make wholesale changes right now. I can't have morale taking a nosedive."

I frowned. "No offense, but it's never bothered you in the past."

His eyebrow lifted and he shrugged.

"I think you don't want potential buyers walking through the newsroom and hearing reporters bitching about working overtime because we're shorthanded."

Ben glanced up at the photo of him on his sailboat off the Keys. "Look, single copy sales have spiked since you've been writing again. I'd like you to be on this teacher kidnapping story full time. I heard this morning that TV crews from New York and Hartford are camped out across the street from the girl's grandmother."

"Who's gonna edit?"

He directed a thumb toward his chest. "I'll edit and Laura offered to come in a few hours early for as long as we need her."

Laura Ostrowski was the night copy editor. She offered to come in early because she has no personal life and her husband is a giant pain in the ass. Better to be working and clocking some overtime.

Even though Ben hadn't confirmed that he was courting a buyer, I was unnerved by the prospect of having new bosses at the *Post*. I've worked on dailies that went through ownership changes. They always look for ways to cut costs and maximize profits. That means cutting pages and staff.

Just as I got back to my office my cellphone rang. Caller ID told me it was Mike Dillon.

"Hey, Mike, what's up?"

"I thought you'd like to know. Theresa Pittman is going to be making a statement to the press at ten o'clock this morning."

"Thanks, I'll be there." I remembered how comforting he'd been at three that morning. "And thank you again for last night."

"Part of the job."

"Above and beyond, Mike."

"We interviewed Eric Decker. He says he has no knowledge of anyone who would want to take a shot at your house."

"Surprise."

"I'll see you at Mrs. Pittman's place. In the meantime, watch your back."

I hate being part of a media circus. I don't like being part of the herd. So, I picked up my personal cellphone and punched up Theresa Pittman, hoping she'd recognize my number.

"Geneva?"

"Hi, Theresa. I hear you're making a statement to the press at ten."

"I am, are you coming?"

"Oh, yes. Is it a zoo outside your place?"

"The police are doing a good job keeping them away from the house, but, yeah, there're a lot of television cameras out there."

"Look, it's going to be hard for you and Nina to come and go. Can I bring the two of you anything this morning? Coffee? Bagels? I'm going right by the East Side Diner on my way over there."

She hesitated. As if she said yes, she'd be making a pact with the devil.

After all, I'm a member of the press.

Coffee and bagels would have been easy. But that's not what Theresa and Nina wanted. They wanted fresh fruit and yogurt. Not the yogurt that I ate, but the Greek kind that was really expensive. I stopped by Stop-n-Shop and picked up some apples, peaches, and grapes as well as two large containers of Chobani.

I had to park two blocks away from Theresa's house. The cops had cordoned off the street, turning it over to the press. Nearly a dozen pop-up tents were in place, as well as vans with colorful logos and incredibly tall, retractable antennas that would beam Theresa's statement up into the heavens, bounce it off a satellite, and send it careening back into thousands of television sets and computers.

With my bag slung over my shoulder, I carried two plastic sacks filled with fruit and yogurt up the sidewalk, steam huffing and puffing out of my mouth as I walked, until I got to Theresa's split-level ranch. Mike Dillon was in the front yard talking with Officer Ambrose when he spotted me. He frowned. "Where do you think you're going with that?"

As if on cue, the front door to Theresa's house opened and Nina popped her head out. "It's okay, Officer. Let her in."

I gave Mike a big grin along with an air kiss, and went up the steps, onto the tiny landing, and into the house.

Nina led me to the kitchen. "Coffee?"

"Sure. Where's Theresa?" I placed the two bags on the table.

She took down a cup and poured. "She's getting ready for her close-up." Nina had a bitter edge to her voice. "You take it black, don't you?"

"Yes, good memory." I took the mug of coffee from her. "Close-up?"

Her mouth twisted for a moment and then she answered. "She's always wanted to be a star…all eyes and cameras on her. Here's her chance." Nina pulled the two containers of yogurt out of the bag and placed them in the refrigerator. "Thanks for all this. What do I owe you?"

I held up my hand. "My treat."

I'll get Ben to expense it.

Nina sat down at the table with me and opened the second bag to see what kind of fruit I brought her.

"Mind if I ask you a question?"

Her brows furrowed. "Okay."

"Do you think that your mother was living vicariously through Bobbi's success? You know, being in the play and all?"

She chuckled. "Hell, yeah. When I was Bobbi's age, she was hoping to live vicariously through *my* show business successes."

"Did you have any?" I hoped that I hadn't come off snarky.

Laughing now. "Hell, no. Even with the acting and voice classes, I never got past the auditions. I never had the natural talent that Bobbi has. But Mom just kept leaning on me to do better…to work harder. Finally, I said fuck it and I ran off with Adam."

The memory of finding Adam's body in the tiny bathroom flashed through my mind again. I shuddered. "I'm sorry about Adam, by the way."

She took a sip of her coffee. "Sooner or later, somebody was going to kill him."

"Because of the gambling?"

"And his borderline sociopathic behavior."

That took me by surprise. "Such as?"

"Other people's feelings never entered into the equation with Adam. Case in point," she jabbed at the table with her finger, "we were about four years into the marriage and already I knew that I wasn't cut out for being a mother. So Bobbi was staying here with Mom while we were trying to make a living in the city. I was waitressing and taking a few classes with the School of Visual Arts. Adam was trying to make it as a photographer. He wasn't making much money, so he became a videographer for a company that shoots porn."

Nina sighed. "He was actually pretty good at it. Tried to convince me to be in some of the videos. He laughed and said it was an opportunity to break into show business."

I cocked my head, waiting to hear what she'd decided.

Seeing me, she answered, "No, I didn't fuck on-camera. What Adam forced me into was much, much worse."

She looked up and gazed out the window over the kitchen sink, silent for a moment. Finally, she said, "I think it was sometime in January, because it was bitter cold out. Two men came to our one-bedroom flat. One of them was Adam's bookie, Nicky Bruno—a fat, little pig who leered at me every time he stopped by to collect money. The other was Tony Giuliano, the guy who breaks bones if you don't pay up."

I reached into the plastic bag on the table and picked off two grapes. "Were they there to collect money?"

She slowly nodded. "Oh, yeah. Adam was in to them for twenty grand."

I whistled.

"Adam told me to go into the kitchen to make coffee. While I was in there, I heard them talking but I couldn't make out the words. Their voices got louder and louder until the talking just stopped. That's when I went back into the living room and asked if anyone was ready for coffee.

"Adam was sitting on our beat-up, old couch, head in his hands. Nicky and Tony were standing in the middle of the room staring at me, arms crossed, smiling, looking at me up and down. I glanced down at Adam and asked him what was going on."

She put her hands on the table and folded them. "He said that they had worked out a payment plan and that he was sorry. Nicky opened his fat face and said that I was going to be working off my husband's debt. 'How,' I asked? Nicky's grin got wider, 'By working for me,' he said.

"I looked at Adam again, who couldn't look me in the eye. 'What's he talking about, Adam?' All he could say was that he was sorry, over and over."

Nina went silent.

"What was he talking about?"

She growled, "For two months, they whored me out, gave me to out-of-town guests they were trying to impress. I'd get a call to go to such and such hotel and they'd give me a room number and time and I'd go have sex with whoever was there."

"Jesus."

Nina looked at me with an expression of defiance. "That same night that Adam offered me up to pay his debt, I had to seal the deal. I had to have sex with fat Nicky Bruno in *our* marital bed, while Adam sat in the living room and listened. Then, when Nicky was done, Tony came in and took his turn."

I didn't know what to say. "I am so sorry."

Nina wiped away tears. "Needless to say, Adam and I divorced soon after."

All I could do was shake my head.

"So, you see, whoever killed him, I'm sure it wasn't because Adam was being a humanitarian."

Chapter Sixteen

Theresa Pittman looked fabulous. Standing on her porch, overlooking her tiny front yard, surrounded by cameras, starkly bathed in the halogen light, she was dressed in a tan, ankle-length skirt, brown leather boots, a white long-sleeved top, and a dark brown vest. She wore a turquoise necklace and earrings.

It all had a Southwest, Native American feel to it.

Her makeup was reserved, lipstick understated, eyebrows perfectly arched.

Theresa's air was one of steely resolve. Make no mistake—Theresa Pittman was one tough mamma.

She stood behind a bank of microphones, one for each station represented in the media gaggle. Theresa's hands didn't shake when she held up the single sheet of paper to read from. She gazed out over the crowd of reporters, newscasters, police officers, neighbors, and curiosity-seekers with a look of satisfaction.

They'd come to see and hear her.

The temperature was cold enough that every time she exhaled, steam drifted from her lips. She cleared her throat, and began. "On Monday of this week, over three days ago, my fifteen-year-old granddaughter, Barbara Leigh Jarvis, got into a vehicle owned by Jacob Addison, an English teacher and drama coach for Sheffield West High School. They have not been seen since.

"The police have informed me that they can only presume that they are travelling together. There's evidence that they may have altered their appearance.

"The police say that the car Bobbi got into is a four-year-old white Prius. The Connecticut license plate reads XVE910. Please be on the lookout for this vehicle and call the authorities if you see it.

She took a deep breath.

Time for the finale?

"I'm pleading now to Jake Addison. Think about what you're doing to my granddaughter's life." A tear appeared and slowly trailed down her cheek, glistening in the harsh illumination of the news lights. "You've already ruined what could have been her best chance at having a career as an actress. You've ruined my life, Jake Addison. Haven't you done enough damage? I beg you to bring Bobbi back home, safe and unharmed."

Another tear appeared and the woman's voice cracked. "And I'm begging the public…" Her voice trailed off as she choked back a sob. "And I'm begging the public to please, please watch for my granddaughter." She held up an eight-by-ten glossy of one of Bobbi's headshots. "And for Jacob Addison." Her face turned grim and her voice nearly a growl. "Who kidnapped my granddaughter and should rot in hell."

She turned without another word, unanswered questions from shouting reporters flying through the air, and disappeared back into her home.

Mike had been standing next to me the entire time I'd been recording her words and taking photos for tomorrow's edition. He got up close to my ear and whispered, "Exclusive to Geneva Chase, we found Jake Addison's Prius."

I turned and looked at him, shocked. "Where?"

"Stamford Train Station, parking lot."

"He took a train?"

Mike glanced around him.

I did the same. The news reporters were busy doing their

follow-ups and were talking into their own microphones, staring at the cameras held by their crew, faces appropriately serious.

"Credit card records say he bought two Metro-North tickets into the city."

"They're in New York?"

He pulled the collar up on his jacket as a brisk wind blew by, throwing dead leaves swirling into the air. "We're checking video at every station between here and there. It's possible he bought the tickets and then they got off before the train pulled into Grand Central, just to throw us off his trail."

"Any chance I can get into Jake's apartment to take a look?"

Mike scowled. "No, of course not. Nothing to see, anyway. We've already tossed it."

Tossing it meant they'd searched the apartment and removed anything that might help them catch Jake and convict him when they did. "Hey, the video you found…?"

"What about it?"

"Was it taken at Jake's place?"

Mike slowly shook his head. "I don't think so. Much of it was digitally obscured. The camera was stationary, focused on the bed. It was difficult to see much of the background except that it was dark blue. Jake's bedroom walls are off-white."

"Were they under the covers or on top of the bed?"

"On top."

"What color is the bedspread?"

"Maroon."

"You sure it's Bobbi in the video?"

"Yeah, sorry, Genie. For sure, it's Bobbi."

I thought for a moment. "Are you sure it's Jake?"

Mike shook his head slightly. "The male in the video was mostly obscured. Didn't seem to be any scars or tattoos we could make out."

It didn't make sense. "If he went to the effort of making a video, why did he essentially take himself out of it?"

Mike glanced at his watch. "Don't know, Genie."

I watched the television crews as they moved their vans as close as they could to pack away their gear and take down their pop-up tents. "You know, yesterday Theresa told me about a phone call she got from Jake the night before Bobbi went missing."

"She told me, too. How he tried to persuade her to get Bobbi to quit the play."

I looked back at the split-level ranch. "What if sometime before she got the part, Jake and Bobbi made this video? For whatever reason, Bobbi was complicit. But then, when Jake didn't get the part, he got pissed, and decided he was going to shut down the production. When he couldn't convince Theresa to pull her out of the play, he blackmailed Bobbi, telling her that if she didn't leave with him, he'd post the video online."

"The reason he obscured himself." He folded his arms across his chest.

"What do you think?"

"You're making a lot of assumptions. You're connecting a lot of dots that aren't there. I got to run, Genie."

He started walking toward his cruiser. I trotted behind him until I caught up. "Hey, why give me the exclusive? I thought we were just friends."

Mike stopped, looked at me sadly, and smiled at me. "It's a friendly thing to do."

I watched him walk away.

Son of a bitch, he feels sorry for me.

If he hadn't given me the exclusive, I think I would have been pissed.

Chapter Seventeen

When I got back to the office, Darcie was working on a piece about an armed carjacking in the parking lot of the South Sheffield Train Station. Before the perp abandoned the vehicle, he sideswiped four parked cars on Ballard Street. The elderly couple who owned the stolen SUV were so shaken up they had to be taken to the hospital.

The suspect was still at large.

I sat down in my cubicle and put together tomorrow's lead story. The six-column headline would be: *Kidnapper's Car Found at Train Station.* Since Theresa's statement to the press would have already run in the six o'clock news, it would be a sidebar.

The journalist in me appreciated the interest level a story like this represented to our readers. As a foster mother, I understood the tragedy of it. When Bobbi and Jake were found—and they would be, sooner or later—her life would never be the same. An older man taking advantage of her like that would leave her forever traumatized.

She'd never be able to go back to school, not West High, anyway.

And what about her role in the play? Was that history?

That thought made me glance at the clock on my computer screen. I had a noon appointment to meet Peter Cambridge.

I felt a tiny thrill. I admit, I had a crush on Peter Cambridge.

Honestly, there probably wasn't a good reason for me to go out to his house in Westport and talk with him. He really wasn't part of this story.

But it's Peter Cambridge.

Around eleven, while I was editing a piece about the Redevelopment Agency, I watched as Ben Sumner came out of his office. I was surprised to see him wearing a tie.

He walked briskly up to the reception desk where a man and a woman, both in their thirties, waited near the front entranceway. They were dressed in impeccable clothing that shrieked "corporate."

The man had on an expensive-looking, well-cut, coal-gray suit, white shirt, and tie. The woman wore a conservative, knee-length black dress, matching jacket, and modest heels. Both carried beige overcoats over their arms.

Ben enthusiastically shook hands, first pumping the man's, then, more gently, the woman's. Then he led them back to his office and closed the door.

Are these the buyers Ben talked about?

Twenty minutes later, the three of them came back out, standing in the doorway while Ben pointed to various areas of the newsroom. Then he pointed directly at me.

They started walking my way.

I did my best to keep my eyes glued to my computer screen, surreptitiously glancing up to watch their inexorable journey to my cube.

Ben almost burst through the door. "Genie, got a minute?"

I was suddenly filled with a sense of dread.

I stood up. "Sure."

"I want you to meet Charlie Johnson and Faith Blair."

Now that they were up close, I saw that the man named Charlie had a widow's peak giving him an unnaturally large forehead that gleamed under the fluorescent lights. He had expressive blue eyes, was clean shaven and he flashed me a warm smile as he shook my hand.

The woman's platinum hair was cut stylishly short. It was one of those expensive cuts that, even when you roll out of bed in the morning, it looked good. She wore simple gold ear-rings and necklace, perfectly accenting her understated outfit. Her eyes studied me carefully, never leaving my face. Her smile seemed forced, though—a show of teeth but no warmth.

Charlie was the first to speak. "It's nice to meet you, Genie. We're with Galley Media. Our whole chain, all twenty-seven newspapers, picked up the story you did last year about those people murdered out on that island. That was impressive work."

"Thank you."

He continued. "And we're following your work on the kid-napping of the high school student by her teacher."

Faith jumped in. "Stories like that sell newspapers." Her voice was crisp and cold.

Charlie's smile broadened. "When I heard that Faith and I were coming down this way to meet with Ben, I wanted to make sure I had a chance to meet you too."

Maybe this…whatever this is…isn't so bad.

For the first time that morning, I grinned.

Faith's smile grew broader but it still struck me as being a fake. "Who knows?" she said. "Maybe we'll all get a chance to work together sometime soon."

I glanced at Ben who stood in the doorway, sheepishly look-ing back at me. "Okay, are you ready to see the pressroom?" he asked.

As they left, heading over to the attached three-story brick annex that housed our press, bindery, and paper storage warehouse, I looked up Galley Media on my computer. A publicly-traded company, they owned twelve television stations, ten radio stations, four magazines and—as the man had said—twenty-seven newspapers. Five of them had been acquired over the last year and a half, two within a seventy-mile radius of Sheffield.

It looked like Galley was having a growth spurt.

Are we next?

I once worked for a newspaper that was acquired by a chain. It was a train wreck. The new owners always talk a good game—better salaries, better benefits, better working conditions. But they do that at the sake of cutting local news and cutting pages, which means fewer local news reporters…and editors.

I glanced at the clock on my computer and nearly broke into a happy dance.

Time to meet Peter Cambridge.

Chapter Eighteen

I don't mind saying that I was still entertaining that tiny thrill while driving to Westport.

I've interviewed dozens of famous people during my career, including a coterie of well-known politicians, writers, artists, singers, actors, and actresses. I was always professional and almost never star-struck.

There were a couple of exceptions, like when I did a piece on Tom Hanks, I got embarrassingly tongue-tied. Same thing happened when I met Harrison Ford. But what can you expect? The man was both Han Solo and Indiana Jones.

Chill, Genie. Be cool.

Peter Cambridge was in that exclusive club. As I drove east on I-95, I could feel the butterfly wings tickle the inside of my stomach lining. I visualized him from the big screen, dangling from a forty-story office building, frantically trying to get inside to save his children. I was on my way to meet Peter Cambridge, the man who played Joe Scott in *Night Challenge*, the psychological thriller that beat out the superhero tripe at the box office that year. When I saw it at the theater, I felt like I was on a wild roller coaster ride, whipsawing back and forth from the action and incredible depth of emotion.

Cambridge was the star in a long line of successful films—*Kill Games, High Heeled, Too Quiet in This Room*, and, of course, the mega-hit—*Night Challenge*.

Angela Owens, his wife, was best known as the playwright for the Broadway hit *Agoraphobic Cocktail*. She'd never written a movie screenplay before. But she'd demonstrated her talent right out of the gate by penning the script for *Night Challenge* specifically for her husband.

At their height, they were the world's hottest couple, Hollywood rock stars.

Then they vanished. It was like they'd disappeared under a rock. No movies, no plays, no scripts, no interviews, no late-night television, no nothing.

Now, out of the blue, she'd written a new play that Peter Cambridge would star in, scheduled to open soon at the Sheffield Playhouse and, with luck, would eventually go to Broadway.

The first thing I saw when I found the address that Theresa had given me was the imposing, ivy-covered stone wall separating the compound from the neighborhood. A metal gate blocked the drive. My instructions were, once I got to the address, to text the number Theresa had given me to announce my arrival.

No sooner had I done that than the gate slowly opened inward, allowing me to drive into the compound. After a short journey along a tree-lined drive, I pulled my Sebring onto the circular parking area in front of the massive two-story Colonial Mediterranean home. With an attached glass serenity patio and multiple bay windows, the house was an example of clean modernity with an old-world feel to it.

The grounds were expansive and manicured, the perfection marred only by the hundreds of multi-colored leaves that had fallen from the dozens of hundred-year-old oak trees lording over the property.

In addition to my car, five other vehicles were parked in front of the house—a BMW, a Mercedes, a Corvette, a Range Rover, and a Bentley.

And then there was my beat-to-crap Sebring.

Before I got to the top step of the massive porch, the front door swung open and I was greeted by a tall man, easily six-four, wearing a cobalt blue shirt, open at the collar, black sport coat, and dark gray slacks. His face and his scalp were both cleanly shaven and he peered at me with intense blue eyes. His thin lips wore only the hint of a smile. "Are you Miss Chase?"

I quickly appraised him. He had a military bearing, standing ramrod straight, hands clasped behind his back, peering at me with interest.

"I am." I glanced at my watch. "I hope Mr. Cambridge still has a few minutes to see me."

"Both he and Ms. Owens are just finishing a meeting. They're about to break for lunch. Please come with me." He closed the door behind us and led the way across the dark-green Spanish-tile floor into an open living area. It was a huge room, populated with leather couches and chairs. Abstract art hung on the walls, white area rugs were scattered about on the floor. A large stone fireplace dominated the far wall. End tables were graced with flowers in silver vases.

Following him, I asked, "Do you work for Mr. Cambridge?"

He stopped, turned and looked me in the eye. "I'm sorry, how rude of me. My name's David LaSalle. I'm house security."

He began walking again and I said, "I see why they need you, it's a hell of a house."

Continuing along, he proudly ticked off its features. "Five bedrooms, seven fireplaces, five full baths, two half baths... three acres of land, six thousand square feet total. The flagstone patio is an additional two thousand square feet. We have two kitchens, one inside, of course, and one outside with a grill and wood-fired oven. There's a gym, a library, and three offices."

"No pool?"

He stopped in his tracks and gazed at me with a bemused expression. "A heated saltwater pool with a waterfall surrounded by a mahogany deck."

David continued to lead as I remarked, "How silly of me. Just out of curiosity, what does something like this go for?"

Was I being gauche?

David LaSalle didn't seem to think so. I believe he was bragging. "Peter and Angela bought this place five years ago for a little over ten million. If they put it back on the market today, I'd guess it would go for around fourteen."

I allowed myself a low whistle. Then I asked, "How big is the staff here?"

He chuckled. "Minimal. Me, of course. Angela's personal assistant, Sarah, and the cook, Mrs. Scolie."

"Do they all live here?"

"Everyone except for Mrs. Scolie."

"Does Mr. Cambridge have a personal assistant?"

He glanced back at me again. "He's a very private person. I guess I'm as close to a personal assistant that he has."

David brought us into a bright, open room with imposing wooden beams and spacious windows that offered a stunning view of the grounds behind the house. There were still vestiges of autumnal foliage but the naked branches of the massive oaks and maple trees rose against the gray, overcast sky in silent supplication, like bony fingers scratching at the clouds. Steam rose lazily off the heated outdoor pool and waterfall.

Seven people sat at a polished teak table. Coffee cups, files, and open notebooks were spread out in front of them. Some were dressed in suits and ties, some in jeans and tee-shirts.

I saw Peter Cambridge straight away. Sitting at the head of the table, he looked up at me when David and I walked through the doorway, and I thought my heart would stop on the spot.

God in heaven, he looks even better in person than he does in the movies.

Yes, I was star-struck.

No, he didn't look like how I remembered him from his last movie. His boyish good looks had matured, become more rugged, masculine. I knew he was in his late forties, his brown hair was longer than in his last film, over the tops of his ears, and shot through with streaks of gray. In every movie I'd seen, he had a sexy two-day stubble, but now he wore a full salt-and-pepper beard.

All I wanted to do was get up close and stroke it like a puppy.

He wore a long-sleeved tee-shirt with a New England Patriots logo on the chest along with distressed, faded jeans and leather sandals.

It was his eyes that always got to me when I saw him in a film. And they were looking straight at me, bedroom eyes, a light gray, gazing at me intently under heavy lids. When he smiled, it was the same thousand-watt grin that lit up the screen at the end of *Night Challenge*.

He beamed at me like he'd known me his entire life and we'd been apart for far too long.

I could literally feel my heart thumping in my chest.

The actor stood to greet me. I was surprised to see that he and I are almost the same height.

Huh, he looks taller in the movies.

"Miss Chase, it's so nice to meet you. Theresa told us that you're working with the police to help find her granddaughter." He shook my hand, putting both of his warmly over my own.

I will never wash that hand again...what, what am I doing? Stop it, stop it, stop it. Quit acting like a freaking teenager. Get a grip.

"Thank you, Mr. Cambridge, for taking time to see me."

"Oh, please, call me Peter."

I felt myself blush. "Okay, call me Genie."

A woman stood up and walked toward me. "We read your story in this morning's paper. The police think that Bobbi ran off with Jake Addison?"

I recognized her immediately as Peter's wife, Angela Owens. I'd seen her in a spread in *People* magazine. She was about the same height as her husband and wore her brown hair long, brushed back. Her bright hazel eyes never left my face as she approached me.

She wasn't a classic beauty. Angela Owens was more of a girl-next-door. Her pert nose and cheeks were spotted with freckles. The only thing glamorous about her was what she was wearing—an oversized brown turtleneck, gold necklace, hoop earrings, black leggings, and leather boots

Oh, and wearing black horn-rimmed nerd glasses that whispered, "I'm an intellectual and a writer."

Pull in the claws, Geneva. You just met the woman and already you're jealous.

I answered her question about Bobbi and her teacher. "I'm afraid so. There's video of her getting into his car."

She frowned. "Pity, she's so talented. Appearing with Peter was going to be the biggest break of her life. To throw it all away is tragic."

"If she's found, you won't let her back into the production?"

She quickly shook her head. "Dear God, no. The play would be notorious for all the wrong reasons."

Peter then spoke, his voice low and serious. "That's why we're having this meeting. We're assessing how much damage she's done."

Angela spoke up. "Let me introduce you to everyone." She ticked off the names of the group at the table. "Sam Buckner, our set designer; Joan Lazarus, musical director; Michael Rice, our publicist; and Larry Cameron, our social media specialist."

As she introduced them, they'd smile, raise their coffee cup and then go back to discussing the subject at hand.

Before Angela finished introducing everyone, a man yet to be named, stood up and came to us. He was of average height, trim, in his thirties, clean-shaven, bright green eyes, brown hair slicked straight back on his head. He wore a dour expression as well as a crisp, designer starched-white, button-down shirt and a red tie.

While Peter made me think of a rugged teddy bear, this man conjured up a vision of a slick weasel.

Peter nodded toward the man. "Geneva Chase, meet our producer, Morgan Stiles."

"Miss Chase," he responded. "I overheard part of the conversation. Bobbi Jarvis will never be part of this production. What she's done is unforgivable. If we don't get a replacement quickly, we're going to have a very difficult time being in New York by next spring."

I'd read about Morgan Stiles. I recalled that he had been the angel investor in a number of Broadway shows—some successful, some not. He was rich by anybody's standards, having inherited a small fortune from his father and then, through savvy real estate deals, turning it into a massive fortune.

There were rumors he was thinking about getting into New York politics.

"We were just getting ready to break for lunch. Would you like to join us?" Peter asked, his voice filled with mellifluous honey. "We can move to that table over there." He nodded with his jaw toward the other end of the room. "It'll give us a little more privacy."

I nearly giggled with pleasure. Instead, I cleared my throat. "Yes, thank you. I'd like that very much."

Angela turned to her associates at the table and said, "Let's take a break. We start again after lunch."

We strolled to the far end of the room to a table seating four, overlooking the broad expanse of lawn, the salt-water pool, and the trees beyond.

I offered, "You have a beautiful home."

Angela acknowledged me with a curt nod.

Peter flashed me a generous grin.

Angela, all business, asked, "How can we help you?"

Then Peter echoed, "Yes, Genie, how can we help you?"

I felt myself blush again. "When's the last time you saw Bobbi?"

"This past Sunday at rehearsal," Peter answered.

"Where do you rehearse?"

"The Sheffield Playhouse."

"Did she seem okay? Did she say anything was bothering her?"

Peter answered. "She seemed fine. She was eager to come back Monday night to run through more of her lines. We became concerned when she didn't show up. We really got spooked when Theresa called us and asked if she was at the theater. That's when she told us she didn't know where Bobbi was."

Angela glanced out the window. "We were very concerned. Now that we know she's with that pervert, Jake Addison…" Her voice trailed off and she shrugged.

The producer pointed a finger at me. "We did a lot to accommodate that kid, and then she repays us by running off and shacking up with that two-bit, talentless drama coach."

"We were rehearsing most of our scenes, at least the ones with Bobbi's character in them, in the evening so Bobbi could attend her classes at the high school," Angela explained.

"Was there an understudy for Bobbi's part?"

The three of them exchanged glances.

Morgan spoke up. "Bad luck there too. Tracey Fine, student at the college. An eighteen-year-old girl who looked like she was fifteen."

Peter's voice was little more than a whisper. "Two weeks ago, she died of a drug overdose."

I recalled editing a piece that Darcie had written. The police said she'd OD'd on Fentanyl, an opioid a hundred times more potent than morphine. The family didn't know who had given it to her. Her mother had found Tracey in her bedroom, unresponsive, when she hadn't gotten up to go to class.

A woman in her sixties came into the room carrying a tray of ceramic soup bowls and cutlery. Close behind her followed David LaSalle with two folding tray stands.

"That's Mrs. Scolie," Peter whispered, tight to my ear. "She's been with us for years. She makes the best stuffed peppers in the world."

Having his lips so close to me made my heart flutter.

David set up the tray stands and left the room. Mrs. Scolie

expertly placed a bowl on the table in front of each one of us along with spoons and knives. I noted that there were no forks.

Peter looked up at her and asked, "What are we having?"

She had hair pinned up on her head. She hadn't let it go gray. Instead, it was a rust-colored auburn, the kind you get in a bottle.

The kind they found in Jake Addison's apartment.

Mrs. Scolie had a round face and gentle eyes and was dressed in black slacks and a white short-sleeved top. She glanced at us and smiled. "It's cold out there today, so I thought I'd make you something hearty. It's my *Coq au vin de Bourgogne.*"

Peter rubbed his hands together and leaned into me. "Melt in your mouth. You came on the right day."

His enthusiasm was almost childlike.

David LaSalle brought in a steaming porcelain tureen and placed it in the middle of our table with a ladle. "This one's for you," he said, glancing at Angela. "I'll bring another for the folks at the conference table."

I noticed that she gave him a half-smile in return.

Peter pointed to the thick stew. "Genie, how about you go first?"

As I ladled out a healthy portion, savoring the deliciously earthy scent, Mrs. Scolie came by with a basket of warm bread. Smiling, she said to me, "Fresh out of the oven. Don't be afraid to dip it into the coq au vin, honey."

David came back into the room with a second tureen for the others at the larger table. Then he stopped by where we sat and asked, "Can I get you all something? Water? More coffee? Wine?"

I smiled up at him. "Just water for me. I'm on the clock."

Peter waved his hand. "Nonsense. David, can you bring us a red? A Southern Rhone would go perfectly with this."

"Absolutely."

Angela and Morgan both mumbled that they'd have more coffee.

Once everyone had filled their bowls, I tasted the coq au vin. Mrs. Scolie had been correct. It was the perfect item for a cold autumn day. Coupled with the red wine that David brought to the table, sitting there talking with Peter Cambridge, it was an afternoon I'd brag about for the rest of my life.

I sipped the muscular red and turned to Angela. "I understand you wrote the play. What's it about?"

"It's called *Darkness Lane*. Have you ever heard the line 'We must pass through darkness, to reach the light'?"

"Sounds familiar."

"It's by Albert Pike. *Darkness Lane* is about redemption. But it's also about how we sometimes must crawl through a black, soul-sucking hell before we can find it. And what the people around you must endure along the way."

"With all due respect, it sounds a little depressing."

Peter's face lit up. "And it would be." He glanced at his wife and beamed. "But Angela has written an absolutely brilliant piece. Oh, it's dark and brooding, but she's infused it with such wit and occasional flashes of humor and irony, that it doesn't descend into depression. There's always that prize, sometimes just out of reach, of hope. We're always stretching for it, grasping for it. I'm not going to give it away, but the ending is absolute genius."

Angela smiled at her husband. "Peter's character is a self-absorbed, alcoholic novelist. He's also the father of a teenage daughter. Mona Fountain plays the mother who is a psychologist having an illicit, self-destructive affair. Have you heard of Mona?"

"Isn't she on *Hell's Highway?*"

I knew she was the lead in a series on one of the streaming channels. The show had something to do with Mona Fountain being a suburban mom doing battle with supernatural forces.

Or some kind of zombie bullshit like that. I don't watch much television.

Morgan cleared his throat and remarked. "Mona is the queen of social media. She has over a million followers on Twitter. Anytime she gets her photo taken, the Internet goes frickin' nuts. This play has everything going for it. Mona Fountain, Peter Cambridge, a brilliant script from Angela. It's a lock that we'll take it all the way to Broadway. For a young unknown actress like Bobbi Jarvis, it's the part of a lifetime."

Angela jumped in. "We're planning on opening in Sheffield on November fourteenth. We know we'll get stellar reviews. We're already fishing for investors to open on Broadway by April."

Morgan blew on his coffee to cool it. "Except we're stalled. We've got no teenage daughter."

"My daughter auditioned for that part."

Did I really blurt that out?

My heart lodged firmly in my throat as they all stared at me.

Peter raised an eyebrow. "She did? What's her name?"

"Caroline Bell."

Morgan's eyes got wide and he suddenly stood up and dashed to the table where the others were sitting. He picked up a notebook and brought it back with him. "Caroline Bell?"

"Yeah, do you remember her?"

Peter glanced at Morgan and Angela, then turned and faced me. "Caroline Bell?" he repeated.

"Yes."

Morgan held up the notebook. "She was nearly neck and neck with Bobbi Jarvis as far as getting the part."

My heart began to thump. "Really?"

Morgan took a laptop off the conference table and placed it on ours, the screen facing where I sat. It took him a moment to find what he was looking for, but then I saw Caroline come up. She was reading lines from a script that she'd just been handed.

Peter whispered, "Listen to this."

I watched as Caroline read from the pages she held, her voice breaking, "Daddy, I'm begging you to stop drinking. You're going to lose Mom and you're going to lose me. Is that what you want? You're trashing your life and, goddamn it to hell, I'm not going to let you trash mine." She looked defiantly into the camera. "I have worth, I have value. Show me that you do, too."

The words were sharp, sad and bitter all at the same time. I almost thought I could hear her saying those lines to me.

It would fit, wouldn't it?

The three of them eyed each other, while the girl on the laptop ran more lines. Peter reached out and paused the scene, saying, "What do you guys think?"

Angela shrugged. "What do we have to lose? We liked her."

Morgan looked at me. "How soon could she start rehearsals?"

"Really? I'd have to ask her. But I'm pretty sure she could start this weekend."

Peter clapped his hands together. "What are the odds? What are the fucking odds?"

Morgan sat back in his chair. "I think I'll have some of that wine now."

On top of an awesome lunch, on top of Caroline getting the part in *Darkness Lane*, Peter by-God Cambridge personally walked me to the front door of his magnificent mansion.

"Thank you for a wonderful afternoon." I glanced at him as we strolled leisurely though the house.

"My pleasure, Genie." His smile was genuine.

Suddenly, it occurred to me that an important point of information I wanted had been forgotten. "Peter, I understand that Jake Addison auditioned for the play but didn't get the part."

Approaching the front door, he stroked his beard. "He did. He auditioned for the part of Mona's secret lover. Did you know that at one time, he was the lead in an off-Broadway musical?"

I shook my head. "I didn't know that."

"Off-off-off Broadway." He chuckled. "It ran for maybe two weeks before it folded. Anyway, I'll bet it got him the gig as drama coach over there in Sheffield."

"But he didn't make the cut for *Darkness Lane*?"

He smiled sadly. "Jake's talents skew more toward screwball comedies than serious drama. He just doesn't know how not to be funny. I've heard Bobbi say that's why the kids at school love him. Hell, what's not to like? I love him. Or I did. Right up until he ran off with our star."

"Did you know that Jake Addison called Bobbi's grandmother last Sunday?"

He frowned. "No. What about?"

"Jake said that he thought Bobbi was in over her head. That her schoolwork was suffering. And that he strongly urged Theresa to pull Bobbi out of the production."

He turned and looked at me. His voice was a soft purr. "I'm so sorry to hear that. I'm afraid that Jake was being childish and was lashing out because he didn't get the part. But Bobbi's a natural. She was quick to memorize her lines. She was comfortable on stage. She took direction well. Bobbi Jarvis doesn't just wear the part, when she's on that stage, she becomes the embodiment of that character. The girl was most certainly not in over her head."

He stepped ahead of me and opened the door, daylight flooding into the hallway. "I'm looking forward to working with Caroline."

"She's going to be thrilled."

"And I'm looking forward to seeing more of you, Genie." He smiled, pulled me close and kissed me on the cheek.

I nearly melted into the floor.

Chapter Nineteen

As I left the house, the skin on my cheek where Peter's lips had lingered felt hot to the touch.

Or is that my imagination?

I drove out of the actor's compound and got back on I-95, heading for Sheffield. I wasn't certain I'd accomplished anything from a journalistic point of view, but I'd managed to help Caroline snag one hell of an acting gig.

Thinking about it again, my first instinct was to drive over to her school to tell her. Deciding that it would be better to celebrate at home, I kept driving.

That's when I noticed that there was a black Ford pickup truck directly behind me.

It looked a lot like the same truck that goon was driving last night when I got the visit from Eric Decker in the company parking lot. The front flat-black bumper guard gave it a belligerent look—like a bulldog with an underbite.

Am I being followed?

I got off on the Saugatuck Avenue Exit and watched my rearview mirror.

The truck followed.

Are you the asshole that fired a shot through my window?

The truck was too far back for me to see who was driving it.

I thought about calling Mike, but what did I really know? That some guy in a truck was behind me? I think I'm being followed?

I'm certain that's the same ape from last night.

For a moment, I considered trying to lose him, but then I remembered what I was driving. No way my Sebring would outrun that powerful engine. And what difference would it make? Whoever it was already knew where I worked and where I lived.

But thinking about someone firing a gun into my front window, where it could have hit one of us…could have hit Caroline…pissed me off.

So, I let him follow me into Sheffield, I let him follow me down to the south side of town. He stayed far enough back that I couldn't get a good look at the driver's face, but close enough that his presence was known. He wasn't trying to hide.

I pulled into the visitors' lot of the Sheffield Police Station and parked.

The truck turned into the parking area and drove slowly past my back bumper. I watched as he cruised to the end of the lot, turned around, and then drove back, stopping right behind my car, blocking my way.

I glanced around the parking lot. Two cops were standing by one of their cruisers, chatting, ignoring me and the pickup.

I'm safe, right? If I do something stupid? I mean, cops are right here.

I pulled my tiny container of pepper spray out of my bag and stuck it in my jacket pocket, then stepped out of my car onto the parking lot. I was facing the driver's side but the windows were tinted. I couldn't tell who was inside or even if the driver was looking back at me.

I stayed by my car.

The driver's side window slid silently down.

It was as if I was staring into the face of a massive Rottweiler—huge forehead, wide-set black eyes that were little more than slits, flat nose, square chin, thin lips. His black hair was buzzed tight to his scalp and he had a dark five o'clock shadow on the lower half of his face. His size was surprising, his head, shoulders, torso filled the cab of the pickup truck. He was wearing the same black leather jacket he had on last night.

His lips curled into a sneer.

"Are you following me?" I glanced over at the cops. They were still ignoring us.

His voice was deep, as if it were coming from inside a crypt, but his words were clear. "Betsy Caviness." There was the hint of an accent.

"What about her?"

"Where is she?"

"I already told your lawyer buddy that I don't know where she is. And I wouldn't tell you if I did."

His tongue snaked out and he ran it across his lower lip.

Gross.

"You have a daughter," he rumbled.

Those words chilled me right down to my marrow. It was a statement, not a question.

"Listen to me," I hissed. "You stay away from her."

His ugly grin grew broader and he raised his right hand, closed his fist except for two fingers and simulating a pistol, aimed it at my face. "We want the notebook."

I glanced at the two cops who, ignorant of what was happening, had turned and were walking through the front doors of the police station.

The driver's side window slid silently back up and the truck rolled forward, pulling out onto the road into traffic.

I could feel my heart racing. My emotions were whipsawing back and forth from anger to fear and back again.

That son of a bitch just threatened Caroline.

Before I left the parking lot, I deliberated about going into the station and telling Mike what had just happened. I could hear his voice in my head saying that he couldn't do anything.

There's no law against pointing your finger at someone.

Instead, seething, I drove to my office where I found a young man sitting in my cubicle, waiting for me.

"Can I help you?" I asked while dropping my bag on the floor, shedding my jacket and hanging it on the back of my desk chair.

He stood up. "Are you Geneva Chase?"

The kid couldn't be any more than sixteen. He was dressed in blue jeans, Nikes, and a white-tee under an unbuttoned long-sleeved flannel shirt. His brown hair was shaved on the sides and long on top, brushed forward, hiding his forehead. The boy had a silver lip ring that looked painful to me.

Except for the face jewelry, he was a handsome boy with even features and soulful brown eyes.

"Yeah, I'm Geneva Chase. Who are you?"

He held out his hand for me to shake. "Tommy Willis. I read your story online about Bobbi and Jake."

We shook hands and I recalled how Mike had called him a white-boy wannabe thug.

Not sure that's how I'd describe him.

"Sit down. What can I do for you?"

We both sat and he answered. "Your story says that everyone thinks they ran off together."

"Yeah?" I let my eyes drift to the screen of my computer, scanning the list of e-mails I needed to answer.

"I don't think that's what happened."

"Oh, no?"

"No, Bobbi wasn't interested in Jake that way. She liked him as a teacher and a friend."

"Have you told the cops that?"

He developed a sly smile. "No, the cops and I don't get along very well."

"Did Bobbi tell you that she only liked Mr. Addison as a teacher and a friend?"

"Yes."

I looked away from my computer and gazed directly into the boy's face. "How old are you?"

"Sixteen."

Sixteen. I shouldn't even be talking to this kid without parental consent.

But he came to see me.

"Did Bobbi like that ring?" I pointed toward his lip.

He reached up and touched it with his fingertips. "She said it made me look like a badass."

I sat back in my chair. "How long were you and Bobbi together?"

He leaned forward, his hands clasped together. "For a long time. Four months."

"Who wanted to break up?"

"She did." Tommy's eyes went to the carpet. He was ashamed that she had dumped him.

"Was it because of another boy?"

He shook his head.

"Why then?"

His face came up and he glared at me. "That goddamned play." It came out a snarl. "Just as soon as she got the part she went all diva on everyone."

Went all diva. I wondered if that would happen with Caroline when I told her *she* got the part.

Tommy continued. "All she wanted to talk about was the play and Peter Cambridge and Angela Owens and Mona Fountain, blah, blah, blah."

I blurted out my next question. "Did you and Bobbi ever have sex?"

His face turned crimson, his eyes were wide and wary. He didn't answer.

"Don't worry. I won't tell anyone."

"You're a reporter. I don't want it to get into the newspaper."

I smiled. "Tommy, two kids having sex isn't front page news."

I'd never tell that to Caroline.

He struggled to get the words out. "Yes, a couple of times."

I sighed. "Use protection?"

He looked at me brightly. "Condoms."

"Good."

It took me a moment to frame my next question because of its delicate nature. "I know you say that they're only friends, but is it possible that Bobbi and Jake may have had sex?"

Tommy chuckled and shook his head.

"What's so funny?"

"Bobbi told me. Jake's gay. Up until recently, he's been seeing Bobbi's father."

Chapter Twenty

The ramifications of Tommy's last two sentences raced wildly through my mind. If true, that meant there was a direct connection between Adam Jarvis and Jake Addison. Was Adam's murder somehow a result of Bobbi and Jake's disappearance? Or vice versa?

And if it's not Jake, who is in the video?

I asked Tommy one more question. "Did you and Bobbi ever video yourselves?"

His face flushed a deeper red than before. "Yes."

"Having sex?"

"Yes." His voice was barely audible.

"Why?"

"Bobbi said she wanted to see what she looked like…you know…while we were doing it."

Narcissism in the Jarvis DNA?

I gave him a small smile. "Romantic." I was pretty sure I'd kept all the sarcasm out of my voice as I said it.

After Tommy Willis left, I toyed with the idea of calling Mike Dillon. Instead, I slipped on my jacket, grabbed my bag, and went out the back door.

I stopped and stood for a moment on the concrete landing everyone used as their smoking lounge. Looking out over the parking lot, I was satisfied there were no shady lawyers in Jaguars and no evil-looking men in big trucks.

Fifteen minutes later, I was parked in front of Jake Addison's place.

The first thing I noticed about the old Victorian was that the police tape was gone.

I climbed the steps and onto the old wooden porch. It could have used a good coat of paint. The front door was locked, so I cupped my hands around my face and peeked through the glass in the door.

All I could see was a carpeted hallway and closed doors to the ground-floor apartments.

I stepped back and turned around, taking a moment to look up and down the street.

No black truck.

Shana's words came back to me.

You can't be too paranoid.

I walked back down the steps and stepped out into the yard, staring up at the old house. Spying the driveway at the side of the building, I followed it into the tiny parking area in back. Only one car, a Toyota Camry, was back there.

I surmised that the other people who lived in the house were all working their day jobs.

Except for Jake Addison, who was in New York City with Bobbi Jarvis?

I climbed up a set of concrete steps leading to a door. Holding my hand up to block out the ash-drab daylight, I peered through the glass into someone's kitchen.

I knocked.

No answer.

I knocked louder.

A face peeked around the doorjamb at the other end of the room. A woman emerged, limped slowly on a cane across the kitchen and opened the door for me. "Can I help you?"

She was in her late seventies and tiny, barely over five feet tall. Her curly white hair was sparse and her blue eyes twinkled behind wire-framed glasses. She wore a bright, floral top, buttoned at the collar and wrists, beige slacks pulled high up above her waist, and white Reeboks. Standing in the doorway, I could see she had a slight stoop to her posture and leaned in to hear me.

"Are you the owner of this house?" I asked.

She frowned. "If you're selling something, I'm not interested."

As she began to close the door, I put my hand out. "No, no, no. I'm sorry. I'm Genie Chase with the *Sheffield Post*."

She shook her head. "I already subscribe. Though there's nothin' but bad news in there. Why don't you people ever print good news?"

I felt myself smile. "Ma'am, I'm a reporter. I'd like to ask you a few questions, if you don't mind."

She stared at me with curiosity. "A reporter, huh? Questions about Jake Addison?"

"Yes, ma'am. How did you know?"

She grinned, false teeth gleaming. "That's all anyone around here wants to talk about."

"Do you know have any idea where he is?"

She appraised me, her lips pressed tight against each other. "I'll tell you what I told the cops: 'Nope. Got no idea.' Want to come in for a cup of coffee?"

She reminded me of my deceased grandmother. Starved for company, she'd invite everyone and anyone into her house for a visit—repairmen, Girl Scouts selling cookies, Jehovah's Witnesses.

I came into the kitchen and immediately noticed the rise in temperature. Air temp outside was in the mid-thirties. Indoors it had to be at least seventy-eight degrees and it smelled like bread was baking.

I walked across a chipped red linoleum floor. Cheap paneling lined the walls, the veneer on some of the countertops was curling at the corners, and a couple of the tiles in the ceiling were stained brown. This apartment had seen better days.

But it was tidy and clean. There were no dishes in the sink, the counters were clear, and the floor was swept.

The appliances were a lime green that was fashionable decades ago, the refrigerator was pockmarked with magnets, and I could see by a tiny red light on the stove that the oven was on.

"Whatever you're baking smells delicious. Mind if I take off my jacket?"

She smiled. "Oh, sourdough bread. Just hang your coat off the back of the chair over there." She motioned toward one of the wooden chairs at her kitchen table. "How do you take your coffee?"

"Black, please."

She turned, opened a cupboard door, and with slow deliberation, took out a mug. "What did you say your name was again?"

"Genie Chase."

As she poured coffee into my mug, the woman turned her head slightly and gave me a look over the top of her glasses. "I'm Maggie Routson."

She handed me the mug and I took a sip. It was good, but then again, I'm always comparing any caffeine I ingest to the crap we have at the office. "Thank you. Nice to meet you, Maggie. So, a lot of folks have been here asking about Jake Addison?"

She sat down at the table. "School principal been here lookin' for him. Cops are lookin' for him. I figured, member of the press shows up at my doorstep, you must be lookin' for him, too."

I smiled at her. "Yes, ma'am."

Maggie shook her head. "Not like him to go someplace and not tell me. I'm the one that collects his mail and waters his plants for him when he goes on vacation."

I got a tingle. "You have a key to his apartment?"

"Sure do. Jake helps me out when I need some heavy liftin' done around here. I'm not as young as I used to be." She smiled. "Gets me groceries a couple of times a week so's I don't have to go out. And in return, if he needs to go out of town on a conference or to visit his friends in the city, I water his plants and get his mail."

"He has friends in the city?"

"That's what he says."

"Do you know who they are?"

She thought a moment and slowly shook her head. "Don't think he ever told me."

"Are you the one who let the police in to search Jake's apartment?"

Maggie took a sip of her coffee before she answered. "Yes, they were all very sweet. I made chocolate chip cookies yesterday and made sure they took some home with them when they were through."

"Would you mind if I took a look?" I asked.

Maggie hesitated. "I don't know."

I held up my right hand. "I swear I won't touch anything."

"Guess you can't make any more of a mess than the police did."

Maggie had been correct. The police had left the place a wreck. Drawers had been pulled out of the kitchen cabinets and emptied. Books had been removed from the shelves and unceremoniously dumped on the living room carpet. The blankets and sheets had been stripped from the bed and, the way the bare mattress was askew, it was obvious that the police had checked underneath it. Sofa cushions were stacked on top of one another on the floor.

I wasn't sure what I was looking for. And in that mess, even if I knew, I wasn't sure I'd find it.

Maggie gazed around her. "Poor Jake. Guess I'll try to straighten things up as best I can before he gets back."

I'm sure that before the cops got to it, the apartment had

been cozy. Posters of movies and Broadway productions hung on the walls. Dark green curtains framed windows that overlooked the street in front of the apartment house. A recliner sat in front of a large-screen television tucked neatly into an entertainment center. There was an old-fashioned record player with dozens of vinyl records placed on wooden shelves.

Sitting near one of the windows was a five-foot-tall yucca plant rooted in a ceramic pot.

Maggie caught me staring at the plant. "Jake calls it Seymour. He says it reminds him of a musical he was in back in New York."

I recalled that Peter Cambridge had told me Jake had a part in an Off-Broadway production. From what Maggie said, I guessed it must have been *Little Shop of Horrors*, a play about a man-eating plant owned by a mild-mannered man named Seymour.

I poked my head into the kitchen—so tiny that two people would have been a crowd. He had a stove, refrigerator, microwave, and counter space, but not much room to turn around. By the way two barstools were positioned, I guessed he ate his meals at the counter, right in front of a window that gave him a view of the house next door.

On the kitchen windowsill sat an African violet and an aloe plant. Both seemed well cared for.

There was a coffee cup, a bowl, and a single spoon sitting in the sink. The counter space was empty except for a drip coffeemaker with a glass pot that was half-empty.

"I should probably clean that," Maggie said, once again following my line of sight.

"Did Jake keep his apartment tidy?"

Maggie beamed. "He was fastidious."

"Not the kind of person who would leave dirty dishes in the sink if he was going on a trip?"

"Doesn't sound like Jake. Of course, none of this sounds like Jake. I can't imagine he would take off with one of his students. Jake had a boyfriend."

I looked at her. "Did you meet him?"

"Oh, yes, he was over here a couple of times." She leaned in close and whispered, "He spent the night."

"Did Jake tell you his name?"

Maggie concentrated. "I'm not as good with names as I used to be. Starts with an 'A'…Alan, Andy…"

"Adam?"

She grinned and pointed at me. "That's it, Adam. But I think maybe they broke up."

"Why's that?"

"I haven't seen him around here for a couple of weeks. Jake said that his boyfriend…that still sounds funny, doesn't it? A man having a boyfriend?"

I glanced at Maggie. In the seven plus decades she'd lived through, she must have seen a lot of changes. But I was pleased at how accepting she was of Jake. "What did Jake say about his boyfriend?" I needed her back on track.

"Oh, yes, that he was having money troubles and he kept asking Jake for loans. I don't think Jake had any extra money to loan him."

We returned to Maggie's apartment, where I collected my jacket and bag, then walked out Maggie's kitchen doorway and back into the cold. The clouds had grown darker. Hitching up the collar of my jacket, I walked around the house to the curb where my car was parked.

Before I got in, I glanced up and down the quiet street again.

My breath caught in my throat.

A black pickup sat idling just up the block, exhaust trailing lazily into the air. *That bastard isn't letting this go.*

Chapter Twenty-one

While I drove, I kept glancing up into my rearview mirror.

Every time I did, I caught sight of the black pickup staying at least two vehicles behind me. He wasn't being obvious, but he wasn't invisible, either.

No, he wanted me to know he was there. He was trying to intimidate me, pure and simple.

I plucked my cellphone off the passenger's seat and punched up Mike's personal number.

Seeing me on his caller ID he answered, "Hey, Genie."

"Three things: Did you know that Adam Jarvis and Jake Addison had been in a relationship?"

I could hear the stunned silence. After a few heartbeats, Mike asked, "What kind of relationship?"

"Well, Adam's ex-wife told me that he was bisexual and Bobbi told Tommy Willis that Jake was not only gay, but was having an affair with her father. I stopped by Jake's apartment and his neighbor corroborated it. You figure out what kind of relationship."

There was another silence while Mike processed the new information. "That throws some doubt on Jake being in the video. But it doesn't discount it completely."

I saw the traffic light ahead of me turn yellow, stole a glance in the mirror, and stepped down on the gas, heard my engine growl, felt the car jerk forward, sailing through the intersection just as the light was turning red.

Looking up in my rearview mirror, I saw truck boy was stuck at the light behind a Volvo SUV.

Heart hammering, my adrenaline level had increased exponentially with the amount of gas I'd applied.

I took a deep breath and willed my heart rate back to normal.

Don't let Mike hear it in your voice.

"That brings me to the second thing I wanted to tell you. Tommy Willis came to see me today."

"He skipped school, nice."

"Relax, tiger. He told me that when he and Bobbi Jarvis were boyfriend and girlfriend, they'd had sex a few times."

"Don't tell me he knocked her up."

"No, they used protection. But on one of those occasions, they videoed themselves."

Yet another stunned silence. Then, "Are you saying that the male in that video is Tommy Willis?"

"Could be."

"Why on earth would Jake Addison have possession of it?"

"Might be it was Bobbi's, and she left it behind."

"So, if Jake's gay, why did the two of them run off together?"

"Good question." I came up to the intersection where I'd need to turn onto Westchester Avenue, but this time didn't get a favorable light. I was stopped at the red.

"You said there were three things you wanted to tell me."

I had planned on telling Mike about the goon following me around in the pickup truck. But instead, I just said, "No, that's it."

"What were you doing at Addison's apartment?"

"Just nosing around, Mike. It's what I do."

"Find anything?" He knew that his team had swept the apartment clean of any evidence.

"Nope, you kids took anything of interest and left a hell of a mess."

"Be careful, Genie."

"Always."

I hit the End Call button and punched up another number.

"Geneva Chase?" Her voice was low, words precisely enunciated.

"Shana Neese, do you remember when you told me you can never be too paranoid?"

The light turned green and I eased into a turn, taking a left onto Westchester Avenue. The truck was nowhere to be seen.

"Yes?"

"I've been followed most of today by a guy in an unmarked black pickup truck. I confronted him in the parking lot of the Sheffield Police Station. He wants me to find Betsy Caviness. More specifically, he wants the notebook."

"Did he threaten you?"

"My daughter, obliquely. He just said, 'You have a daughter,' then pointed his finger at my head as if it was a pistol."

"What did he look like?"

I was coming up to the *Sheffield Post* parking lot. "Big. One of the biggest guys I've ever seen. Head like a cinderblock. Buzz cut, tiny eyes, thin lips, massive jaw, nasty five o'clock shadow."

"Bogdan Tolbonov. They really want to get their claws on Miss Betsy. You rarely see him on the street."

"For good reason. He's scary lookin'. Shana, it's one thing if someone threatens me. In my line of work, it happens more often than you might think. But I'm not good with someone threatening my daughter." I took a right turn into the company lot, drove down the alley, and into the employee parking area. I was relieved not to see any trucks or Jags back there.

"How about I send someone to keep an eye on you?"

"What do you mean?"

"Do you remember the man in the parking lot of the Metro Sheffield who checked to make sure you weren't being followed?"

"Yes." I pulled into a spot and turned off the engine.

"I'll send him to watch out for you. You'll like him. His name's John Stillwater. He's an ex-cop."

"Let me take that under consideration."

There was a moment of silence, as if Shana was expecting me to say something else. Finally, she said, "Okay, let me know. But be careful."

It was the same thing Mike had told me only moments before.

●　●　●　●　●

As I got to my cubicle and took off my jacket, Darcie rushed into my office. "What's up?" I asked.

"I was going to ask you the same thing." She sat down uninvited in one of my office chairs. "Everybody's wondering who the two people are in Ben's office. They've been in there all day with the door closed."

Involuntarily, I glanced up and saw that she was right.

Was it possible that the two corporate predators from Galley Media were still in the building? I glanced at my watch. I'd met them shortly before noon and it was nearly four o'clock.

Ben Sumner, you'd better not be signing away my career.

They hadn't asked me to keep any secrets for them so I told Darcie who they were. "They're from Galley Media. I've got a feeling they're going to be our new owners."

Darcie looked stunned, unconsciously rubbing her stomach. I knew what she was thinking. What changes would they make? Would she keep her job? Would she have health insurance when she gave birth?

"Hey, look," I said, "this is all going to work out, okay? Don't worry about it. Just keep working."

"Yeah, yeah," was all she could get out.

I regretted telling her about the sale.

Everyone is going to find out sooner or later.

After she left, I noticed that the red light to my voice mail was blinking. I listened, surprised. "Hey, Genie Chase. It's Peter Cambridge. You know, I don't have your cellphone yet, so

I called your office. I hope you don't mind. I had our attorney get a contract together for Caroline. I'd like to go over it with you if you have time. There are details that I need to get from you—her social security number, date of birth. And, as her mother, I need you to sign a waiver. Can you call me on my cell?"

And then Peter Cambridge gave me his personal cellphone number. Forgetting all else, I called him on the newspaper landline.

He must have recognized the number because he started out, "Is this Genie?"

"Yes, it is," I answered, slightly out of breath.

"Excellent. You got my message. Thank you for calling me back."

"My pleasure." And it *really* was.

"I'd like to get some paperwork taken care of and I'd love to do it sooner rather than later."

"Of course."

Whatever you want, Peter Cambridge.

He asked, "What are the chances that we can get together after work?"

"What time are you thinking about?"

With the tiniest bit of hesitation, Peter answered. "Well, what about dinner? Say seven?"

Yes.

"Got someplace in mind?"

"I feel like Latin. Do you like Latin?"

"*Muy bien.*"

"Do you know where Orinoco is? They do a mean Latin-Caribbean fusion."

"Absolutely. Will anyone else be joining us?" I was thinking specifically of Angela Owens.

"No, I'm afraid you'll have to put up with just me." He chuckled.

I smiled and my voice dropped. "I'll see you there at seven."

After he hung up, it took all my self-reserve to keep from jumping up and down in another happy dance.

But as elated as I was, my mood blackened almost immediately when I saw the door to Ben's office swing open and he and the two corporate drones appeared. All three were grinning broadly. Ben shook Charlie Johnson's hand first and then Faith Blair's. The two of them slid into their overcoats and, carrying their briefcases, walked briskly toward the front exit.

Ben caught me staring at them. He waved me over.

By the time I got to his office, he was seated at his desk. A half-dozen folders were stacked next to his computer terminal. Having any clutter at all on his desk was extremely unusual. For Ben, a tidy desktop was an empty desktop.

"Sit down."

I seated myself. "Did you sell us out?"

He frowned. "Our attorney will send over the paperwork to their home office."

I felt dread brush over me like a cold wind under a black storm cloud. "How long do we have?"

Ben rubbed his eyes. "This isn't a death sentence. The newspaper is changing owners. All that will happen is you'll have someone new to answer to."

"Should I be looking for another job?"

His expression was serious. "Listen, Genie. They've done extensive research on everyone who works here, including you. They're favorably impressed with your writing and editing skills. They're particularly impressed with how you handled the Connor's Landing murders. And they love the way you're all over this teacher student kidnapping. But they also know that you have a history of drinking."

Ouch, so we're being blunt here.

"There are people employed by Galley Media that have worked with you at other properties. Apparently, you have a colorful past."

The dread was only growing colder.

Ben continued. "Take my advice. You've been sober for over a year now. Stay that way."

The mind is a playful puppy. Just as he said those words, I recalled there was still some vodka in my commuter cup in the car.

Chapter Twenty-two

At six-thirty, Jessica Oberon's mother dropped Caroline off at the house.

When I heard the front door open and close, I was upstairs having my secret after-work cocktail. I chugged the last few swallows and rinsed away the boozy scent with mouthwash.

I left the glass in my bedroom, rather than take it back to the kitchen and risk an eye roll from Caroline.

When I got downstairs, she was in the living room, sitting on the floor, playing with Tucker. She looked up. "Hey, Genie." She had on black leggings, sneakers, and a gray sweatshirt with the New York Giants logo on it.

I was a Patriots fan and I think Caroline wore it just to piss me off.

I reached the bottom of the steps and realized that I had a very pleasant buzz on. "How was your day?" I asked, hoping my lush flush wasn't too obvious.

"All anyone could talk about today was Bobbi Jarvis and Jake Addison. Everyone's wondering how long they'd been having an affair and if they'd ever done it in any of the classrooms at school. Or had they done it in the community center or the Playhouse? Jake has keys to both."

She doesn't know that Jake Addison is gay.

I sat down on the couch and watched as Caroline rough-housed with our dog. "I have a question for you. Does Tommy Willis have any close friends at school?"

She looked at me with curiosity. "No, not really. He keeps to himself mostly. I think that's what attracted Bobbi to him when they were together. She said that Tommy has an air of mystery to him. He has secrets."

He'd kept the one about Jake.

"Hey, sit up here with me. I have something to tell you." I patted the seat cushion next to mine.

She got up slowly. Tucker looked up at her expectantly, tail wagging, hoping for more play time. "What did I do?" There was an adolescent whine in her voice.

"I have news."

She sat on the couch next to me and stared down at the dog.

"I interviewed Peter Cambridge and Angela Owens this afternoon. I had lunch with them, actually, at their house."

She turned her head toward me, her blue eyes wide, jaw dropped. "Really?"

"Yeah, and I learned something. When you auditioned for the part in their play?"

"Yes?"

"Did you know that Bobbi only beat you out by this much?" I held up my index finger and my thumb, demonstrating a tiny distance.

She blinked, wondering where this was going. "I didn't know that."

"Okay, this next part is bad news, good news."

"Okay."

Her hands were resting in her lap. I put my hand over hers. "When Bobbi and Jake surface, no matter what, the producer won't take her back. She's off the production permanently. That's the bad news."

"What's the good news?"

"You got the part."

It took three full seconds before she understood what I was saying. But then, she literally shot up, pushing herself up with her legs, into the air. A shrill, ear-piercing shriek tore through the room as she celebrated, fists in the air, jumping up and down.

That's when I discovered I was doing the same thing. Squealing, shouting, jumping, hugging. Even Tucker got into the act, barking, leaping into the air.

Eventually, we wore ourselves out and suddenly we were both very still, gazing at each other.

She said something, but it was so faint, I couldn't understand what she'd said. I asked her, "What?"

Caroline repeated herself. "I got the part because Bobbi made a mistake."

Yeah, well, it was a whopper.

"Look, this is going to sound awful, but that's not your problem. You didn't make Bobbi and Mr. Addison vanish into the night together. They made that decision."

She chewed at her bottom lip, thinking.

I said, "This is a huge break for you, sweetie, whether you want to be an actress forever or not. Just the fact that you're getting a chance to work with such talent, this is once in a lifetime. Your father would be so proud."

At the mention of her dad, she smiled again. "Do you think so?"

I grinned at her. Then I glanced up at the duct tape on the front window. "Hey, I'm actually having dinner with Peter Cambridge in about an hour. He wants to walk me through some paperwork. I called your Aunt Ruth. Would you mind spending the night there tonight? I really don't feel comfortable with you being here alone."

She glanced over at where the bullet had pierced the glass. "Will she take me to school in the morning?"

"She said she would."

Another glance at where the bullet had bit into the wall across the room. "Aunt Ruth's it is."

While Kevin was alive, Aunt Ruth and I competed for his attention and his affection. I'd suspected that Ruth Spence had the hots for her dead sister's husband.

She and I didn't get along at all.

Things changed after Kevin died. There wasn't anything to squabble about. She was the only family that Caroline had left, so every other month we'd have Ruth over for dinner. On occasion, we'd drive to Darien and dine with her in her magnificent stone home.

Ruth had married well, but she had divorced even better. She got the house and a jaw-dropping settlement

When we ate at her house, it was always an expensively catered affair. When we had Ruth over to our place, it was either takeout or what I could find in the freezer, defrost, and nuke.

I'd called her when Peter had invited me to dinner. There was no way I was leaving Caroline home alone. When I asked Ruth if she could let her stay overnight, her answer was, "Of course, dear. Are you planning on staying out late?"

Just because we didn't squabble anymore didn't mean she couldn't be catty.

"Not really, but I but I'd like to know that Caroline is someplace safe."

I could visualize Ruth pursing her lips while she thought. "Why wouldn't she be safe at your house?"

That's where she had me. Caroline would tell her anyway. "Someone took a shot at our house last night. Bullet came through the front window and hit the wall in the living room."

Her voice took an edge. "Even when Kevin was alive, I told him that he was in a bad neighborhood. That's no place to raise a daughter."

There's nothing wrong with our neighborhood other than we don't have a single millionaire living in it. I honestly prefer it that way.

"I'd just feel better if she was with you tonight. I know she'll be safe."

Lay it on, Genie.

"Of course she can stay here tonight. Do you want to stay here as well?"

The thought of sleeping overnight at Ruth's house made me cringe. The animosity I'd harbored for her hadn't completely dissipated. "Thanks, Ruth. I'll be fine."

I thought about that while Caroline was in her room packing and I was sitting on my bed, having another vodka over ice.

Pace yourself, Genie. You don't want to pass out while having dinner with the world famous actor every woman in America drools over.

Thinking about it brought the butterfly wings back to life in my tummy. It made me smile.

I was going to have dinner with Peter Cambridge. I was so excited.

But then I took a long breath.

I've learned from my relationship with Frank, haven't I?

Chapter Twenty-three

The Orinoco Café is right on the waterfront, overlooking Sheffield Harbor. In the summertime, you can sit out on an expansive wooden deck and watch the boats go by. In late October, the inside was cozy with logs blazing in a stone fireplace.

The chairs were made of teak and the tables were covered with red linens. The floors were a dark-stained hardwood. Gaily colored tapestries covered the walls. Lamps hanging over the tables had an old-time Tiffany feel to them.

The last time I'd been to Orinoco had been with Frank. I recalled that after we'd finished eating, we adjourned to the Hilton for dessert, our code name for sex. Low in calories, highly satisfying.

However, I was meeting a different man. Let me clarify, I was meeting a different *married* man.

Is this becoming a pattern?

I asked that question and then rationalized it by reminding myself that I was there to look over paperwork for Caroline's role in *Darkness Lane*. I wasn't there to seduce anybody.

Just as I was pulling into the parking lot, Peter Cambridge texted me that he was already inside the restaurant. As I got out of my Sebring, I felt a chill breeze blow in off Long Island Sound and I pulled the collar up on my black Burberry trench coat.

I rarely wear it. It was a gift from Frank. I'd looked it up online. That coat sells for over a thousand dollars. Much, much too nice for everyday use.

But that night was special because I was having dinner with a world-renowned movie star. It wasn't just the coat I was wearing. I had on a black dress cut low in the front but not so low as to overemphasize my cleavage, but just enough to let Peter Cambridge know I had boobs. And the hemline wasn't so high that I looked like a streetwalker, but it offered a nice view of my legs.

No, maybe I haven't learned anything from my time with Frank.

Walking into the restaurant, I felt the warmth of the room wrap itself around me like a familiar, cotton blanket. The colors were subdued and the smells were delicious, a medley of warm bread, baking chorizo, and frying plantains. The place was packed with customers; there was low hum of discordant conversations and forks and knives clinking against plates.

It took me a moment to spot the lone figure in the room, his back to me, seated at a table, gazing out the window. Even though it was dark out, the lights of the city reflected off the harbor surface, bobbing and floating like tiny, multi-colored neon leaves that had fallen into the water.

The hostess at the door asked if I'd be dining alone. I told her that I was joining someone for dinner and nodded toward where Peter was sitting.

The woman blushed and whispered. "Oh, you're dining with Mr. Cambridge. You're so lucky."

"Does he come here often?" I unbuttoned my coat.

She smiled. "Oh, yes. He's one of our favorite customers."

"Is he always alone?"

"Sometimes he's here with a group of show business people. Sometimes he comes alone. I think he likes looking out over the water."

So charming.

I negotiated my way across the room and around the other tables. He must have seen my reflection in the window because, as I got closer, he stood up and turned around. He opened his arms, coming toward me, enveloping me in a warm hug.

I hugged him back.

It felt good. There had been a lack of physical contact over the last month or so. Up until that moment, I didn't realize quite how much I missed it.

"Genie, I'm so glad we could get together this evening."

He was dressed casually, black jeans, deck shoes, long-sleeved shirt, cuffs rolled up at the wrists.

The first thing I noticed about him was his face. He'd shaved his beard. The face looking at me was the face of the hero in *Night Challenge*. Steely eyed, strong jaw, pronounced cheekbones, hearty smile.

I liked the beard, but I loved the clean-shaven Peter Cambridge even more. Less cuddly, more studly.

"You shaved." I reached out and touched his cheek. I felt myself blush.

He grinned. "Yeah, it had to come off. My character in the play doesn't have a beard. Do you like it?"

He's asking me if I like the way he looks?

I stared at him. "Oh, yeah."

Does my voice have a carnal rasp?

"Here," he said. "Let me help you off with your coat."

Once he had it off, he seemed a little confused about where to put it. The restaurant hostess had been watching us and swooped over. "Mr. Cambridge, may I take that and hang it up for you?"

He smiled at her and handed her my coat.

Peter held my chair while I sat. "Does that happen all the time?"

"What's that?" He sat down opposite me.

"Women falling all over themselves to do things for you?"

He answered by offering me a shy grin.

"I'm sorry that Angela couldn't join us tonight."

Did I sound sincere?

"She wanted to rework some of your daughter's lines."

A young man wearing a white shirt and bow tie came by, lit the candle on our table, and took our drink orders. Peter asked for Glenfiddich on ice and I ordered an Absolut and tonic.

"Something I should make clear, Peter. Caroline's not my daughter. I'm her guardian. Her father and I were engaged to be married when he passed away."

He propped his chin in the palm of his hand, resting his elbow on the table, his full attention on me. "You're her *legal* guardian. You can sign papers?"

"Oh, yes."

He frowned. "I'm sorry to hear about your fiancé. How long has it been?"

"A little over a year."

He surprised me by dropping his hand away from his chin and laying it on top of my own. "It must still be painful for you."

"I won't lie, I miss him."

"I understand. I know what loneliness is like."

The young man came by with our drinks and asked us if we needed a few more minutes to decide.

Peter looked up at him. "We'd like to finish our drinks and then we'll decide. We have a little business to discuss."

The waiter smiled at the two of us. "Of course."

I took a sip of my drink and watched Peter do the same. He closed his eyes. I know that feeling when the alcohol spreads its love through your body, that familiar warmth, the feeling of well-being.

I remarked on his earlier statement, continuing his line of conversation. "A man as famous and successful as you are, lonely? It's hard to believe you'd ever even be alone, let alone lonely."

He smiled, but then it faltered. "I'm alone more than you know, Genie. You can be alone even in a crowd of people."

I held up my glass as if to toast what he'd just said. "Amen to that. But you have Angela."

He shook his head, sighing. "Angela and I have been drifting apart over the last few years. Up until when we started working on this play, we were barely speaking to each other. And as far as a physical relationship, we decided that we're better friends than lovers. We have separate bedrooms. We haven't been intimate in a long, long time."

I felt myself redden. This man, whom I idolized, was giving me the most personal, confidential information about himself that he could possibly share. I wasn't sure what to say.

Peter suddenly looked up into my eyes, grinning. "But we're not here to talk about that. We're here to talk about Caroline." Then he reached down next to his chair and brought up a black leather briefcase. Opening it, he took out a large, tan envelope, closed the briefcase, and placed it back onto the floor.

"Let's see what we have here." He opened the envelope and took out a thick sheaf of papers. "First of all, here's the script. But when you give it to Caroline, warn her that it's a work in progress. The way Angela writes, it changes almost daily."

I took it and held it in my hands. The cover page was blank except for the words "*Darkness Lane.*"

Peter continued by handing me more pages. "I'm going to give you these to read at home. It's the contract. If you can bring it back Saturday morning when you bring Caroline in for rehearsal, that would be great. The only paper I need signed tonight is the waiver."

I sipped my drink and watched him while he explained the paperwork. In the dancing candlelight, his face became even more handsome. "Waiver?" I asked, not really caring.

He smiled, catching me gazing at him.

Do you ever get used to it, women staring at you?

"You're giving us permission to work with Caroline. Because she's a minor, we need you to say it's okay." He slid it over to me and handed me a pen.

I gave it a cursory glance and signed my name, dating it, and handing it back to him. "Is Caroline going to need an agent?"

"Eventually. At this stage, she'll be making actors' equity scale of 976 dollars a week. I'm sorry that it's not more. If we take *Darkness Lane* to Broadway, it'll be substantially higher."

My eyebrows shot up. "Hell, that's more than I make at the paper."

Peter's eyes glimmered in the light. "Actors and actresses can do very well…when they're working. Unfortunately, we're not always working."

"Do you mind if I ask you a question?"

He picked the briefcase back up and placed the waiver inside. "I just told you all about my personal life. Why would I mind if you asked me a question?"

"After *Night Challenge*, I don't recall seeing you in anything else up to now. How come?"

He turned his gaze to the window again, staring out at the night and our reflection in the glass. "Before we met, Angela taught creative writing at Columbia. After she wrote *Agoraphobic Cocktail*, she quit teaching and started working on a movie. It was around that time that we met and started going out. Long story, short, we got married, and the movie she wrote was *Night Challenge*."

"You were brilliant in that film, by the way. I absolutely fell in love with you in that movie." I hoped that I wasn't gushing.

He turned and flashed me an adorably boyish grin. "Thank you, Genie. That means a lot. Anyway, one of her old students from Columbia sued Angela, me, and our production company for plagiarism. The woman claimed that she had submitted an outline for a screenplay to Angela for one of her classes. That case, and keeping it out of the newspapers, took years of our time and cost us a fortune."

He put his hand back over mine again. "This is all off the record, okay?"

"This whole evening is off the record. Did you win?"

He frowned. "I read what Angela's student had submitted. It was essentially the same movie. We lost the settlement. Damn near bankrupted us. All the while, Angela cranked out amazing screenplays, but no production company would touch us. We were poison. We had to sell the house."

"What house?"

He looked down at the tabletop. "The house we're living in."

"I don't understand."

"We sold the house to Morgan Stiles." He looked up at me, the tears in his eyes glistening in the candlelight. "At that point, we were days from being foreclosed on and homeless."

I reached out and took his hand. "Oh my God, Peter."

"Morgan bought the house for substantially less than market value, but we needed the cash. He's letting us live there, subsidizing us with the understanding that Angela would churn out a hit play and I'd do the lead."

"All because your wife plagiarized one of her students."

He nodded.

I took another sip of my drink. "I'm a little surprised that you two are still together."

"Because of our deal with Morgan, Angela and I don't have any choice in the matter. We're forced to work together, even if the marriage is a sham."

"Wow. I haven't seen anything about this in the media."

"And I hope I can trust you to keep it that way."

"Cross my heart."

He squeezed my hand and held up his glass. "How about we toast Caroline and the play?"

We touched our glasses together.

Then he offered. "And how about we toast us as well? I have a feeling we're about to have a very nice evening."

We clinked glass again and drank.

I agreed.

Chapter Twenty-four

Peter had the Ropa Vieja and I had the Lobster Ceviche accompanied by a bottle of excellent Alto Moncaya. Over dinner, Peter told me about his childhood—a father that was never home and a disapproving, emotionally distant mother. He'd gone to college as a pre-med major but decided that it was much too much like work.

Peter changed his field of study to the theater arts and his mother went ballistic. As it turned out, Peter was very good at it but before he'd made it to stardom, his mother passed away, still branding him as a bitter disappointment.

He told me about his career, dropping names along the way like De Niro, Redford, Eastwood, Bullock, and Streep. By the time he got to the present, I was not only star-struck but seriously buzzed.

When it was my turn, my long litany of jobs and three husbands sounded like the unsavory fairy tale of a woman on a runaway roller coaster.

As I talked, I noticed his eyes never left my own.

I could feel my heart pounding.

I should have considered my mind-set during that evening. Mike Dillon, the man I'd been seeing off and on, had kicked me to the curb. Frank Mancini was a bad habit I'd broken.

I was lonely.

That and vodka make for a dangerous combination.

Peter called for one more round of drinks, another scotch for him and vodka for me. Then he switched conversational gears. "So, are you seeing anyone?"

That took me by surprise. I looked down at my glass, beads of condensation reflecting the candlelight. I gave an honest answer. "No."

"I like you a lot, Geneva Chase."

I gazed back up into his eyes. "I like you, too."

Oh, it's way more than like, Peter Cambridge.

He reached over and took my hand. "I feel a connection to you. More than I've felt in a very long time. I feel like we've established a friendship, but I'd like to take it further than that."

"Oh?"

"I don't want to be alone tonight."

Oh God, neither do I.

"You're married, Peter." My voice was soft. I really didn't have the heart to make a cogent argument.

"In name only. Please stay with me tonight. When I come here," he stopped and glanced around him, "to this restaurant, I'll often take a room at the Hilton. It's within walking distance." He pointed toward his glass. "That way I don't have to worry about driving home. Be with me tonight, please?"

I can't tell you how many times I've heard a married man tell me that he and his wife don't sleep together, they're married in name only, that he's lonely, that he doesn't want to be alone.

It's always bullshit.

But because it was Peter Cambridge?

I said, "I don't want to be alone tonight either."

● ● ● ● ●

Peter put his briefcase in the trunk of his BMW 320i sedan and we left our cars in the restaurant parking lot. Then we walked along the waterfront, Peter's arm around my waist. My arm was around him as well, as much for warmth as for proximity.

There was a sharp, autumnal bite in the air. I breathed it in, hoping it might clear my head.

Am I making a massive mistake here?

With Caroline being in the production, I was going to be seeing this man a lot. And worse, I'd be seeing his wife as well.

How awkward is this going to be?

"Having second thoughts?"

His question surprised me. I wasn't used to men being so aware.

"A little." My voice was little more than a whisper.

"Why?"

"You're married," I repeated, again.

"You've never been with a married man before?"

I chuckled. "I have. That's why I'm having second thoughts. It can get really messy."

He squeezed my waist. "It doesn't have to be. It doesn't have to be messy. And every time I see you, like when I'm running lines or rehearsing with Caroline, I'm going to smile inside with warm memories."

"How do you know? We haven't done anything yet. I might be lousy in the sack."

He made an odd sound that came out 'feh'. Then he said, "For all you know, I might be lousy in the sack."

I doubted that.

I growled at him. "Well, now we *have* to find out."

He was very good.

The hotel room was like almost any other I've been in—king-sized bed dominating the middle of the room, bureau, desk, entertainment unit complete with wide-screen TV, window overlooking the harbor, tiny bathroom.

We'd stopped off at the bar downstairs to purchase two snifters of brandy to bring up to the room with us. We walked into the room with them and I went straight to the window, gazing out at the lights reflecting off the black surface of the harbor.

He came up behind me and put his arms around me, the front of his body pressed against my back. Peter caught my line of sight. "The harbor's pretty at night."

"Pretty during the day, too. Let me get my coat off." I turned around to face him.

He leaned in.

Peter Cambridge kissed me on the lips, softly at first, gently. Then he pulled me close and the kissing became harder, lips open, tongues touching, probing.

He stepped back slightly, gazing into my eyes, and then we kissed again, harder, breathlessly. I felt his hands unbuttoning my coat.

I let my thousand-dollar Burberry drop to the floor in a heap. Turning, with my back to him, I purred, "Unzip me."

He did, slowly, and I shimmied out of my black dress, letting it fall to the carpet as well. I turned back to face him, wearing stockings, panties, and bra.

He gave me his boyish grin and whispered, "Your turn, unzip *me*."

I got up close, looking him in the eyes, my lips inches from his. Then I reached down, feeling him. He was hard, pushing against the fabric of his jeans. I slowly slid his zipper down. Then I reached inside, pushing his underwear aside, until I could wrap my hand around him.

He moaned. Again, his lips pressed against mine. Our mouths were open, tongues exploring with renewed urgency.

I felt his arms envelop me, his fingers probing along my back until they found the clasp of my bra. It, too, found its way to the floor.

"Let's do this on the bed," I whispered.

"Good idea."

"And let's turn off some of these lights."

"No, I want to see you." His voice was raspy and his breathing labored as my hand caressed him, stroked him.

Getting the rest of his clothes off, my hands and mouth appreciated his body, but so did my eyes. He was beautiful. All muscle, smooth skin, and he was rock hard.

I'd seen his body, parts of it, on the big screen. But you don't know if what you're lusting after in a movie is the real deal or a body double. The man exploring my body with his lips and tongue was very real.

At first, I was self-conscious with the lights on. But I'm proud to say that my tummy is still flat, my legs are toned, and my ass and boobs are still as pert as when I was in college. It's the running, the workouts, and the occasional stress that keeps me shape.

Once I got used to it, having clear sight of the man you're having sex with increases the heat.

He was patient, using his hands and lips and tongue in all the places that needed attention. Peter was also remarkably agile. That man was putting himself, as well as me, into some very interesting positions. He was inventive, eager to please, and he had stamina.

In the end, it was the old-fashioned missionary position that brought him to a moaning, groaning climax.

I'd managed three of my own before we got there.

He wasn't the best I'd ever been with. But he was one of the most imaginative.

No, the best was still Kevin. I was in love with him.

That night, with Peter, it was pure animal lust.

When we'd finished, Peter turned off the lights, we climbed under the sheets, and he held me close.

For a long time, we didn't say anything.

Finally, Peter whispered, "Thank you."

I patted his leg and listened to him breathing. Before long, he fell asleep.

But I was wide awake.

I just shagged Peter Cambridge.

I would have loved to have taken a selfie of me in bed with him, but like I said, in Fairfield County, that sort of thing isn't cool.

I knew that I'd never be able to get to sleep in that hotel bed, so I quietly got up, put on my clothes, and wrote him a note.

Peter—I have to get up early in the morning so I left while you were sleeping. I think you wore yourself out. I'll see you when I drop Caroline off for rehearsal on Saturday morning. Let me know what time we should be there. You have my number.

Yeah, he had my number, alright.

Walking along the waterfront back to the restaurant where my car was parked, I glanced at my watch. It was only a little after ten.

No wonder I couldn't sleep.

Peter Cambridge. What the hell was I thinking?

I'd been buzzed and it had seemed like a good idea at the time. By the time I'd gotten to the car, I was feeling the shame.

I wanted to go home and take a shower.

Oh, and kill the last of the Absolut.

Chapter Twenty-five

The nonstop chirping of my cellphone woke me up.

I reached out to the headboard and scrabbled for it. The time on the tiny screen told me it was six-thirty, too early to get up. The Caller ID said that it was Mike Dillon.

"Hey, Mike. What's up?" My voice had a throaty late night, vodka growl.

"Jake Addison's dead."

Adrenaline hit my system like a jolt from a cattle prod. "What?"

"A jogger found his body on one of the hiking trails in Vet's Park. I'm heading over there now. Thought you'd like to know."

"Yeah, yeah. What about Bobbi Jarvis?"

Is her body out there too?

"I don't know, Genie. This isn't good."

"See you in a few minutes."

I grabbed Tucker up from where he'd been snuggled up next to me. Carrying him toward the steps, I poked my head into Caroline's bedroom. Better she find out about Jake from me rather than from the Internet.

The room was empty, the bed was made.

Oh yeah, she's at Aunt Ruth's.

I went downstairs and let Tucker outside to run and do his business in the backyard. I hustled back upstairs to shower, brush my hair, and get pretty in the shortest amount of time possible.

Dressed in jeans, sweater, and hiking boots, by the time I let the dog back into the kitchen and had my quilted jacket on, it had taken me only twenty-five minutes from the time of the phone call with Mike. All of it done with a major hangover.

That's the mark of a professional.

On the way to the park, I swung through the drive-thru at Dunkin' Donuts and got a large black coffee and a bagel with cream cheese. I skipped having it toasted. I was in a hurry.

Chewing at the bagel like a starving rat, I pulled my car into the parking lot of the Sheffield Playhouse. The only other vehicles there were cop cruisers and an ambulance. A police officer was engaged in conversation with two of the EMTs. No one was in a hurry. They weren't trying to save someone's life. They were there to take away the dead.

I glanced at the theater. It was a massive, wooden barn-like structure painted red to resemble the way it looked back in the thirties when it really was a barn. That was when the Hawkes family still owned the land. They were theater buffs and turned the barn into a theater where actors and actresses performed anything from musicals to vaudeville. The original structure had burned down in 1981 and the city received state and federal grant money to rebuild the theater into its present form.

Able to seat 450 patrons, it boasted state-of-the-art lighting and acoustics. There was a full bar in the lobby and a wrap-around porch outside, complete with rocking chairs. I'd spent a few intermissions on that porch with a glass of wine. Of course, that was when the weather was warm and agreeable.

On that morning, it wasn't. The sky was a depressing gray, the temperature hovered near freezing. Steam came out of my lungs when I identified myself to the cop and asked where I'd find the crime scene.

He pointed. "That trail right there. Stop when you see the yellow tape." He laughed at his own joke.

Smart ass.

While I walked, I punched up Caroline's number.

She obviously recognized my number. "Hey, Genie. How'd it go last night?"

"Good. I got the paperwork signed and you're ready to rock 'n' roll. Your first rehearsal is going to be tomorrow morning. I got a text from Angela that I have to get you there by seven a.m."

"Wow, it's all really happening, isn't it?"

"Sure is. Did your aunt cook dinner last night?"

Caroline laughed. "Of course not. She had dinner brought in from Rinaldi's—lasagna, one of my fave's."

"Awesome. Look, there's something I need to tell you. I don't want you finding out on the Internet, okay?"

Her voice took on an audible quiver. "What, Genie? You're scaring me."

"I don't have all the details yet. All I know is what Mike Dillon told me over the phone about a half hour ago."

"What?"

I'd just gotten to the mouth of the trail where it entered the woods. "They found Mr. Addison's body in Veteran's Park."

There was a horrified moment of silence as Caroline digested what I'd just said. Finally, in a tiny voice, she asked, "He's dead? What about Bobbi?"

I took a breath of the chill air. "I don't know yet, sweetie."

"Was Jake…you know…like Bobbi's dad?"

"Murdered? I don't know that either. Look, do you want me to call the school and have you excused today? Stay with your aunt?"

I could almost hear her shaking her head. "No, I want to be with my friends when the news breaks. Will you be the one writing the story?"

"Yeah, looks like I'm on the crime beat again. Can you keep a lid on this until I get it online?"

"I'll try. Although, the other kids are going to wonder why I'm walking around like a sad zombie."

I tried to lighten the mood with a joke that fell flat. "Say you're practicing for the dress rehearsal of Death Mansion."

"Oh, I forgot to tell you that I let Mrs. Ortiz know I couldn't do Death Mansion anymore, that I was going to be rehearsing with Peter Cambridge."

Her voice had cracked, like she was close to crying.

"You sure you want to go to school?

"Yes."

Wondering if telling her about Jake Addison over the phone had been a good idea, I told her to call me if she needed me, and I started hiking. There was still enough foliage on the tree branches overhead to make it like entering a tunnel, the gray light dimmer, a grim, dusky footpath laden with dead leaves.

The trail was reasonably flat and free of any fallen tree limbs or protruding roots, and it was well marked. Joggers loved it. I'd gone running through this park a few times.

But if you wandered off the path, you'd find yourself in thickets of tangled branches that would tear at your clothing, and fallen moss-covered trees and limbs rotting on the wet ground.

There was a sudden breeze that rustled the trees overhead, ripping the dying leaves away and dropping them down around me like brightly colored snowflakes.

The smell that time of year was a pungent mix of wet earth, mold, and decomposition.

Other than Jake, I wonder how many dead things are rotting out here?

Ten minutes on the trail, less than halfway between the Playhouse and the community center at Hawkes Manor on the other side of the park, I spotted the yellow tape. Not directly on the trail, but off to the side in a clearing, the police barrier was tied to tree trunks in a rough trapezoid.

Inside the tape, police officers, all in dark blue windbreakers, were taking photos, shooting video, and combing the ground for clues. Every one of them wore paper booties on their shoes and latex gloves to keep from contaminating the scene.

Mike stood off to one side, notebook in hand, interviewing

a woman in black leggings, quilted vest, pink running shoes, and a pink baseball cap, behind which trailed a blond ponytail. When she talked, her hands were animated—waving, pointing, shrugging, fingers touching her face.

Seated on the ground next to her feet, patiently watching her hands moving in the air, was a golden retriever. Every now and then, its big tail would thump against the ground.

Mike spotted me, gave me a quick wave, and held up his index finger—indicating that I should give him a minute.

I nodded and turned my attention to the crime scene. A low white tent had been erected in the middle of the clearing. I've been to enough of these to know that it was hiding the body from curious eyes, like mine. I watched as Dr. Foley crept out from underneath. In his sixties, five-seven, heavy in the gut, with a full head of white hair, sporting a gray handlebar mustache, he reminded me of a walrus.

He had on latex gloves and a tiny microphone attached to his collar. A wire from it snaked down the front of his nylon jacket and into a pocket, where I knew a recorder rested. His knees were mud-stained from when he'd been kneeling to examine the body.

I saw Mike finish his interview and walk purposefully to the medical examiner.

While the two of them conferred, the jogger came toward me, dog trudging alongside.

I lifted the tape for her and she ducked under.

"Thank you," she said.

I nodded toward the tent. "You're the one who found the body?"

She glanced back and shuddered. "Yes." Her voice was little more than a whisper. "Well, really Elmo did." She pointed toward the Retriever.

"My name's Genie Chase. I work for the *Sheffield Post*. Do you mind if I ask you a couple of questions?"

She shook her head.

I pulled my notebook out of my bag. "What's your name?"

"Patricia Gravato."

"And this is Elmo?" I leaned down and scratched the dog behind his ears.

"Yeah, I was running along the trail, listening to some tunes." She pulled an iPhone and earbuds out of the pocket of her quilted vest. "When I got just about there." She pointed back to the path. "Elmo jumped off the trail and ran into the woods."

The woman stopped and glanced back at the white tent again. "I went after him and I saw he was pulling at something that was partially buried in the ground. When I got up to him, I saw that Elmo had a man's hand in his mouth."

The woman shuddered again. "I called 911."

"All you could see was a hand?"

She shook her head. "Oh, no. It looked like there'd been other animals digging around where the body's buried."

"Why is that?"

She held the screen of her iPhone up so she could see it and started to scroll with her finger. Then she showed me a photograph. "Something had dug up the dirt around his face."

It was gruesome. It was little more than a filthy, muddy mask peeking out from the wet earth. Something had made a meal of the man's eyes and parts of his lips and ears.

I held up my hand. I'd seen enough. "You took a picture?"

She stared at the screen. "Yeah."

"Why?"

"Don't know. Makes it more real."

"Did you post it anywhere?"

She shook her head.

"What are you going to do with it?"

She glanced up at me, back at the tent, then down at her screen again. She whispered, "Delete it."

"That's a good idea." I saw Mike coming toward us.

She saw him too. "I'd better get going. My husband's going to start worrying."

I watched as she picked her way back to the trail and started off at a slow trot in the direction of the community center. I estimated it was about a quarter mile from where I stood.

"Hey, Genie."

I turned. "Hey, Mike. Is it really Jake Addison?"

"No wallet, no phone, no ID, other than our visual. But, yeah, it's Jake Addison."

"Robbery?"

Mike folded his arms. At a moment like this, our friendship ended and our relationship returned to stark professionalism. "Possibly."

"How did he die?"

"One gunshot to the back of the head, execution-style. From the entry angle, he was most likely kneeling. Then to be sure, someone pumped two more bullets into his back. I won't know for certain until we get the state forensics team in, but I'm guessing they came from a handgun, most likely a nine-millimeter."

I glanced over at the white tent, under which the body of Jake Addison reposed. "Then what, someone buried him out here?"

"Obviously not deep enough."

"Was he killed out here or somewhere else?"

"We don't know yet."

I gazed around me, looking into the woods. "Do you think Bobbi Jarvis is buried out here someplace?"

He kicked at a rock. "I hope not. But we've got over two hundred acres of wooded parkland to search. We're asking Hartford to send us cadaver dogs."

The whirring scream of a helicopter interrupted us as it quickly became the loudest noise in the forest. We both stared up into the sky, seeing something appear then disappear behind clumps of foliage. When it found us in the clearing, I could clearly make out the logo from the CBS affiliate out of New Haven.

Mike gave me his "pissed off" expression. "Better set up a perimeter. This place is going to be crawling with you reporters."

I gave him a half grin. "Yeah, but none of them as hot as I am."

He grinned right back. "Damned right, Geneva Chase. Not even close."

Watching him go back to the crime scene, I felt a momentary flush of shame over what I'd done with Peter Cambridge at the hotel.

Mike broke up with me. Gotta keep that in mind.

I slowly picked my way back to the path, careful not to trip over any stray tree roots, then along the trail back to the parking lot at the theater. As I walked, I kept glancing around me, wondering if Bobbi was buried out there somewhere.

How sad and lonely is that?

To be out here all by herself?

The thought made me want to cry.

Chapter Twenty-six

When I'd left my car in the Sheffield Playhouse's parking lot, the only other vehicles there were cop cruisers and the ambulance. Walking out of the woods, I now saw four more cars in the lot—a Mercedes E-Class sedan, a BMW Z-4 Roadster, a Range Rover, and a Lexus hybrid.

Curious, I climbed the steps to the theater's wraparound porch. On either side of the glass doors were windows, eight feet high, allowing light to pour into the lobby. I pulled on the metal handle and the door swung open.

The lights were off and the only illumination came from the slate-gray daylight filtering through the windows. Walking quietly across the thick red carpet in the lobby, I saw the empty ticket counter to my right. Ahead of me, at the end of the long room, was the concession counter.

I veered to the left and opened one of the double doors that led to the theater.

The house lights were on, the theater seats were vacant, the curtains were open and there were four people on the stage. One of them, I easily recognized as Angela Owens. She was dressed in an oversized sweater and black, tailored slacks. A second woman looked familiar to me. I guessed she was Mona Fountain, one of the leads on *Hell's Highway*.

The other two were men I didn't recognize.

The stage was set with furniture that might have come from someone's living room—couch, recliner, coffee table, bookcase.

I started to walk down the aisle toward the stage when I detected movement behind me.

"Miss Chase?"

I wheeled and found myself face to face with Peter Cambridge's security guy, David LaSalle. Dressed much like he'd been at the house, he had on a powder-blue button-down shirt under a navy-blue blazer, black slacks, polished shoes. The house lights glistened on his shaved head.

"Mr. LaSalle," I acknowledged.

Angela, seeing the two of us at the back of the theater, disappeared backstage. Seconds later, she emerged from a doorway and quickly came up the aisle to where we stood. Her expression was serious. "Geneva Chase, what are all the cops doing in the woods?"

I waited until she was closer. Then I replied, my voice somber. "They found Jake Addison's body out there."

"Jake's dead?" Angela's hand went to her mouth. "Oh, my God."

David blinked. "What?"

"He'd been shot. It looks like someone tried to hide the body."

"Oh, my God," Angela repeated. "Do they know what's happened to Bobbi?"

"They'll be searching the park using cadaver dogs." That simple sentence struck me as being excessively grim.

"They think she's dead, too?" Angela's voice went high.

"They just don't know yet."

David shook his head. "Bobbi's father...and now Jake. It's awful, awful."

"Wait until Peter hears this," Angela said. She glanced up at me, suddenly remembering something. "Did you sign the paperwork last night?"

The vision of her husband, naked and on top of me, flashed in my head.

"Yes," I answered. "Is he here?"

Angela studied me through her black rimmed glasses. "No, he hasn't gotten here yet. Where did the two of you have dinner?"

Suddenly I felt deeply ashamed. I cleared my throat before I responded. "The Orinoco Café."

"Of course. Whenever he goes there, he drinks way too much and then walks to the Hilton and stays the night." She studied my face. "Did he say anything to you about staying the night at the Hilton?"

She knows.

"I don't recall that being part of the discussion." I lied.

"Did he look like he was getting hammered?"

I shrugged. "I'm not a good judge of that sort of thing."

She sighed and glanced at her watch. "He'll show up eventually. Look, if you hear anything about Bobbi, will you let us know?"

With another flash of guilt, I realized that I knew how to reach Peter, but not Angela or David. "Of course. Can you give me your numbers?"

● ● ● ● ●

Driving back to the office, I had a chance to think about the affairs of the last twelve hours. I'd bedded a world-famous movie star last night. That was pretty cool.

But he was married. That sucked.

After being with Frank so long ago, I know that there's nothing good that can come out of this.

Plus, I was sure that Peter's wife at least suspected I'd slept with him.

Then waking up this morning to find out that Caroline's English teacher and drama coach was dead. The same man who everyone thought had disappeared down a rabbit hole with Bobbi Jarvis.

Dear God, don't let Bobbi be buried out in those woods.

Jake Addison, the man having a gay affair with the bisexual Adam Jarvis. Both of those men murdered.

Were their deaths connected? Or was it a random coincidence?

Other than their affair, what did they have in common?

Bobbi Jarvis, of course.

Where are you, Bobbi?

Pulling into the newspaper parking lot, I was pleased to see that there were no vehicles parked back there that I didn't recognize. I'd been checking my rearview mirror. There hadn't been any pickup trucks behind me.

I no sooner got to my cubicle and hung my jacket on the back of my chair when Ben fairly exploded into my office. "Tell me you got the story."

"I got the story. And photos of the cops at the crime scene."

He pumped his fists into the air. "Hallelujah. How fast can you hammer it out? I want to get it up online before anyone else."

I saw Darcie staring at me from her desk out in the newsroom. "I have to get quotes from Bobbi Jarvis' mother and grandmother, and we'll be good to go."

"Then don't waste time talking to me." He gave me a thumbs-up and walked out into the newsroom. Then he exclaimed with a single clap of his hands, "And that, ladies and gentlemen, is how it's done."

I whispered to myself. "You're going to miss this, Ben Sumner."

As I was sitting down, Darcie trotted over. "Got a minute?"

"Kind of busy here."

"I'm giving my two weeks' notice."

Now what?

I waved her to sit down. "What's up?"

"I took a job as staff writer with the *Bridgeport Times*."

I rubbed my eyes. "Why?"

Seated opposite me, she crossed her arms and cocked her

head. "If Ben is selling this place, I don't want to be the one who turns off the lights. I'm being proactive."

I glanced around the newsroom. "Who else is looking for a job?"

"Everyone."

My stomach did a sick twist and I felt sweat under my arms. The last thing I needed was a mass exodus. "Okay, put it writing for me, will ya'? I can't worry about this right now."

"I heard. You were the first one at the Jake Addison crime scene."

"And I need to be the first one to get it up and out."

Darcie left and I punched in Theresa Pittman's number.

"Theresa, it's Genie Chase."

Her voice was shrill, nearly hysterical. "They're coming back, Genie."

"Who?"

"Those vultures with the cameras. They're setting up across the street. The cops have put up barriers again. What's going on? Have they found Bobbi?"

I took a second before I delivered the news. No matter how you looked at it, it wasn't good. "They found Jake Addison's body this morning in Vet's Park. He was murdered."

There was an ominous silence.

It was replaced by Nina's voice. "I'm sorry, Mom had to sit down. She handed me the phone. Jake Addison's dead?"

"I'm afraid so."

"What about Bobbi?"

"No sign of her so far."

There was another poignant silence. Then, "Do you think she's still alive?"

"Yes, I do."

"Jake and Adam. Are they connected somehow?"

It was my turn to hesitate. "They were lovers."

"Oh, my dear God."

"You don't think Bobbi's buried in that park someplace?"

"I don't. Do you have any theories?" I needed a quote.

I could tell she was trying to formulate some idea where her daughter might be. "Nothing I want to think about."

I could make that work as a quote.

"Off the record, Genie."

"Okay."

"I'm worried that Adam might have done something stupid."

Fear clutched at my gut.

"Remember, back when we were married and he owed money to a bookie, the bastard pimped me out to pay his debt?"

I really didn't want to hear this.

"Yes, you told me."

"Adam was into this bookie for even more money. He was worried enough that he was thinking about running. I just hope he didn't do the same thing with my daughter." Her voice finished the sentence with a bitter edge.

"If he did, it didn't keep him alive."

"I know. Plus, there was video of Jake picking up Bobbi at the gas station." She was doing her best to talk herself out of a horrible theory.

There was a distant muffled noise coming from Nina's end of the conversation, someone talking in the background.

"I didn't hear that," I stated.

"It was Mom. She said that maybe Jake caught wind and was trying to protect Bobbi. Maybe that's what got him killed."

Chapter Twenty-seven

I finished writing the piece about the late Jake Addison and hit the button to send it to Ben to edit and post online. Then I leaned back in my chair and wondered where this would all go now.

The police had over two hundred acres they were going to have to search. Even with cadaver dogs, that would be daunting. Would they elicit volunteers from the community to go through the woods looking for the body of a fifteen-year-old girl?

I shook my head. It was counterproductive to wonder what was out in Veteran's Park.

I'm going to assume that Bobbi Jarvis is alive. The alternative is simply too ugly to think about.

I picked up my cellphone and called Shana Neese.

"Hello, Geneva Chase? Is everything okay?"

It was a valid question. The last two times I'd talked with her, someone had shot through my front window and I'd been followed and threatened by a man the size of bulldozer. "I'm fine. But I need your advice."

"I'm listening."

"I'm following up on the disappearance of a fifteen-year-old girl."

"Is this the one who was kidnapped by her teacher?" Her voice was tense. This was obviously a sore subject for her.

"Yes, Bobbi Jarvis, except there's been an unexpected twist. The teacher turned up dead, buried in a shallow grave."

"And no sign of the girl?"

"None."

"Police have any theories?"

"None that they're sharing." I took a sip of the coffee that I'd gotten earlier that morning at Dunkin' Donuts. No surprise, it was ice cold.

"Didn't I read in your newspaper that the girl's father was murdered as well?"

"Yes, but her dad was tortured and beaten to death. The teacher was shot execution-style, one in the head, two in the back."

I listened to the silence as the woman thought that over. "Still, it's a hell of a coincidence, isn't it?"

I tapped a pen against my desktop. "I was told that Adam Jarvis, the dad, owed his bookie a ton of money. I was also told that a couple of weeks ago, two guys got out of a truck with a Wolfline logo carrying baseball bats. Owners of the coffee shop next door thought they were there to scare a payment out of him."

"That's ominous. Is there more?"

"Another coincidence, the father and the teacher were lovers."

"A connection between the two murders? There's video showing the girl getting into a car with the teacher, isn't there?"

"Yes. Look, the girl's mother has a theory. She thinks the girl's father was going to pay off his gambling debt by pimping out his daughter. Somehow the teacher heard about it and picked up the girl to keep her safe. It looks like everything went to hell somewhere."

"And you think that Wolfline has something to do with that?"

"I think someone at Wolfline was taking Adam's bets."

I heard her sigh. "Then it's possible that they have the girl."

I rubbed my forehead. I couldn't tell if my headache was from the hangover or if the subject matter was really getting to me. "Yeah."

"Okay, let me make some inquiries."

"I appreciate that." I was about ready to wind our phone call up, but I had one more question. "Would it be worth my while to talk to Valentin Tolbonov?"

"Do you really want to be on his radar?"

"I'm already on his radar. You put me there with the Betsy Caviness interview."

"I doubt he'll see you."

"Any suggestions?"

"You can try his jewelry store in Greenwich. I understand he's there most of the time. Oh, Geneva?"

"What?"

"Are you still being followed?"

"Not that I've seen."

Shana was quiet for a moment while she considered that. "It makes me wonder what they're up to."

I hit the End Call button, stood up, and stretched. As I did, Darcie grabbed an envelope off her desk and came across the newsroom and into my cube. "Here's my resignation letter, Genie. I hope there are no hard feelings."

Taking the letter, I answered. "I'll never stand in the way of someone who's looking to better their life."

"Thanks, you've been a great teacher and mentor."

"Well, I've got you for two more weeks. What are you working on now?"

"It's a weird one. According to the police, there's a couple of homeless guys who got their hands on a whole slew of credit card information. They've been buying things like pizzas and Chinese takeout. Bought some camping equipment at Costco—cooking utensils, small gas stove, blankets, blow-up bed. And listen to this. They're getting around by Uber."

"Multiple homeless guys?"

"Got three different descriptions."

I glanced over at Ben's office. He didn't know that Darcie was leaving. I changed the subject. "Did you tell the HR people at the *Bridgeport Times* that you're pregnant?"

Her green eyes widened. "No. I don't have to, not legally, right?"

I sighed. "Right."

The surprise will serve them right for stealing one of my writers.

"Ben doesn't know yet, does he?"

"Nope." I nudged her out of my doorway. "I'd better get this over with."

Ben greeted me as I walked into his office. "Want to have lunch?"

The look of surprise on my face must have been obvious. "Lunch?"

He frowned. "Yeah, just my way of saying good job on the Jake Addison piece. I just posted it online. Almost seven thousand people have already seen it. We've gotten over a hundred comments."

"Oh, well, thank you. Maybe another time." I still remembered how he'd asked me out a couple of times when I'd first gotten hired. Even though I was drinking hard, I knew it was a bad idea to bang the boss. "There's another angle I want to check out on the Bobbi Jarvis story."

He rubbed his hands. "Do what you got to do."

"Look, there's something I need to tell you." I held up the envelope. "Darcie resigned. Effective two weeks from today."

"Because of the sale?"

I nodded.

"It's not even final."

"I know. She got spooked."

"Who else is spooked?" His voice was only slightly sarcastic.

"According to Darcie, they all are."

"I can't have a stampede out the door. It'll queer the deal." He gazed out onto the floor where about a dozen people sitting at desks, were tapping away at keyboards. "Gather up the news staff. Tell them we're going meet in the lunchroom. I want to talk to them. I'll do advertising, production, and circulation later this afternoon."

I did as Ben asked and got the troops together in our lunchroom. Twelve of us squeezed into the kitchenette. There were three tables and enough chairs so that everyone had a seat with a few left over.

The room had a tiny counter, a full-size refrigerator, and a microwave. In the corner stood a large plastic garbage can that should have been emptied at least a week earlier.

Ben walked in after everyone had sat down, his sleeves rolled up, a serious look on his face.

I stood, leaning against the cinderblock wall in the back of the room.

The publisher clapped his hands together. "Okay, I guess everyone has heard about our pending sale to Galley Media."

There were a few collective nods, but most of the staff sat stone-still.

Ben continued. "Galley Media owns twenty-seven newspapers, twelve television stations, ten radio stations, and four magazine companies. They offer their employees top-notch health-care insurance, paid vacations, and a matching 401K plan. They've won dozens of awards in journalism, including three Pulitzers."

Ben made it a point to make eye contact with everyone in that room before he began again. "You all know that every other newspaper here in Fairfield County is owned by a chain. We simply can't compete as an independent. They have economies of scale. We don't. I wish I didn't have to do this, but in the end, everyone will be better off."

I've heard Ben when he's given a speech. And he can be one of the most eloquent, silver-tongued orators I've ever experienced.

This wasn't one of those times.

This time, Ben doesn't believe his own bullshit.

I raised my hand. The least I could do was help him out a little. People are afraid of the unknown. "What's the time frame on the sale?"

He flashed me a half-smile. "I'm glad you asked, Genie. It's not going to happen overnight. Galley has done its due diligence and they have the contract our attorney sent over. It'll take a couple of weeks for their attorneys to amend the paperwork, and then our attorney will look at it again. All told, probably two months before the sale is complete.

I raised my hand again. "We should probably break the story before one of our competitors gets wind of this."

He blinked. "Yes, yes. Genie, can you do that for me?"

I gave him a nod and a thumbs-up. I wouldn't publicly humiliate Ben. But I was going to make him eat that sandwich. Ben was going to have to write his own damned story.

Our business writer, Dan Fisher—white hair, graying mustache, steel-rimmed glasses, and short-sleeved shirt—asked a question. "How many of us are they going to keep on?"

Ben shifted his weight from one foot to the other. "That's another good question. I've included an addendum in the contract that they keep everyone who is presently employed at this newspaper working here for at least twelve months."

Dan, who is nobody's fool, countered, "You said their attorneys may amend the contract."

"If they take that out, it'll be a deal breaker."

I watched as heads bobbed and there was a low murmur of approval.

Ben glanced at me. I nodded.

I didn't believe him for a moment, but everyone else did. Hopefully, it would stanch any mass stampede to other properties.

As everyone shuffled out and back out into the newsroom, I caught Darcie. "Still want to leave?"

She motioned toward Ben, who was at the other end of the

lunchroom talking to Tony Larson, one of our sports writers. "Do you believe him?"

"Sure, why not? If I didn't, I'd be sending *my* résumé out."

She took a couple of beats, then made a decision. "Okay, I'll let them know I've changed my mind. Think Ben will be okay with me staying?"

I gave her a wan smile. "You're the reason he called this meeting."

Chapter Twenty-eight

When I got back to my desk, I saw that the light was blinking on my phone, letting me know there was a message waiting for me. I listened and heard the voice of Angela Owens. "Genie, I know this is short notice, but Morgan, our producer, reminded me that we are way behind. Would it be at all possible for you to bring Caroline to the theater after school to run lines with Peter and Mona? We'll have pizza here so she can have dinner with us."

She left me her cellphone number.

I immediately did something I never do. I texted Caroline at school, asking if she wanted to rehearse at the playhouse once school let out.

As I left her the message, I recalled that the Drama Club was supposed to be doing a dress rehearsal for the opening of Death Mansion at the community center out at Vet's Park.

Caroline said that she'd told Mrs. Ortiz that she couldn't do Death Mansion, that she had a part in the Peter Cambridge production.

My cellphone chirped. Instead of texting me back, Caroline had called. I answered, "Hey, baby."

"Hey, Genie." Her voice sounded mighty chipper. "Damn right I'll rehearse tonight. "

I winced. I don't like when Caroline swears. I know she's trying to get a rise out of me, so I usually take a low-key approach and ignore it. Unless she drops the f-bomb. She knows that's over the border. "Cool," I answered. I'll duck out of work around three-thirty, pick you up at school, and take you over to the theater."

"Great."

"Hey, what's the reaction to the news about Mr. Addison?"

"Same one I had when you told me—shock. Then, of course, the natural question comes—where's Bobbi?"

"Anybody have any theories?"

"A few are circling right back to Tommy."

Hearing that, I'd have to ask Mike if they went back to the ex-boyfriend's house again. "Are they still doing the dress rehearsal thing for Death Mansion tonight?"

"Out of respect for Mr. Addison, they've decided to push the opening night off a week."

I noticed she'd called him Mr. Addison and not Jake.

Caroline added, "There was some talk about forming a group of kids and teachers to go out to Vet's Park and look for any sign of Bobbi. But the principal killed that. She said she'd talked with the cops and they're worried we might fuck up their own search."

Ouch. "Really?" My voice dripped acid. "That's really what the principal said?"

I think I heard her grinning over the phone. "See you at three-thirty."

I spotted Ben going into his office, so I raced across the floor and caught him before he sat down. "Darcie changed her mind. She doesn't want to leave anymore."

He raised an eyebrow and appeared satisfied with himself. "Good."

"Now, if you can watch the shop, I've got a lead I want to run down regarding Bobbi Jarvis."

"Get on it."

"Oh, and it was all bullshit, what you were saying in the lunchroom. Right?"

He frowned. "Go, work. Write something."

"Oh, and that story you want me to put together about our pending sale?"

"Yeah?"

"I ain't doin' it. Get on it."

• • ● • •

Fairfield County is extraordinarily affluent. Names like Westport, Darien, New Canaan, and Ridgefield are equated with wealth.

But Greenwich, Connecticut, is in a class all of its own. The town is home to the rich and the uber-rich. There's a specific area in Greenwich, known as the Golden Triangle, where the median household income is in excess of six-hundred-thousand, the richest neighborhood in America.

Some of the finest and most expensive retail shops outside of New York City are clustered along Greenwich Avenue, known as the "Rodeo Drive of the East Coast." Handbags, couture, electronics, home furnishings, and jewelry are available for purchase—at a price.

If you can afford it.

The most exclusive jewelry shop, however, was not on Greenwich Avenue, but on the next block over, on Wyndham Street, in an inconspicuous two-story brick office building.

Before I'd left my cube, I looked up Tolbonov Diamonds' website on the Internet. It claimed to be the ultimate in superlative craftsmanship, all jewelry handmade onsite, every diamond hand-cut personally by Valentin Tolbonov, guaranteed to be unique and of the highest clarity.

There was an abbreviated sampling of what might be ordered from Tolbonov Diamonds. The least expensive was a bracelet that retailed for twenty-five-thousand dollars. The most expensive was a necklace that went for eight-hundred-thousand.

Slightly beyond my newspaper salary.

I hit a button at the top of the homepage titled "About Us." It took me to a page called the "Tolbonov Diamonds Story." The dominant feature was a large, professionally done color photo of Valentin Tolbonov, smiling into the camera lens. He was dressed impeccably in a white shirt, lavender tie with a perfect knot, closely cropped rust-colored beard, every hair in place, piercing brown eyes directed right at the photographer.

The accompanying text told a story about how he and his half brother Bogdan were smuggled out of the then Soviet Union by their mother, Darya Tolbonov, a pediatric physician. They settled in Queens, New York, where the boys grew up.

Valentin went to the Columbia School of Business, where he earned his MBA. Then he spent five years in New York learning the diamond business, taking numerous trips to Africa to see the mining operations firsthand.

Any blood diamonds, Mr. Tolbonov?

After graduation, he married his longtime sweetheart, Elaine Harris, of Greenwich, Connecticut. They settled in Greenwich, where Valentin started his business, Tolbonov Diamonds, and are raising their two children.

The only mention of half brother Bogdan is when they're smuggled out of Russia.

I read through the text again. Could this man really be a ruthless gang boss? A family man, a father with two children, a successful businessman?

I returned to the home page and looked for the address and the hours. It read, "By appointment only."

I've never let that stop me in the past.

I drove along Greenwich Avenue, cruising by storefronts that I couldn't afford, until I found Wyndham Street. I took a right and parked in front of an innocuous, squat, two-story, brick building. Throwing my bag over my shoulder, I walked up to the glass front door, opened it, and found myself in a short hallway.

On the wall to my right was a plaque listing all the companies in the building. The first floor hosted a hedge fund, an insurance company, a literary agent's office, and an attorney.

Of most interest to me was discovering that one of the offices belonged to Wolfline Contracting.

Nowhere on the plaque was a listing for anyone on the second floor. It was as if the space was uninhabited.

I walked up the hallway until I found a doorway marked with the Wolfline logo.

I tried the door.

Locked.

I guess nobody's working today? Well, when your company is a shell corporation, you don't need much of an office staff.

I turned and went to the elevator, stabbing the Up button with my finger. The door slid open and I rode to the second floor.

The elevator opened into a claustrophobic, windowless anteroom, empty save for a metal doorway right in front of me. There was a small, dignified sign off to one side that said, "Welcome to Tolbonov Diamonds. By appointment only."

There it was again.

Next to the door, a buzzer and a small speaker box was affixed to the wall. Above the door, in the ceiling, was a closed-circuit television camera.

Am I being watched?

I pushed the buzzer.

"Yes?" came a disembodied voice.

"I'd like to see if I can speak to Mr. Tolbonov."

"Do you have an appointment?"

For a moment, I felt like Dorothy, standing at the doorway to the Emerald City, trying to get audience with the Wizard of Oz.

"I don't."

"I'm sorry, we're by appointment only."

The box went silent.

I pushed the buzzer again.

"Yes?"

"My name is Geneva Chase. I'm a reporter from the *Sheffield Post* and I'd like to ask Mr. Tolbonov a few questions."

The box went silent again and I waited. While the seconds spread out into long minutes, I punched up the *Washington Post* app on my phone to see what the latest silliness was coming out of our nation's capitol.

Finally, the voice abruptly returned. "Mr. Tolbonov wants to know if you're pretty."

I put my phone away and smiled up into the camera. "Dazzling."

I heard the door unlock with an electronic click and it opened inward. The man standing with his hand on the doorknob was tall, a little over six-feet, and broad in the shoulders and chest. He wore a dark-blue blazer, gray slacks, white shirt, and a red tie. He was clean shaven and wore his blond hair in a tight, military buzz. His blue eyes studied me intently.

"Pretty, yes." He nodded in approval and offered a tight-lipped smile. Then he turned. "Please follow me."

We were in another short hallway. Off to my right was a small metal desk where an open laptop rested. A counter behind the desk, against the wall, held four computer monitors, three offering views from outside the building. One showed the hallway where I'd just been waiting.

Interesting, they already knew what I looked like. Somebody was toying with me.

At the end of the short hall was another door. This one had a keypad on the wall.

Standing between me and the keypad, the man punched in a code and then opened the door.

I was amazed.

The room was massive, but then again, I recalled that Tolbonov Diamonds occupied the entire second floor of the building. Glass cases ran all along the perimeter, and cases were positioned strategically on the floor.

Walking behind my guide, I trod upon thick, luxurious, dark blue carpeting. Track lighting in the ceiling accented many of the gleaming showcases, where necklaces, bracelets, rings, and watches glistened and glimmered. Standing behind the glass cases along the wall, were women, all drop-dead attractive, all wearing the same uniform—a black dress, low in the front, high in the hemline, simple gold necklace, earrings, and bracelet.

Some talked quietly to clients, some watched as customers silently studied the glittering inventory.

All told, there were eight female attendants ready to wait on buyers, and ten customers. The age-range of the clientele was from late twenties to early seventies. You could smell the scent of money in the room. Every one of the customers was wearing expensively tailored, name-brand clothing, shoes, and accessories.

I, on the other hand, was wearing my quilted jacket, jeans, and hiking boots. I felt woefully out of place.

At the other end of the expansive showroom stood two men, dressed precisely the same way as my guide, in blazers, gray slacks, and polished black shoes. They were side by side, eyeing me with interest, blocking the front of yet another doorway. I had no doubt there were guns under their sport coats.

We walked toward them and the two men stepped aside. Once again, my guide punched in a code and opened the door for me.

This room was dark. Shadows around the perimeter prevented me from judging the size of the interior. Two men sat at worktables off to my left. One of them wore dark goggles and was using what looked like a small blowtorch on an item held by a metal press. White hot flame blew against a tiny metal object that the workman painstakingly turned from one side to another.

The other had a soldering iron in his hand and was dabbing gently at an object, smoke rising, on the table under a harsh light, mere inches from what he was working on.

Off to my right sat a table in an island of illumination, a bright lamp hanging low over its surface. Sitting, leaning into the light was a man wearing a jeweler's loupe. In front of him, glittering under the illumination was a tiny pyramid of diamonds on a black, velvet cloth. He held one of them in a pair of tweezers and was studying it with great interest.

The man slowly looked up when he saw the two of us walk into the room. He removed the loupe and stood, watching us approach. Now that he was no longer under the light, I couldn't see him well. He was standing in the shadows.

My guide stopped and I did the same.

The man at the table came around, emerging into the light. He was tall and trim, with a full head of curly red and gray hair. He was in his mid-forties.

His face was all angles, high cheekbones and a sharp, patrician nose softened by a closely cropped beard, rust-colored with hints of silver, like his hair. Thick eyebrows accented his piercing, dark brown eyes.

His attire was immaculate, gray slacks cut perfectly to his ankles and waist, a pale blue shirt, a bright red tie, polished shoes reflecting the light from above his table. I noted that a matching suit coat was draped over the back of the chair in which he'd been working.

He came close to where we stood and he smiled, teeth exposed, wolf-like. "Yes, dazzling." His voice was low.

A compliment like that should have made me smile. Instead, the way he said it made the hairs on the back of my neck stand erect. I'd been seen…and balanced against a vast room filled with diamonds, rubies, and emeralds, all glittering under spotlights. I'd come into this place woefully unprepared, outclassed.

"Miss Chase. So nice to meet you. I'm Valentin Tolbonov."

Chapter Twenty-nine

Valentin Tolbonov.

I suddenly recalled the story that Mike had told me, the one in which Valentin and his brother had brutally killed a man's family before his eyes and then buried him alive. All because he'd been a competitor and had beaten Valentin in a deal.

He and his brother had grown up on the streets of Queens close to Brooklyn, the epicenter of Bratva, the Russian Mafia. Vying for control in Queens? I'd done a piece on it when I worked in New York. In addition to multiple Italian Families, were the Albanian, Korean, Black, and Latino gangs.

I'd discovered that out of all the crews in that part of the city, the Russians were the most ruthless. They weren't afraid to get bloody.

I knew all this and yet I still walked into this shadowy spider's web.

Tolbonov reached out and took my hand, cupping it in both of his own. They were dry and rough, like the skin of a snake. "Can I get you something to drink?"

His voice was deep, and I noted that he didn't seem to have any hint of an accent.

"No, thank you."

Letting go of my hands. "Oh, I insist." He turned and slid back into the dark shadows.

My guide gave me a light touch on my shoulder and motioned that I should follow.

My eyes were adjusting to the lack of light and I could just make out Valentin Tolbonov's dark form as he moved easily across the room. I watched him disappear though an open doorway.

Light suddenly burst through the shadows from a small kitchenette. The walls were brick, probably the original building material of the room. On the right, a gleaming, stainless-steel stove and refrigerator stood against the wall. To my left was a granite countertop that included a microwave, toaster, blender, juicer, and espresso machine.

Not at all like the lunchroom at the newspaper.

Valentine took a crystal-faceted tumbler and a gleaming wineglass out of a polished oak cupboard, opened the freezer, and brought out a bottle of vodka, pouring the glass half full. Then he dropped in two ice cubes. From the refrigerator, he found a plastic container of clear liquid, pouring it into the same tumbler. Then he handed it to me. "Vodka and tonic. I believe that's your beverage of choice."

How did he know that I drink vodka and tonic?

I blinked and felt a tiny, electric charge of fear humming through my nervous system. "Thank you. It's a little early for me."

He made a show of looking up at the diamond-shaped clock on the wall. "Nonsense, it's nearly noon. And I insist that you taste the vodka. I know you enjoy Absolut, but try this."

He even knows what brand of vodka I drink.

"It's Tsarskaya. Its formula is based on the vodkas that were served on the tables of the Russian tsars from the Romanov dynasty. It's particularly good with caviar and rye bread."

Then, while I wordlessly took possession of the icy glass of alcohol, he turned and picked up a bottle of Cabernet on the countertop, removed the stopper, and poured it into a Baccarat wineglass. "I find that a little red wine in the middle of the day brightens my mood."

He turned and held his glass out for me to toast with him. "To good health."

A little stunned, I reached out and we touched glass. I repeated, "To good health."

He sipped his wine. "Now, how can I help you, Geneva Chase?"

I took a quick sip of my own while clumsily fishing the recorder out of my bag with my free hand. Finding it, I glanced back at him.

The man was frowning. "I'm sorry, Miss Chase, but this entire conversation must be off the record."

Disappointed, I put the recorder back in my bag. "Off the record," I repeated.

"I'm sorry. I must always worry about the reputation of my business. Sometimes an errant comment to the press can be taken the wrong way, yes? A phrase taken out of context can cause irreparable harm."

I nodded. "Of course." Glancing back into the dark room from which we'd come, I said, "You have a unique business here. I've never seen a jewelry showroom quite like yours."

Start out with a friendly, non-adversarial compliment.

He gave me a predatory grin. "Thank you. It's taken me years to build the business to what it is today. We cater to a very discerning, exclusive clientele."

"I can see that. Is this your only business?"

He cocked his head. "I have a diverse portfolio."

"Do you actually own any other companies?"

"No, Miss Chase." He gestured for me to sit down at the tiny table in the middle of the kitchenette. Its surface was covered by white linen. A single rose in a slim, silver vase sat in the center.

I sat down and he did the same.

He explained to me as if I were a child. "The only company I'm directly responsible for the day-to-day operations is this one." He waved his hand at his surroundings. "But I have investments in many other companies. Companies that have competent management and a good rate of return."

I took a tentative sip of my drink. It was light on the tonic, heavy on the vodka. "Such as?"

"Very diverse—real estate, retail, hospitality, food service, pharmaceuticals, construction, shipping, banking."

"Construction. I see there's a company downstairs called Wolfline Contracting. Is that one of yours?"

"Yes, I have a financial interest in that company."

"What does Wolfline Contracting do?"

He shrugged slightly. "All I know is they make money."

"I tried the door. There was nobody there."

He took a sip of his wine. "They rarely are. It's a satellite office. They're often on the road. Like you, Miss Chase. With our laptops and our smartphones, your office is anywhere you happen to be. I'll bet you spend a great deal of time in your car."

I felt another pinprick of fear. Of course, Valentin would know exactly how much time I spent in my car. His brother had been following me around for days.

I decided to take another path. "Did you know a photographer by the name of Adam Jarvis?"

His heavy eyebrows knitted together and he rubbed the whiskers on his chin, giving the appearance that he was searching through his brain cells for a reference. "Adam Jarvis? I don't recall anyone of that name."

"Mr. Jarvis liked to gamble. He owed a bookie a great deal of money. Witnesses said that they saw a Wolfline Contracting truck park in front of Mr. Jarvis' studio a few weeks ago and two guys went inside with baseball bats to scare a payment out of him."

Valentin shrugged again. "Like I said, I don't have anything to do with the day-to-day operations of any business other than my own."

I pressed ahead. "Two days ago, his body was found in the back of his studio. He'd been tortured and beaten to death."

Body found by me. Sitting in a pool of blood, fingers and arms at unnatural angles. Skull caved in.

He shook his head. "That's terrible. Do they know who killed him?"

"No. Plus, his daughter is missing. Her name is Bobbi Jarvis. Have you ever heard of her?"

He pointed at me. "Fifteen years old. I saw it on the news. She ran away with her teacher."

"The teacher's body was found this morning in a shallow grave in Sheffield."

He picked up his wine and swirled it in his glass, giving it a sniff, then a swallow. Still holding the stem of his glass, his voice was somber. "Oh my, so many bodies."

"The girl is still missing."

He leaned forward with a concerned look. "Do you think the two murders have anything to do with her disappearance? Do you think that the girl might have killed them?"

"We don't know what to think, Mr. Tolbonov."

"Please call me Valentin."

I didn't make a similar offer of familiarity. I got to the point. "I have sources who claim that Wolfline Contracting is a front for illegal activities."

He leaned forward, his eyebrows raised. "What kind of illegal activities?"

"Illegal bookmaking, for one." I ticked off a list, watching his face. "Drugs, extortion, weapon smuggling, prostitution, human trafficking."

His eyes never left my face. "I assure you, Miss Chase, I have no knowledge of any illegal activities. Is that what you came to talk to me about? I sell diamonds and jewelry. I have no reason to be involved with any illegal activities."

I was suddenly aware that the man who had met me at the front door was still standing directly behind me. I glanced back. He stood, feet slightly apart, hands clasped behind his back.

He'd been staring at me, the back of my head, the entire time.

Creepy.

Valentin saw me looking at the man and said, "That's Dmitri. He heads up my security team here at the shop. You've seen some of the inventory out there. We'd make quite a target for thieves. But I never give it a second thought while Dmitri and his men are on duty."

I glanced back at him again.

He grinned and gave me a curt nod.

I turned back to face Valentin.

He gently tapped the table with his finger tips. "So, Miss Chase, what specifically did you come out here to talk to me about?"

I locked directly onto his dark brown eyes. "I'm looking for Barbara Jarvis. I thought you might have some idea where she is."

He nodded slightly. "Yes, she's good friends with your ward, isn't she?"

That set me back in my chair. Fear tightened in my chest. *He didn't read that in the newspaper.*

He continued. "What's her name? Caroline?"

I remained speechless.

He pursed his lips. "I'm afraid I have no idea where Miss Jarvis is. I wish I could help you."

Still stunned by his mention of Caroline, I tried to think of a way to wind this up and get the hell out.

Valentin wasn't finished. "Since we're talking about people we'd like to find. I believe you've met with Eric Decker?"

"Yeah, he ambushed me one night in my company's parking lot."

"He's an attorney. Sometimes they can be aggressive." He shrugged. "Mr. Decker told me about the untimely death of one of Wolfline's employees, a Mr. James Caviness. I understand he was incinerated by his wife."

His eyes were unblinking, relentlessly staring into my own. "Mr. Decker has told me he's trying to locate Mrs. Caviness. It seems she has some intellectual property that belongs to Wolfline."

The notebook that Jim Caviness kept.

His words became loud, emphatic. "Mr. Decker would like to have it back."

It was jarring. Throughout the conversation, Valentin Tolbonov denied any day-to-day involvement with Wolfline. But then he brought up Caroline and the notebook.

How extensive is his reach? How slick is his operation?

Dread was turning to terror.

Who knows that I'm here? No one. Am I making bad decisions because I started drinking again?

This man cuts diamonds, the hardest objects on earth. He trims them, shapes them.

What could he do to human skin? What could he do to one lone woman here in his shop?

When I didn't respond, Valentin continued, his face dark. "I know that the Friends of Lydia posted Mrs. Caviness' bail. I'm guessing they're the ones who are keeping her whereabouts a secret. Do you have a way to contact them?"

I slowly shook my head.

He nodded and took another sip of his wine. "How much do you know about the Friends of Lydia?"

I cleared my throat and searched for my voice, "Not much." The trembling timbre of my voice betrayed my fear.

He brought both hands up, palms out, then placed them slowly on the tabletop. "I thought not. Did you meet Shana Neese?"

I was going to answer, but then thought better of it.

"Did she tell you what she does for a living? What she does when she's not rescuing the downtrodden?" He formed air quotes with his fingers when he said that.

How much should I share?

"She said that she's a physical therapist." I whispered.

He coughed out a dry laugh. "Is that what she told you? That's hilarious. Shana Neese is a professional dominatrix. She owns a very successful dungeon in Manhattan. I understand that she actually employs ten ladies who will beat the living hell out of you…for the right price."

I blinked, hoping I'd think of something to say. But nothing seemed appropriate.

"Did she introduce you to her partner?"

The man in the parking lot at the hotel who had watched to see if I'd been followed?

Valentin continued. "No? I'll tell you his name. He's John Stillwater, a New York cop, unceremoniously kicked off the force. Have Shana tell you that story. It's illuminating."

I pushed my glass forward, the cut facets sparkling in the light. It was still half full but I wanted to get the hell out of there.

Valentin drained his own glass and set it on the table. "Do you know who Lydia was?"

I nodded. "Tragic story."

"Tragic, indeed. Knowing who Lydia was explains the passionate involvement of Miss Neese. Lydia was her younger sister." He looked directly at me. "It's a dangerous world, Miss Chase."

I felt sick. I wanted to leave. I needed to get out. I couldn't breathe. "Thank you for your time, Mr. Tolbonov. I'm on deadline." Pushing the chair back, I stood up and slid my bag onto my shoulder. Even though my legs were shaking, I was determined to walk out gracefully.

Message received, Mr. Tolbonov, but I'm still standing.

Valentine stood as well. "Dmitri will show you out."

I looked up into his face. He wore a dark, serious expression, his eyes little more than slits. "Miss Chase, unless you intend to make a purchase, I'm confident that I won't see you again. At least, not here."

Chapter Thirty

I sat in my car until my hands stopped shaking. Even in the short walk from the building to my car, the cold air had chilled me to the bone.

Or had it been my encounter with Valentin Tolbonov?

The man knows way too much about me. And has the resources to do anything he wants.

I started the engine and cranked up the heat as high as it would go. I put my hands in front of the blower vent to warm them up. It took a few moments, but I felt the heat in my fingers and palms, my arms and shoulders loosening, more relaxed.

Then, breathing easier, I pulled out onto the road and headed back to I-95. I glanced down at the center console where my commuter cup was nestled. I knew that it was empty and that I didn't have any vodka in my bag. If I wanted a drink, I'd have to stop off somewhere, either a bar or a liquor store.

That was when I realized that I didn't have a single friend to talk to.

Someone to talk me out of buying another bottle of vodka.

I wonder if I still have my AA sponsor's number in my phone?

Cultivating friendships really wasn't in my DNA. Because I interact with so many people, often under stressful conditions, I appreciated my time alone.

Don't get me wrong. I liked being with Caroline, even with her being a teenage angst-ridden pain in the ass.

But she was in school and I don't think sharing my concerns about Bobbi Jarvis and Valentin Tolbonov was a particularly good idea. And I certainly wasn't going to talk to Caroline about stopping by the liquor store.

I couldn't talk to Ruth. She'd use it against me. There was no one on the staff I could turn to, and Ben was selling us out.

I'm utterly alone.

Getting to the entrance of the highway, I glanced at the digital clock on my dash—twelve-thirty. One hand on the wheel, I reached into my bag and rummaged blindly until I found my phone. Then I punched in a number.

"Genie?"

"Yes. Hi, Frank."

He hesitated before he said anything. Then, "This is a surprise. Is everything okay?"

When I'd run into him by accident at the pub, I hadn't been particularly friendly.

No wonder he's surprised.

I took a deep breath, the first since leaving Valentin's presence.

"Got time for lunch?" I hoped that I sounded stable.

There was a moment of shocked silence. Finally, "When?"

"Quarter after one? Black Sheep?"

"I have a meeting but, for you, I'll move it. See you at Black Sheep."

Really? Really? Frank Mancini? There's no one else in the world that you can call a friend?

I drove past the wrought-iron gate to the entrance of Vet's Park and found a spot for my car. The parking lot had filled up with news trucks and camera crews. Cops had put up barriers and police tape blocked entrance into the woods. Two officers stood at the entrance of Hawkes Manor, looking slightly ridiculous as two full-size plastic gargoyles crouched with menace, silently snarling next to them.

I wondered if the Drama Club's fundraiser would open at all this season. How would they pay for any of their productions?

I was struck with yet another sudden sense of dread.

If the paper's sold and the new owners judge me unfit, how will I pay my own bills?

A dozen pop-up tents had gone up since that morning and there were cameras and talking heads all over the place. Two helicopters hovered over the trees in the vicinity where Jake Addison's body had been found.

So many bodies.

Valentin's voice was in my head.

Off to my right, I watched as three crews sat, transfixed to monitors, watching the live feed as their drones skimmed the tops of the trees.

Past the barriers, I saw Mike under a pop-up tent of his own, working with state investigators, pouring over maps on a card table.

Got to get my head on straight, get back to work. Do the job.

The Sheffield cop standing at the barrier keeping the news horde at bay was Officer Rodney Shore. Back when I was on the beat, I wrote a piece on him getting a citation from the mayor for exceptional conduct in the line of duty. He'd rescued two children and a German shepherd from a burning van.

He barely got the dog out before the damned thing blew up.

I walked up close to the barrier where he stood guard. "Hey, Rodney."

Recognizing me, his face exploded into a grin. "Miss Chase." Then he noticed the crowd of reporters behind me and his smile disappeared. "I can't let you across the tape, I'm sorry." He shook his head.

I waved my hand. "No worries. Can you do me a favor, though? Can you tell Mike Dillon I'm here?"

He smiled again. "Oh, yeah, sure."

I watched as he trotted across the grass until he got to the tent and tapped Mike's shoulder. They conferred a moment, Rodney pointed in my direction and Mike caught sight of me.

Mike nodded and Rodney walked briskly back to the police tape. "He said to give him a minute."

While I waited, I checked the *Sheffield Post* website on my smartphone. Ben had given the story about Jake Addison a headline that screamed, "Teacher Found Dead in Shallow Grave".

Properly gruesome.

"Hey, Genie, what's up?"

I looked away from my phone and saw that Mike was standing inches from me, the two of us separated by yellow tape. As a blue helicopter with an NBC logo swooped overhead to join the other two, the *whop-whop-whop* noise was almost deafening.

Mike glanced up and shook his head. "Freaking circus."

I leaned in over the tape to get closer to his ear. "Anything new?"

He shook his head, knowing I was talking about Bobbi Jarvis. "Nothing so far. We've got a dozen dogs out there, but there's a hell of a lot of ground to cover."

"Would it be worthwhile to check out Tommy Willis again?"

"The ex-boyfriend? Way ahead of you, Genie. Right after we found the body this morning, we got a warrant to search his house. Got nothin'."

"Crap."

"I showed him a still photo from the video we took from Jake Addison's apartment."

"And?"

"He claims that's not the video that he and the girl shot. Kid got pretty steamed when he saw some other guy having sex with his ex-girlfriend."

Who the hell is the guy in the video?

I heard a faint whirr as a drone buzzed just over our heads, slowing and hovering near the police tent. Mike spotted it. "I'm about on my last nerve. I'm going to shoot one of those goddamned things out of the sky before this is over."

• ● ● ● •

I got to the restaurant before Frank arrived. The atmosphere was deliciously warm and comforting. Black Sheep boasts a wood-fire oven and the faint scent of burning oak and maple wood hung in the air alongside curry and basil. A young man, wearing a long-sleeved, blue pinstriped shirt, tie, and black apron, met me at the door and escorted me to a table overlooking the Sheffield River.

Calling it a river was generous. It was little more than a rushing creek. But the restaurant cozied up to its banks, and the water washing over a clutch of large rocks was mesmerizing. I sat and stared out the window, watching the current gurgle by, thinking about my meeting with Tolbonov.

Escaping the suffocating, tightly controlled environment that Tolbonov owned, I was as cold as the water below, chilled to bone by the hard surface of Valentin's icy resolve and intellect.

What was I hoping would happen?

That my mere presence would rattle Valentin enough that he'd make a mistake and blurt out that he'd killed Adam Jarvis and Jake Addison?

My God, had I been wrong.

I was outclassed, outgunned, outmaneuvered. A waif in hiking boots among the diamonds and the predators.

The way he looked at me reminded me of a documentary I'd seen years ago about wolves hunting in Siberia. They'd wait for hours in the snow, motionless, watching their prey for weakness.

He'd brought up Caroline, knowing she was my weakness.

"Genie?"

Hearing Frank's voice gave me a start.

"I'm sorry." His voice was slow, warm honey. "Did I frighten you?"

I smiled nervously. "No. You don't scare me." I stood up and we hugged.

Then we sat down at the table. Frank cocked his head. "It was a nice surprise to get your lunch invitation. When we ran into each other at the bar, it didn't go well."

Before I could answer, a second young man, dressed like the one who had seated me, asked if we'd like something to drink.

I answered first. "God, yes, vodka, rocks."

Frank raised an eyebrow. "Jack Daniels over ice, please."

The boy scurried away and I turned back to Frank. "I need to talk to a friend."

"And when you couldn't find one, you called me?"

I scowled. "Why say that? I hope the hell I can call you my friend."

"I always considered us more than friends. At least, we were."

I reached out and took his hand in mine. "We're still more than friends. But right now, I need a friend, not a lover...a friend."

He squeezed my hand. "All right. Friend."

The young man swooped in with our drinks and asked if we were ready to order. Frank looked up at him and said that we'd be a little while.

Once he left, I took a deep swallow of my vodka and let it rush through my body. The stress of the day didn't disappear, but it grew less distinct, the harsh edges less painful.

Frank was patient. He didn't push me; he didn't hurry me. We sat at that table sipping our drinks, holding hands, watching the river rush by. Finally, I started. I told him everything. I told him about Bobbi going missing that past Monday on her way to school. About how I found Adam Jarvis in his studio with his skull crushed.

"Oh, my dear God, Genie," Frank uttered. "I didn't know that it had been so gruesome."

Then I outlined how the police found evidence that Bobbi and Jake Addison had run off together, finding Jake's car at the Stamford Train Station, how he'd purchased two tickets to New York.

But then his body was found locally, apparently shot execution-style. I told Frank about how Adam Jarvis, years ago, had sold his own wife into prostitution to pay off his gambling debts and how she had a suspicion that he might have done the same thing with his daughter.

My words poured out like the burbling stream rushing over the rocks.

I went on to tell him about how the coffee shop owners had seen a Wolfline Contracting truck pull up in front of Adam Jarvis' studio and two men went in with baseball bats to scare money out of him.

Finally, I recounted my ominous meeting only an hour earlier with Valentin Tolbonov.

Shaking my head, remembering. "There's no way I can describe how I felt while I was sitting across from him. The impact it left on me. The sheer evil I felt emanating from that man. His world, under his control."

I stopped talking and took a deep breath. It felt good to unload.

Frank had been mostly silent during my monologue. "I'm not sure that your visit with Mr. Tolbonov wasn't..."

While he searched for the right word, I finally interjected, "Wasn't stupid?"

He smiled. "I was going to say, wasn't well advised. Don't you think you should leave this line of investigation to the police?"

I sounded frantic. "That's not where they are. They think Bobbi's dead and buried somewhere in that park."

He scowled. "Other than the fact that she's Caroline's friend, aren't you taking this girl's disappearance too personally?"

I sat back in my chair. I was about to tell Frank something I had never shared with anyone, none of my husbands, not even Kevin Bell. "When I was fourteen, my Uncle Jessie hit a low point in his life and needed a place to live until he got back on his feet. He'd been living with us for about a month when he came into my room for the first time. I'd been sleeping. I smelled him before I saw him. The smell woke me up. He smoked and he reeked, like nicotine and cancer."

Frank stared at me. He knew something bad was coming.

"He slid in under my sheets without saying a word, put his hand over my mouth. He said that I wasn't a child anymore. He was going to make me a woman. He told me not to tell anyone or he'd hurt me and my mom."

Frank shook his head. "I'm so sorry, Genie. How long did it go on for?"

I could feel tears burning in my eyes as my vision went foggy. "Once or twice a week for over a month. Until I snuck a serrated butcher knife out of the kitchen and brought it to bed with me. The next time he slid into bed with me, I held the blade up to his thigh and told him that if ever touched me again, I'd cut his off his balls. He got out of bed and he never tried it again."

Frank was silent.

I gazed out the window as the water gurgled and roiled and rushed to fill Long Island Sound. My voice dropped to little more than a whisper. "To this day, the smell of cigarette smoke turns my stomach."

"I'm glad to see you've still got yours."

I glanced at him. "I've still got my what?"

He offered up a tiny smile. "Balls."

Chapter Thirty-one

Caroline tossed her backpack into the backseat of the Sebring and then slid into the front with me. "I need to change clothes before I go to the theater."

No "hello". No "how was your day?" No "any news about Bobbi Jarvis?"

She was flexing her teenage "rude" muscle.

Rise above.

"So how did everyone handle the news about Mr. Addison?"

Her hands lightly tapped the tops of her knees. "Like I said on the phone, everybody's in shock. Tommy Willis was in school when the cops came by to talk to him again. When he got back in class he was really pissed off. He said that the cops told him they were searching his parents' house."

"What else did Tommy say?"

From the corner of my eyes, I could see her turn and stare directly at me. "Tommy said that a cop called Mike Dillon showed him a still photo from a video found at Jake Addison's apartment."

My stomach knotted.

Caroline continued. "Apparently, Bobbi starred in a sex tape. The cops had asked him if the guy in the video was him. It wasn't. Tommy was royally pissed."

I could see that Caroline was too. "Mike was just doing his job," I said.

She didn't answer.

Change subjects.

"Are you excited about starting rehearsals?"

She glanced behind her, at the backpack on the seat. "I started reading through the script at lunch. Powerful stuff."

"Oh, yeah?" I kept my eyes on the traffic.

She ticked off the subjects by holding up her fingers. "It's got everything—adultery, lies, death, failure." Caroline looked at me and jutted out her chin as she named the last subject in the script. "Alcoholism."

Ouch.

She's aimed that knife right for my heart.

I cleared my throat. "When Angela Owens told me about the play, I thought it sounded depressing."

"I know, right?" She held out her hands. "But it's not. It's got biting, intense moments of humor, bordering on black comedy."

"Do you like the character you'll be playing?"

I could see her grinning. "Oh, yeah. The character's name is Karen and boy oh boy, is she a snarky smart-ass."

My turn to smile. "Right up your alley."

While Caroline took a few minutes to change into jeans and a long-sleeved top, I had fully intended to sneak a drink in my bedroom. But I had Caroline's voice still in my head, making the one-word statement, "Alcoholism."

Instead, I opened the back door for Tucker. Then I stood out on the porch and watched while he ran back and forth across the yard, sniffing and stopping, then taking off at trot again. Finally, he lifted a leg.

I folded my arms across my chest, feeling the chill of the air. Kevin's old wooden picnic table still sat in the yard, although last winter had taken its toll. Some of the boards in the table top were dry and splitting. I promised myself that when spring came, I'd sand it down and paint it with sealant.

I smelled smoke in the air—a wood fire. I glanced around at the houses behind and next to ours. Someone had a fireplace going and the scent was delicious. Perfect for the time of year.

It was still light, but the days were getting shorter and, even at four in the afternoon, the sun was low in the sky. The leaden clouds that had effectively shut down the sun all day, opened slightly to offer an otherworldly golden glow.

"I'm ready."

I turned to see Caroline standing in the doorway behind me. Her long blond hair was brushed back and pulled into a ponytail. She wore eyeliner and lipstick and looked so mature and beautiful, I almost felt like crying.

Kevin, I'm so sorry you're not here to see this right now.

"Look at you," I said, without thinking. "You're all grown up."

She frowned.

"I'm so proud of you right now."

Then she did something that surprised me. She came out through the door onto the porch and hugged me.

It was something she hadn't done in a long time. Something I sorely missed.

● ● ● ● ●

I pulled into the parking lot of the Playhouse and cut the engine. "Mind if I come in with you?"

"Help yourself," she answered, holding the script in one hand and opening the car door with the other. Without waiting, she started across the lot to the wooden steps leading up to the theater's front porch.

Rolling my eyes, I followed behind, up the steps, across the porch, and through the glass-paned doorway. Inside, I found Caroline, stopped dead in her tracks.

A few lights were on in the dim lobby. Off to our right was the ticket counter. Ahead of us were carpeted steps leading up to additional lobby space.

Catching up to where she was standing, I asked, "Are you okay?"

She turned her head and stared at me with wide eyes. "This is real. This is serious."

I felt myself smile. "As a heart attack. C'mon, baby. You've got this. Let's go in there and knock 'em dead."

I took her by the hand and began to lead her to the theater doors. No windows here. The only light allowed in the theater was what was provided by the storytellers. Her hand fell away from mine as I pulled open the door and went inside.

Once again, the seats were empty, save for the man sitting in the back row—David LaSalle. I waved at him and he smiled back at me.

The spotlights were focused on the stage where Peter Cambridge, Mona Fountain, and Angela Owens stood looking over the script. The set had changed. That morning, the stage and its furniture resembled the living room of an apartment.

Now it appeared to be someone's bedroom, complete with queen-sized bed, lamps, night tables, chest of drawers, and a mirror hanging on a faux wall.

While we walked up the aisle toward the stage, I glanced back at Caroline. "Hey, how many set changes does this production have?"

Staring up at the high-powered stars on the stage, she mumbled, "According to the script, four. Apartment, parents' bedroom, Karen's bedroom, mother's office."

Noticing us coming down the aisle, Peter held a hand up to his eyebrows to shield his eyes from the spots. He saw us and offered a wide grin. "Geneva Chase and our newest member of the *Darkness Lane* team, Caroline Bell."

He proceeded to clap his hands together and the other two women did the same.

Angela shouted, "Welcome to our little corner of the universe."

Caroline and I got to the edge of the stage and climbed the steps. Peter reached out with both arms and took our hands. "Come, come. Have you met Mona yet?"

As he led us across the platform, it occurred to me that the last time I saw this man, he was naked, sweaty from our lovemaking, and asleep.

No, this isn't awkward at all.

Mona Fountain was slightly shorter than me and very thin. Her dark hair was shoulder-length and she had bangs that nearly reached her eyebrows. Her almond-shaped brown eyes gave her a slightly exotic appearance. She wore black jeans and an off-white sleeveless top. I was surprised to see the toned musculature in her arms and shoulders. I recalled hearing that she did most of her own stunts in her television series.

When the woman smiled, she offered a brilliant display of artificially whitened teeth. She held out her hand. "I'm Mona Fountain."

Caroline got to her first. Pumping hands, she said, "I've seen all the episodes of *Hell's Highway*. You're a fantastic actress."

I was next to take her hand. "It's nice to meet you. I'm Geneva Chase."

Angela moved closer to Caroline. "Ready to get started?"

She nodded eagerly.

I suddenly realized that Peter was standing directly behind me. He leaned in and said, "You're welcome to stay if you like."

The way he said it made my heart flutter.

I turned to face him. "I've got to get back to the office. What time should I come pick Caroline up?"

Angela spoke up. "Oh, we'll most likely knock off around ten, but we'll have David drive her home."

She'd said it loud enough that the entire theater could have heard it.

In the shadows in the back of the expansive room, I watched as the dark figure raised his hand in acknowledgment.

"That okay with you?" I glanced at Caroline.

Caroline, star-struck by being with both Peter Cambridge and Mona Fountain, had now just been told that she'd have a driver take her home. Nodding, she gave me a thumbs-up. "Oh, I think that will be fine."

I left the stage and walked back through the theater. As I did, I heard Angela say, "Okay, what we're going to do is run lines directly from the script. Caroline, feel free to over-emote while we're doing this. Don't be afraid to ham it up. I want you to be comfortable with the energy and power of the script."

I took one last look behind me—the four of them standing on stage, holding scripts, saying their lines in the spotlights.

So proud of Caroline.

Then I walked through the door and into the lobby, nearly bumping into the rushing figure of Morgan Stiles.

"Mr. Stiles, I don't know if you remember me."

He attempted a smile. "Of course. Did you bring your daughter?"

I didn't correct him. "She's running lines as we speak."

He rubbed his hands together. "First break we've had this week. If your daughter is as good as Angela and Peter say she is, with some luck, we can be ready to open before Thanksgiving."

"Fingers crossed." Then I recalled my discussion with Peter at the Orinoco Café. "Mr. Cambridge told me something curious while we were having dinner last night."

His eyebrows shot up. "You had dinner with Peter?"

And sex. Is that what you're wondering?

"He said that you own the house they're living in."

The man glanced around the lobby to see if anyone was within earshot. "He told you that? How much did he have to drink?"

I shrugged.

Morgan scowled and shook his head. "He's not supposed to be blabbing about that."

"But it's true?"

"Off the record, Miss Chase, this has to be off the record."

"Okay." Peter had actually already confirmed that, but I couldn't imagine that I'd personally use it in a story for the *Sheffield Post*. The *National Enquirer* maybe, but not the *Post*.

"Peter Cambridge and Angela Owens don't have two nickels to rub together. I'm paying the freight for everything—rent, their cars, the cook, this theater, even their freaking groceries."

"Peter told me they lost everything from a lawsuit over *Night Challenge*. That Angela had plagiarized the script from one of her students."

The producer studied me. Then he said, "Yeah, that works."

Not the affirmation I'd expected. Something's not right.

I let his answer slide. "I see why it's so important that this production is successful."

"Like you said, Miss Chase, fingers crossed." Then he disappeared through the door and into the dark theater.

Walking out into the cold afternoon and across the parking lot, my cellphone chirped. I looked at caller ID and saw that it was Shana Neese. "Hello?"

"Genie, I think we found your girl."

Chapter Thirty-two

"Tell me." I couldn't keep the urgency out of my voice.

"Not over the phone." She sounded very tired. "Look, it's been a hell of a day. Where can we go that's quiet and we can get a drink?"

I glanced at my watch. It was almost four-thirty. "Have you heard of a place called Brick's?"

"Yeah, pizza joint near the waterfront. See you there in half an hour," she said, then disconnected.

I stood outside my car and called the office to see if Ben needed me back for anything. "Are you still working the Bobbi Jarvis story?" he asked.

"Yes."

"I hear the police are keeping everyone out of the park. The scuttlebutt is they're convinced Bobbi's dead and buried out there."

I involuntarily glanced up at the woods beyond the parking lot of the Playhouse. There was a cop standing at the edge of a trail that, I knew, eventually led to the Community Center on the other side of Vet's Park. I hadn't seen him when we'd first parked the car, but then again, I hadn't been looking for him.

Studying the cloudy sky, I noticed that the news 'copters were gone. I'd take a quick spin around to the other side of the park and check out the Community Center parking lot. But I was certain that all the reporters with their pop-up tents and news vans were gone as well, working on other stories, confident that they'd be back when the cops found another body.

I spoke into the phone. "Well, I'm not convinced she's dead."

Especially now that Shana Neese told me they might have located her.

● ● ⬤ ● ●

Brick's was a hole in the wall not far from my old apartment on the south side of Sheffield. They served pizza, lasagna, and beer and wine and the place reeks of garlic and oregano. It only had eight tables and a bar along the back wall. Appropriately, the red brick walls gave the place a New York feel.

I missed that I wasn't within walking distance any more.

When I got there, Shana, wearing a black sweater and form-fitting blue jeans, was already sitting at a table with a man who looked familiar to me. As I approached, the man stood up.

Shana nodded toward him. "Geneva, this is John Stillwater, one of my associates. The day you came to interview Betsy Caviness, John was the one watching the parking lot."

He nodded and pulled my chair out for me. "It's nice to meet you, Miss Chase. I see your byline all the time."

He was in his forties, tall, about six feet, and I guessed he weighed in at about two-twenty. He had on a button-down, navy blue shirt, rolled up at the wrists and tucked neatly into a pair of faded, well-worn jeans. John Stillwater was clean-shaven, had a strong jaw, a pleasant smile, and blue eyes that appeared fatigued, like he'd seen much more than he could ever possibly forget. The lines around his eyes and the sides of his mouth gave him character. The way his full head of brown hair fell over his ears and the back of his collar, I figured he was about two weeks overdue for a trim.

The square, black-rimmed glasses he wore gave me the impression that he was both intelligent and vulnerable.

I sat and then he did as well. Shana had a glass of chardonnay in front of her and John had a chilled mug of beer.

A young lady wearing black slacks and a sleeveless, brown top stopped by the table and took my drink order. I skipped the usual and went for a chardonnay.

I watched her walk to the back of the restaurant, smiling at a young man behind the bar. Then I turned my attention to Shana. "Speaking of Betsy Caviness, shouldn't the two of you be babysitting her?"

John and Shana briefly glanced at each other. Shana was the first to speak, her words measured and precise. "I'll tell you about Mrs. Caviness in a moment. But first, let's talk about the young girl you're looking for." Shana leaned forward. "We made some discreet inquiries and found out that one of our local pimps has managed to procure a teenage white girl."

"Bobbi Jarvis?"

John Stillwater picked up his mug with one hand and wiped condensation off the tabletop using a napkin. "Names are hard to come by, Miss Chase."

"Call me Genie. But it *could* be Bobbi Jarvis."

Shana glanced around the room. There were two men at the bar and a man and woman sitting at a table on the other side of the tiny restaurant, near the fireplace. Shana spoke in a low voice. "The pimp we're talking about, his name is Del Randall, also known as Loose."

John interjected. "As in Lucifer."

Shana pulled up the sleeve of her sweater and pointed to her forearm. "He has a tattoo of the devil right here."

"Nice fashion statement." Just then the woman brought my glass of wine and asked if we wanted to order any food.

We all shook our heads and she headed back to the bar.

Shana pulled her sweater back down to her wrist. "Loose specializes in trafficked girls. Mostly imports from places like Nigeria, Libya, Pakistan, Syria, Mexico, and El Salvador."

John said, "Mostly women of color."

Shana took a sip of her wine. "So, when a white girl comes up for sale, it causes some street buzz."

"How does this guy get his girls?"

John's nostrils flared and he said, "He buys them from an importer. Loose likes to keep his stable fresh so he changes inventory on a fairly regular basis. When he gets tired of them, he sells the girls back to the importer who sells them again to another pimp."

I took a sip of my wine. Talking about girls like they were things, like they were property or animals to be bought and sold, was making me queasy. I cleared my throat. "An importer," I repeated. "You mean smugglers."

Shana nodded. "Our friends at Wolfline have trucks, they have airplanes, and they have access to ships. They're very good at transporting things from point A to point B, all the while bypassing customs or nosy Homeland Security agents."

"How do they get their hands on these girls?"

Shana explained, "Multiple methods. Their families are poor, and I'm talking really poor, so it is not uncommon that parents sell off a daughter or two. Or a young lady is promised a good job if only she finds a way to get to America. But once here, Geneva, it's a very different story."

John drummed his fingers on the tabletop. "And sometimes there's a special order and a girl is flat-out kidnapped off the street."

"Wolfline is full service. When a pimp wants to change up his stock, they'll buy back inventory and resell to other buyers," Shana added. "Plus, they take a percentage of the action."

"Just to be clear, when Lucifer the Pimp wants new girls to prostitute, he goes to Wolfline and they'll buy back the old ones and sell him new ones." I heard the bitter edge in my own voice. Looking at my glass of wine, I wished I'd ordered something stronger.

Shana's tone was modulated. "And when the girls get older and cycle out of the sex trade, then Wolfline sells them to domestic agencies as household help."

"So, what we're talking about is twenty-first century slavery." I was having a difficult time keeping the anger out of my voice.

John leaned in. "That's exactly what we're talking about. Between fifteen and eighteen thousand people are trafficked in the United States every year. One third of those are used for manual labor, two-thirds as sex slaves. Human-trafficking is the third-largest criminal enterprise, behind only drugs- and weapons-smuggling. Globally, it's a one-hundred-fifty-billion-dollar business."

"Treating people like animals."

He took a sip of his beer. "Very much. Keeping them locked up during the day. Pimping them out at night. Not much of a life."

I felt the bile rising in my throat. "Is that what they're doing with Bobbi Jarvis?"

"We don't know for sure that it's her," she said. "But it's a hell of a coincidence that your girl disappears and a white teenager comes on the market all in the same week."

I asked a question. "How involved is Valentin Tolbonov in all of this?"

John shook his head. "The reason he stays off the radar screens of so many law agencies is that he rarely gets his hands dirty. He leaves that up to the hired help."

Shana sneered. "And to his brother, Bogdan. It sounds like you two have met. He leaves a hell of an impression, doesn't he?"

"This morning, I met Valentin Tolbonov as well."

Both of them went wide-eyed.

John asked, "What did that look like?"

I felt myself smile. "He is one scary son of a bitch."

Shana agreed. "They're both very scary, Geneva. Tread carefully. Did he ask you about Mrs. Caviness?"

"Yes. And he told me that he wants the notebook."

John took off his glasses and rubbed the bridge of his nose.

"They got to Mrs. Caviness' sister. They threatened to kill her, her husband, and their two kids if Mrs. Caviness doesn't give up the notebook."

My gut tightened. After my meeting with Valentin, I had no doubt that's what took place. "When did this happen?"

He answered, "No more than an hour ago. Mrs. Caviness made the decision that she didn't want us to look after her anymore. She said that she was going to put the notebook into the hands of someone who would keep it safe. She said she'd leave instructions that if anything happened to her or her family, the notebook would be given to the police."

Shana looked away from me. "Then she asked us to leave."

"Will she be safe?" I asked.

Like anyone would know for sure.

"Honest to God, Genie. I think she's making a mistake. Once she goes public, she's at risk. And if she's tortured and gives up the name of who has the notebook, that person is at risk as well."

I recalled how the poor woman had looked when I talked with her in the hotel room. Sad, tiny, and beaten, both physically and mentally. I directed a question to Shana. "You don't think she'll hurt herself, do you?"

Shana's hands rested on the tabletop, her face thoughtful. "You mean commit suicide? She didn't do it during the twenty years her husband was beating her. Suicide? No. But I think she's going to plead guilty to premeditated murder and spend the rest of her life locked up. And, honest to God, I don't know how safe she'll be in prison."

Damn it. I hate that she's still getting beaten.

Shana offered up a tiny smile. "As we were leaving, Miss Betsy gave me a hug and said that it was a Mexican standoff. The notebook wouldn't go to the cops as long as nobody hurt her or her family. But Wolfline wouldn't get it either."

"Did she give it to her attorney?"

"I don't know who she gave it to."

I had to pull it together. "What's our next step with Bobbi Jarvis? Do we go talk to Lucifer the Pimp?"

John stole a look at his watch and shook his head. "He's out working the girls already. Our best bet is to find out where he's housing them and then pay a visit sometime in the morning."

"What's that mean, working the girls?"

John's hands balled up into fists. "He's getting them to the motel rooms or to their spots on the street or into some massage parlor or spa. Loose will work them until sometime around two in the morning. Then he'll bring them back in and let them sleep."

The thought of Bobbi Jarvis turning tricks out on the street or in some cheap motel was nauseating.

It was difficult to talk through clenched teeth. "And you think you can find where this pimp is keeping them?"

John raised his eyebrows and adjusted his glasses. "We're going to give it a try, Genie."

"Once you find out where this Lucifer is keeping the girls, are we telling the police?"

Shana shook her head and directed her attention to me. "We work privately. If we can get the girls out safely, we'll protect them. The cops would deport them back to the hell holes they came from to start all over again."

John tapped the tabletop with a finger. "We give them sanctuary, a chance at starting a whole new life."

I relaxed my jaw and smiled at him. I liked his style. "I heard you used to be a cop."

He grinned back. "Once."

Shana asked, "Did Tolbonov tell you that?"

I glanced at her. "Yes."

She was staring back at me with a bemused expression on her face. "Did he say anything about me?"

"He said that you're a professional dominatrix."

She leaned forward. "Did he? What do you think about that?" Her lips were slightly apart, her teeth showing.

"I'm jealous. It sounds like great fun."

Beating the crap out of men and letting them pay for it? Hell, yeah, it sounds like fun.

Shana asked, "Then why are you frowning?"

"Silly bit of irony," I answered. "The woman rescuing a teenager from being a sex worker is a…" I let my sentence dangle in the air.

Shana smiled and slowly shook her head. "What we do isn't against the law, Geneva. We can humiliate, beat, and dominate our clients and, as long as we don't have sex with them, what we do is legal…more or less."

I did a story about a dominatrix when I was in Boston. She'd been fascinating. The woman had taken me for a tour of her working areas. Walls festooned with whips, manacles, collars, chains, crops, and paddles. Furniture consisted of spanking benches, stocks, and an X-shaped structure called a St. Andrew's cross.

She was versatile. Set pieces included a dungeon, of course, as well as a school room, and a hospital examining room.

And the costumes. Oh, my God, so much leather—skirts, hot pants, studded bras, corsets, thigh high boots.

I recall that she did extremely well financially.

"How many employees do you have working for you?"

"Ten, plus me. Although, these days I rarely go into the office. I have a wonder woman who runs things for me when I'm not there. Her stage name is Mistress Frost. Smart and tough, she's perfect for our line of work. What else did Tolbonov say?"

"He told me how you're related to Lydia."

She slowly sat back in her chair, a forlorn expression on her face. "Yes, she was my sister."

"I'm sorry, Shana."

She held up a hand. "It was a long time ago."

I watched John lean in and put his arm around her shoulder. When this was over, when we had more time, I was eager to know more about these two.

Chapter Thirty-three

Before I left Bricks, I grabbed a takeout order of their chicken chili and garlic bread. Then, knowing that the bottle in my panty drawer was getting low, I stopped by Bev-Max to pick up some Absolut.

Shopping complete, I went home and let Tucker outside.

While he did his business, I set up my laptop on the kitchen table.

It felt odd. Whenever I do any kind of newspaper work at home, I do it in my bedroom upstairs. The kitchen was shared space with Caroline, not work space.

But Caroline was at her first rehearsal and the whole house was mine. She was going to be out of the house a lot. I had to adapt.

The first person I looked up was Del Randall, AKA Loose, short for Lucifer. Arrested once for aggravated assault and twice for promotion of prostitution, he'd never done any actual time. He'd gotten off on time served, a fine, and probation.

Low level thug.

I looked at his mug shot. The man staring back at me was in his fifties and was wearing an orange jumpsuit. His oily, gray-blond hair was slicked back away from his forehead. The man had thick jowls and wore a smirk, as if he knew his lawyer wouldn't let him spend any real time in jail.

The thought of Bobbi having anything to do with that worm made me shudder.

I had already attempted to look for information about Valentin Tolbonov, but it had been from my office where there were relentless distractions. As I sat at my kitchen table, eating my chili and drinking vodka and tonic, I took my time.

When I still came up with nothing, I stood up, stretched, and then let Tucker back in. I was surprised that the little guy was wet. Glancing out the door, I saw that it was raining. I picked up my terrier and walked him into the laundry room where I kept a towel for wet dogs.

After I dried the little guy and set him down on the floor, it was as if I'd goosed him with a firecracker. He set off at a dead run, an animated cartoon, running in circles and acting like he was a puppy.

Where do you get the energy?

Letting Tucker run himself into exhaustion in the living room, I glanced up at the duct tape covering the bullet hole in the front window and then I went back into the kitchen, poured myself another drink, and punched up Tolbonov Diamonds on my laptop. I'd already seen this website, but it was before I'd met Valentine Tolbonov face to face.

I pulled up the photo of Valentin that I'd seen in my office. He was smiling into the camera...a practiced public grin, one that he'd offer to his exclusive customers. Non-threatening, avuncular, he appeared friendly, his eyes almost sparkled.

Not the man I'd met.

The Valentin I'd encountered was the epitome of evil. Even in my own home, I felt the grasp of icy fingers of fear clutching at my arms. By his sheer malevolent presence, I knew he was capable of inflicting horrible pain.

I took a healthy swallow of my drink and shifted gears, punching up Peter Cambridge. I'd seen it all before—a long list of television and movie roles, awards, and accolades.

I did the same with Angela Owens and saw much of the same. The Internet brought up her achievements, which included a Tony Award-winning Broadway play and the blockbuster movie *Night Challenge*.

But what I hadn't looked at was her earlier life. A Wikipedia entry told me that she'd been born into abject poverty as Angela LaSalle in Leesville, West Virginia, to a coal miner father and a mother who died when Angela was only six. Her father was an alcoholic that she wrote about in a magazine article published in *The New Yorker* magazine while Angela was still in college. It was the milestone that established her as a writer. Shortly thereafter, she changed her name to Owens, her mother's maiden name.

What caught my eye, though, was that she was one of two siblings. Angela had a younger brother named David.

So, Peter Cambridge's security guy, David LaSalle, is Angela's brother?

I briefly wondered how Angela's brother would feel if he knew that Peter was screwing around on his sister.

There was scant mention of David LaSalle other than he'd been in the Marines and had served in an intelligence role in Afghanistan, achieving the rank of captain before he retired from the service.

I tabbed down through the numerous mentions of both Angela and Peter and only found one brief mention of a lawsuit regarding plagiarism with a former student of hers. The piece had run in *Variety* and had ended by saying the matter was settled out of court for an undisclosed sum.

According to Peter, it had bankrupted them.

I then went to Facebook and typed in Bobbi Jarvis. I immediately found her page. She'd used her glam shot as her profile picture. Behind that, her cover photo was of the stage at the Playhouse. The curtain was open and the houselights were on, so it was clear to see there weren't any people on the platform, but the faux furniture was there. It was a picture of the living room set from *Darkness Lane*.

I scrolled down through her timeline. It was filled with posts from her schoolmates, wishing her well, hoping she's okay, telling her that she was missed.

One of them was from Caroline. It said, "Missing you horribly, Bobbi. Please come home."

She'd written it before she'd been offered the part in *Darkness Lane*.

I looked, but there hadn't been any timeline entries from Bobbi since the day she went missing. Before that, she'd posted multiple photos and entries about being in the production and how great Peter Cambridge, Angela Owens, and Mona Fountain were.

Then abruptly, late Saturday night, she wrote something both ominous and cryptic. "I hate it when life turns to shit. Why do people hurt each other?"

That was the last thing she'd written.

I hit the private message button. I wrote a note to her that only someone with access to her account could read. "Bobbi, this is Genie Chase. I'm worried about you. Where are you? Tell me where you are and I'll come get you."

I waited.

There was no return message.

At about ten-thirty, I heard a vehicle pull into the driveway and a car door closing. I went into the living room and peeked through the curtains, past the duct tape. I saw Caroline scoot around the hood of a dark green Land Rover, bathed in its headlights. She threw the driver a wave and walked up our steps.

Tucker went nuts when she came through the front door, yipping and jumping until Caroline scooped him up into her arms.

"How did it go?"

Did I just slur my words?

She studied me for several heartbeats before she said anything. "This is going to be so intense, Genie. They want to get started at seven tomorrow morning and they're not planning to wind it up until around ten in the evening. They said they'll get some Thai takeout for dinner tomorrow night." Her words were coming out in an enthusiasm-infused jumble.

Carrying the dog toward the kitchen, she continued. "They are such professionals, very exacting, precise down to the last inflection of every word. Where your eyes should be focused, how you should be standing. How you should react to what other actors are saying or doing."

She stopped at the doorway and smiled at me. "I…love… this…so…much."

Then she disappeared into the kitchen. Before I could follow, I heard a sharp disapproving shout. "Genie."

My heart did a slow roll when I realized what was happening. Coming into the kitchen, I saw she was holding the bottle of Absolut—two-thirds empty.

Really? I drank that much tonight?

I wasn't sure how to react. One part of me was horrified. I felt like a teenager who'd been drinking on the sly and then got caught by her parents.

The other part of me was pissed. I was the parent, not Caroline.

She placed the vodka on the table. "I'm disappointed. Aunt Ruth told me she thought you might be drinking again."

"It's not your place, or Aunt Ruth's, to lecture me about drinking."

Oh yeah, slurring.

Her voice level rose. "Oh, I think it is. I remember what Daddy was like when he was drinking. It almost killed him and it damned near ruined us. It's one thing if you want to trash *your* life, but I'm not going to let you trash mine, goddamn it."

Without another word, she brushed past me and went upstairs to her bedroom.

My anger passed.

I was ashamed.

All too familiar.

Chapter Thirty-four

The next morning was spent in awkward silence. Caroline bustled about making herself a bowl of oatmeal.

I went about my business making coffee, toast, and staying quiet.

The drive to the Playhouse was equally wordless. It wasn't until we got through the wrought-iron gates of the park that Caroline finally said something. "I'm sorry I yelled at you last night."

"I understand how you feel. We can make this right."

"I know. I don't want things to change between us, Genie."

"Your Aunt Ruth has been talking to you about this." A statement, not a question.

"Your drinking?"

I nodded. The fact that the two of them would talk about this felt like a knife to my heart.

"She wants me to live with her." She turned and looked at me. "I don't want that to happen, Genie. Please don't make that happen."

And then she opened the door and she was gone, heading up steps to the theater's front porch.

I don't want that to happen either, sweetie. What am I going to do? I've tried to quit drinking.

I went back home and, not wanting to be alone with nothing to do, put on a pair of leggings, a base top, and a hoodie.

Then I went for a long-overdue run. The sky was dark, the clouds swollen, pregnant with precipitation. The temperature hovered near freezing. The fresh, cold air rushing in and out of my lungs was cleansing. With each steamy breath of condensation exhaled, I felt as if I was purging my body of its sins. The burn in my knees and calves was atonement for hurting Caroline.

And myself.

I managed to get down to the waterfront and back in about an hour. Not bad for being out of shape. A hot shower, some time in front of the mirror, and a soft pair of well-worn jeans along with a warm flannel shirt made me feel like a new woman.

I poured a cup of coffee and sat down with my phone, punching up Mike Dillon's personal number. It was Saturday morning and I didn't know if he was working or not.

"Genie?" he answered, recognizing my number.

"Hey, Mike. I hope you don't mind me calling you on a Saturday morning."

"Nah, I'm out here in the woods again. I don't know how long we'll be here, though. Temp is supposed to drop below freezing. Weather is calling for sleet sometime this afternoon. Roads are supposed to get bad. I can't have the dogs and men out here in an ice storm."

"Still haven't found anything?"

"Nope. I'm not sure we're going to."

"Hey, I've got a question. When you searched Jake's body, did you find a tiny, pink container of pepper spray, maybe on his keychain?"

He answered immediately. "Jake's pockets were picked clean. No phone, no wallet, no watch, no keys, no nothing."

"So, it was a robbery?"

"Anything is possible. Someone might have killed him, stolen his keys, taken his car, used his credit card to buy a couple of tickets to New York."

"You're not suggesting that Bobbi did that?"

"All I'm saying is we've got a hell of a lot of loose ends. And that doesn't even factor in Adam Jarvis' homicide."

My phone suddenly pinged. I looked at the screen and saw that I'd just gotten a text from Shana Neese.

"Anything else I should know?"

He answered. "Yeah, be careful with the Tolbonov brothers. They play rough."

"Understood. Hey, Mike?"

"What?'

"I'm sorry if I've hurt you."

I could almost hear him smile over the phone. "We're fine. Neither one of us is ready for a relationship."

"True. But don't completely count us out yet, okay?"

"Have a good weekend."

I moved my phone away from my ear and checked out the screen. My heart jumped when I read Shana's text. *We found where Loose is keeping the girls.*

I hate texting, so instead of tapping out my answer, I called her.

She answered. "Geneva."

"You found out where Bobbi is?"

"We don't know if your missing girl is there. All we know is that John has a source who said Loose has a new girl. She's supposed to be white and about fifteen years old."

She was warning me not to get my hopes up.

It wasn't working. "Okay, what do we do?"

"I'm going to give you the address of a convenience store in Bridgeport. Meet John and me there in half an hour."

● ● ● ● ●

Bridgeport is Fairfield County's poor stepchild. The largest city in Connecticut is also the most impoverished.

Fighting hard to make a comeback, Bridgeport can point to a few successes. But the city still has neighborhoods that look like they could be located in a third world country. Crumbling factories shuttered for decades, foreclosed homes with plywood nailed over the windows, dark, empty storefronts on streets devoid of any traffic other than to sell drugs.

It was into one of these neighborhoods, near the I-95 overpass, that I met Shana and John in the parking lot of a Fuel-Rite convenience store. They were in a white, unmarked panel van idling in a parking place directly in front of a silver ice machine, exhaust drifting in the bitterly cold air.

As I pulled up next to them, Shana motioned me to get out and at the same time, I saw John vacate the passenger's seat of the van and disappear into the back. I slid in where John had been only seconds before.

Shana had the heat cranked up high. Settling into the passenger's seat, I was pleased that it was so warm inside.

"Ready?" she asked.

Not knowing our game plan, I answered anyway. "Absolutely." I glanced behind me. The interior of the van was windowless and dark. There were two rows of bench-style seats, like you'd see on a shuttle from a hotel to an airport. John sat in the one closest to me.

He smiled.

I grinned back and then noticed that he was wearing a shoulder holster, complete with handgun, under an unzipped windbreaker. I nodded toward it. "Do you think we'll need that?"

He shook his head slightly. "No, but it doesn't hurt to have a little insurance."

Leaving my car where it was, Shana drove the van out of the parking lot. A few minutes later, we parked on the street in front of an abandoned brick building—graffiti-covered, windows broken, the property encircled by a metal fence topped with barbed wire to keep out the homeless and addicts.

Across the street was an empty lot strewn with weeds and debris that included busted televisions, a stained mattress, and the burned-out carcass of a pickup truck. From where we sat, I could see empty, boarded-up storefronts and a few houses, sorely in need of repair.

"Let's go," Shana announced, opening her door, taking with her a clipboard and a blue windbreaker.

Once we were out, she glanced around the neighborhood. Satisfied that we were the only ones on the street, she handed me the clipboard and the jacket. "Leave your coat in the car and wear this."

Slipping out of my denim jacket, I saw that Shana was wearing a windbreaker just like the one she'd just handed me. Over her heart was an official-looking insignia and the words, Municipality of Bridgeport, Public Works.

Putting it on, I asked, "What's this for?"

"Do you think they're going to let you in if you announce that you're a reporter?"

"No." I glanced at the van. "Is John coming?"

She shook her head. "I don't want to spook whoever is inside. Two women working for the city is pretty benign." Shana pulled something out of her pocket that was about the size of a cellphone.

"What's that?" I pointed to the gizmo in her hand.

She smiled. "You'll see."

As we walked past the dark, abandoned factory, I shivered. The sky was silver-gray and the temperature was dropping. After I talked with Mike, I'd checked the weather report. It had predicted an early freeze and the possibility of precipitation, making for icy conditions later in the day.

We walked past empty storefronts that, according to their fading signs, used to be a beauty shop and a liquor store.

The house we were looking for was just ahead of us, a squalid, single-story Cape Cod, set upon a tiny yard that consisted of weeds, old magazines, and loose bricks. The white vinyl siding, gone to gray, was missing in more than a few spots. The windows were all covered from the inside with towels and sheets. A windowless van, similar to the one we'd arrived in, was parked in the driveway.

Wordlessly, we trudged up the steps to the cinderblocks that served as a front porch. Shana knocked hard on the door.

There was no response.

She did it again, using the bottom of her right fist.

Out of the corner of my eye, I saw the sheet hanging in the front window twitch, as if someone was eyeballing us.

Shana knocked one more time, hard and with urgency.

The door swung open and a tall man, about six-two, stood in front of us. "What?"

I recognized his face from the mug shot I'd seen on my computer last night. He looked like he might have just gotten up out of bed, oily hair tricked out in all directions, creases along one side of his jowly face, eyes red. He was wearing a wife-beater tee-shirt, green boxer shorts, and white socks. He reeked of tobacco smoke.

Just like my fucking uncle.

What I couldn't have seen in the mug shot, was how muscular Del Randall was. He had a gut that stretched his tee-shirt and fell over the elastic of his shorts, but his arms and shoulders were huge, thick with muscle.

Shana spoke up in strong, steady voice. "We're with the city. We're checking out a report of a natural gas leak here in the neighborhood."

He stood up straighter, his bushy eyebrows knitted together. "Gas leak? I don't smell nothin'." His voice had the gravelly rasp of a smoker.

She held up the small contraption she'd taken out of her pocket. "You won't. That's what this is for. We've got to come in and check your house."

He thought for a moment, staring at our official looking windbreakers and the clipboard in my hand. "Look, I've got guys who worked construction out on I-95 last night sleeping in the back bedrooms. I can't let you come in and wake them up."

"We'll be quiet."

He held up his hand. "No can do."

Shana reached out and poked him in the chest with her finger. "Look, pal. This isn't up for debate. If we don't find that gas leak, the next time you light up a cigarette you're going to turn this whole fucking house into a fireball. Now move aside."

His eyes got wide and his mouth opened like he was going to argue, but instead, he stepped back and we went past him through the doorway.

We were inside the living room. Off to one side was a brown, stained, cloth couch, the arms ripped and worn beyond repair. A large-screen television hung on the wall at the end of the room. A faux-leather recliner, also torn, tufts of stuffing peeking out, was situated right in front of the TV.

Weight equipment, resting on a rubber mat, dominated the rest of the room—adjustable bench, flat bench, two-tier dumbbell rack, kettle bells, power lifting rods, and plates.

I glanced again at the man called Lucifer, clearly seeing the red and black Satan tattoo on his right forearm. The only light in the room came from the television where NASCAR racers were screaming silently around a track. But it was enough illumination to see how strong the man's arms, shoulders, chest, and legs were. Lucifer would be ripped if it wasn't for the beer gut he'd developed over the years.

Shana made a show of holding the tiny machine in front of her eyes, studying a gauge. She shook her head. "Nothing in this room. Gotta check the rest of the house."

Without asking, she walked into the kitchen.

Keeping one eye on Loose, I followed her. The smell was overpowering. A swirling cocktail of onions, spoiled milk, jalapeños, and mildew punched me hard.

Shana gave me a look while holding her hand over her mouth and nose.

The garbage can was overflowing; dirty dishes filled the sink; pizza cartons and old containers of Chinese food fought for space on the counter.

Loose watched us from the doorway as Shana "tested" the kitchen for the nonexistent gas leak.

Shaking her head, we both went out into the living room. "Okay," Shana said. "Now we check the rest of the house."

The big man stepped between us and the hallway. "I said no. There's guys sleeping in there."

"Move, or I'm callin' a cop." Her voice crisp and sharp, feet apart, fists on hips, it was clear that Shana was well practiced in being obeyed.

For a moment, he appeared to be uncertain.

I saw movement in the darkness behind him. A person, not very tall, a little over five feet with long hair, peeked around a doorway. Eyes glittered in the darkness.

Heart racing, I shouted, "Bobbi?"

Seeing my line of sight, the man turned away from us to look behind him and I pushed past where he stood.

In an eyeblink, he shoved me hard from behind, my head snapped back, hurled through the dark hallway, legs tangled.

Crashing into a wall, shoulder impacting, breaking a fall with hands and elbows.

On the floor, on my side, dazed, smelling mold from the carpet.

Sitting up, stunned, I peered into a bedroom. It was only illuminated by the muted daylight coming through the threadbare towels over the windows.

Four sets of eyes were staring back at me, all girls, sitting on mattresses and mounds of bedding on the floor.

"Bobbi?" I managed to whisper.

One of the girls responded in a tiny voice. "*Que?*"

Remembering Loose, I quickly turned, frightened, and looked back up the hallway. There in the entrance, the big man was on his back on the floor, jerking and twitching in irregular spasms.

Shana stood above him, holding a second box, a taser the size of a pack of cigarettes. This one had two long wires attached to it. The other ends of those wires were barbed hooks embedded in the side of Lucifer's neck.

She was talking into her phone.

Using the wall, I pushed myself up on uncertain legs, my shoulder on fire, throbbing.

Putting her phone in the pocket of her windbreaker, she shouted, "You okay?"

I leaned my back against the wall to steady myself. "Yeah, there're girls here."

Suddenly, John was in the doorway next to Shana. In one swift movement, he knelt, binding Loose's wrists together with plastic zip ties. He did the same with his ankles.

Then he stood up and came quickly to my side. "You okay?"

"Yeah," I repeated, nodding toward the bedroom.

John stood in the doorway of the bedroom. "Do you ladies speak English?"

Four voices said, "Yes," all at the same time.

"Awesome. We're getting out of here. You have thirty seconds to grab your things."

There was an immediate scramble of young bodies. Dressed in a wild mix of pajama bottoms, sweatpants, and tees, the four girls were a blur, picking up clothes, rushing into the bathroom, gathering up cosmetics.

"Bobbi?" I asked again.

John turned toward me and shook his head sadly. "Looks like our intel was bad. They're all Hispanic."

Shit.

Shana came toward me but then disappeared into another bedroom on the opposite side of the hall.

I followed her. Up against the wall was an unmade, queen-sized bed. Off to one side was a chest of drawers. Another television, much smaller than the one in the living room, hung on the wall. This was obviously Lucifer's bedroom.

Shana picked something up from the bureau, a metal tube, maybe two feet in length. "See this?" She snarled, smacking it in her hand.

Rubbing my shoulder, wishing I had an ibuprofen, I answered. "Yeah, what the hell is it?"

"Cattle prod."

"What?"

"Just in case there was a night one of the girls didn't want to go to work."

That son of a bitch.

John announced in a loud voice. "Let's go."

I watched him lead out four young women. They all had long hair that needed brushing and carried plastic bags of what clothing and makeup they could grab. And they were all still dressed in what they had been sleeping in.

They'd never asked a question or wondered where they were going.

Any place is better than this hell.

Chapter Thirty-five

The girls stood together in the living room, glaring at Loose as he lay helpless on the floor. One of them muttered something guttural in Spanish, barely under her breath.

The others chuckled nervously.

Shana whispered in my ear. "She just told the others that all Loose needs is an apple in his mouth and he'd look like a pig ready for the spit."

While we waited for John to bring the van to the house, I studied them. They looked to be between sixteen and nineteen. Even without makeup and with bed-head hair, they were all very pretty.

And very young.

"How long have you girls been in the Unites States?" I asked.

"Two years," one of them said.

"Too long," whispered another.

"Where are you taking them?" I asked, leaning into Shana's ear.

"There's a place in Hartford."

"Friends of Lydia?"

She smiled slightly. "Friends, let's leave it at that. If the girls want to go home, they'll get them there. If the girls want to stay, they'll get them IDs and find them places to live, places where they don't have to sell their bodies."

I glanced back at the pimp called Lucifer, who glowered at us from the floor. "What about him?"

"We'll call the cops once we're on the road. They'll come, find him tied up, find evidence that he was harboring illegals, take him in for questioning, and then let him go."

"Any concern that the Talbonovs are going to be pissed?"

"Technically, the girls belong to Loose. We've put *him* out of business, at least temporarily. What will be of concern for Valentin is that we're mucking around in his backyard."

"It'll make a hell of a story," I whispered.

Shana glanced at the pimp to make sure we were out of hearing range. Then she turned and looked directly into my eyes. "Think hard, Geneva. Are you sure you want your name on this? Up until now, Loose only has physical descriptions of the three of us. Valentin will figure out that John and I were here. He knows us. But he won't know that it's you until you put your byline on it."

Of course I filed the story. I included a grim photo of the squalid room in which the girls were forced to sleep, the cattle prod Loose used to persuade the girls to go to work on cold nights, and one from behind the girls rushing single-file to the unmarked van.

Because we were shorthanded, for the last few months, Laura and I had alternated working as editor on weekends. This was Laura's turn to work Saturday. When she read the piece, she looked up from her cubicle and gave me a thumbs-up.

I involuntarily glanced over at Ben's office. The door was shut, locked.

When this place is sold, who will be sitting in your office, Ben?

The clock on my computer screen told me it was nearly twelve-thirty. I contemplated going home to make a sandwich, but brought up Facebook again on the slim chance that Bobbi had answered my private message to her.

She hadn't.

But Caroline had posted on *her* timeline. Up until then, she had refrained from writing about being in an Angela Owens production alongside Peter Cambridge and Mona Fountain. She'd said that listening to Bobbi bragging about it had pissed off a lot of the kids at school.

But there it was, along with a photo taken with her phone—a selfie of Caroline, Peter, and Mona, all smiling into the lens. Caroline captioned it: *Rehearsing with Peter Cambridge and Mona Fountain. Such nice people. So excited for being given this chance!*

I smiled. I was very proud of her and my heart ached that her father wasn't there to see it all.

My phone pinged.

I picked it up off the desk and was shocked by what I saw on my screen.

Bobbi's phone is on, the tracking app is live.

According to the tiny map, she was at 1320 East Avenue.

I quickly looked it up. That was the address of the Cornerstone Diner.

Grabbing my denim jacket, I rushed the door to the parking lot.

By the time I'd gotten into my car and turned on the engine, the tracking app was gone. Bobbi had removed the battery from her phone again.

Squealing my tires, I zoomed down our alley and into the street. I made the drive in twelve minutes.

The Cornerstone was a gleaming throwback to another era. The inside of building was an homage to the sixties— all chrome, glass, and leather. I pushed open the glass door of the restaurant and stood in front of the cash register, studying the room.

It was lunchtime and the place was packed—executives in shirts and ties, blue-collar workers in jeans and work shirts, retirees dressed much like I was—in comfortable slacks, flannel shirts, and sneakers. The air was heavy with fried foods, sautéed onions, and low murmurs of conversation.

I don't see Bobbi.

"Can I help you?" The question came from a middle-aged man of Middle Eastern descent. He wore a practiced smile and a disingenuous expression of interest. He was holding a laminated menu, anticipating my request for a booth.

"I'm looking for a fifteen-year-old girl who was just here. Did you see her?"

He blinked. "Just now?"

"Yes, no more than a few minutes ago." I pulled a photocopy of her picture out of my bag and held it up for him to see.

He shook his head. "I'm sorry. Nobody here like that. The only person we had in here was a young man back from Afghanistan."

What?

"Are you sure?" I could hear the desperation creeping into my voice.

"I'm certain. The only person who has left here in the last few minutes is the man I told you about. He said he's a veteran, but I think he's homeless. He ordered ahead, online."

"Online. How did he pay you?" I suddenly recalled the piece Darcie had written about the homeless men on a buying spree, using stolen credit information.

"He paid online when he ordered the food."

"What makes you think he's homeless?"

"His clothes look like they could use a good cleaning. And he doesn't own a car. He came by Uber. Had the car wait for him until he got his lunch."

"Maybe his car is in the shop."

The man leaned on the counter and pointed at me. "And I told him that we deliver. Next time he could save the carfare. He told me he didn't know where he'd have it delivered to. Sounds homeless to me."

"What did this guy look like?" I pulled a notebook out of bag.

"Not very tall. Maybe in his twenties. Had on a stocking cap, black waist-length coat, camo pants."

"Any facial hair?"

The man glanced around him to see if anyone was close enough to hear him. "He's disfigured from the war. He said he'd been in a truck that had been attacked. The truck had overturned and burned." The man shuddered and he pointed to his cheek. "His face was all scarred and discolored from the fire. It's very hard to look at him."

Not willing to give up. "This young man, did he make a phone call while he was here?"

He thought a moment and pointed in the direction of a leather couch against a wall. "While he was waiting for his food, he pulled a laptop out of his backpack. He saw something on his screen that agitated him. I saw him typing and then he threw his hands up in the air. He reached into his backpack, pulled out a cellphone, inserted the battery, and made a call."

"What did he do when he was finished?"

"He took the battery back out and put everything into his bag—the phone, the laptop, everything. He got his meatball sub and left."

My pulse quickened.

I thanked the man and went back out to my car, standing by the driver's side door, breathing in the cold air. It was starting to get misty, drops of precipitation too small to see with the naked eye. I could feel it on my face and my bare hands.

I thought it through. The man, a disfigured war veteran, who may have been homeless, became agitated at the same time that Caroline posted online that she was enjoying rehearsal with Peter Cambridge and Mona Fountain.

Over the last few days, there had been a rash of reports about homeless men using stolen credit card information—ever since Bobbi had gone missing.

This particular homeless man was in possession of Bobbi's phone. He was disfigured, difficult to look at.

Caroline had told me that Jake Addison had access to both the Sheffield Playhouse and Hawkes Manor. Jake had keys to both.

There's not a lot of room to hide out at the theater, but plenty of places to hole up in at the mansion where the Drama Club had a supply of stage clothing and makeup.

I took my phone out of my bag, brought up Facebook, and tapped out a private message.

Bobbi, I know where you are. Unlock the front door for me, sweetie. I'm on my way.

Chapter Thirty-six

By the time I pulled out of the diner's parking lot and onto the street, the mist had become sleet pellets bouncing off my windshield and hood like tiny meteorites. The temperature on my dash told me that it was now only thirty degrees. I knew that before long, the roads were going to become a dicey mess.

Glancing up at my rearview mirror, I half expected to see Bogdan Tolbonov's truck behind me. The only traffic behind me was a Volvo SUV, a Lexus sedan, and a Range Rover.

I thought about Betsy Caviness for a moment. About how the Tolbonovs had put enough pressure on her that she was willing to spend the rest of her life in prison. About how she handed over the notebook to someone she trusted enough to keep it safe—unless something happened to her.

Mutual destructibility. She'd called it a Mexican standoff.

No, Bogdan Tolbonov was no longer interested in me.

The roads still hadn't iced over by the time I drove through the wrought-iron gates of Vet's Park. The stone mansion stood silently ahead of me as I came up the driveway, turning right to park in the lot. Mine was the only vehicle there.

Mike had been true to his word. He'd pulled his men out because of the bad weather. Yellow tape still hung in front of the trail leading into the woods where, some two hundred feet away, Jake Addison's body had been found.

I got out and studied the building. Two stories, built of

stone, imposing stained-glass windows; it was more haunted house than Community Center. The Drama Club had chosen well for its Death Mansion.

I rushed through the stinging pellets of sleet, up the stone steps until I got to the portico. Up under the roof, on either side of the porch entrance, were two statues—six-foot gargoyles. Even though I knew they were plastic props, weighed down by cinderblocks hidden inside their bases, they made for a spooky entrance.

I stepped up to the arched, wooden double doorway and reached for the handle.

Did she get my message?

I turned the knob.

If she didn't, or I'm wrong, it's back to square one.

Unlocked.

I pulled the door open and stepped in. I'd been to Hawkes Manor many times, mostly for fundraisers and cocktail parties, so I knew that I should have been stepping into a big open room. On the opposite side of the expansive space would be a large set of steps, roped off, off-limits to visitors, that led up to the second floor.

Instead, I was looking at a short, dark hallway, barely three feet in width, with a low ceiling, constructed from what looked like black burlap. My claustrophobia kicked in.

The door closed behind me and I was wrapped in the dim red illumination that emanated from the "Exit" sign mounted over the entrance behind me.

I called out. "Bobbi."

Silence.

I stepped forward, eyes straining against the darkness, and called out again. "Bobbi."

"Genie."

I couldn't tell where the voice had come from, but my heart was beating wildly. Bobbi was alive.

"Bobbi?"

"Lock the door." Her voice came from somewhere ahead of me, somewhere where it was still pitch-black.

I reached behind me and twisted the deadbolt, hearing it click.

"Where are you, sweetie?"

"Keep coming."

The further down the hallway, the darker it got. I reached out in front of me, hands touching air. "Where are you?"

"Right here."

A flashlight came to life under her chin.

I jerked backward, heart misfiring, a tiny yelp escaped my lips.

She was still wearing the makeup she'd had on when she'd gone to the Cornerstone Diner, something out of a horror movie. A face filled with scars, burnt, discolored flesh, lips missing.

"Oh, my dear God." I was still trying to get my heart rate somewhere near normal.

"Sorry, Genie." She smiled, but because of the prosthetics on her face, it turned into more of a snarl. "You didn't give me enough time to get this crap off my face. C'mon."

She turned and started walking. Bobbi was wearing a black coat, camo pants, work boots and her hair was all tucked up under a black knit cap. She carried a plastic Cornerstone Diner bag that held her meatball sub.

"Wait a minute," I shouted.

Bobbi stopped and looked at me.

I didn't know whether to be pissed off at her or relieved that she was alive. So, I rushed up to her, reached out, and hugged her.

She hugged me back. We held each other like that for a long time.

"Everyone's been so worried," I told her.

"I know, I'm sorry."

In the glow of the flashlight, I could see she was crying, tears trailing down the thick layer of makeup.

"I've got to get this off," she whispered, pointing to her face.

I followed her through the Death Mansion maze, past dungeons, graveyards, rat-filled prison cells, electric chairs. "How long you been living here, Bobbi?" I asked, glancing around me.

"Since Wednesday. How did you know I was here?"

"I put it together when the guy at the diner described your face. Burned beyond recognition. Difficult to look at. You were always good with stage makeup. I knew that the Drama Club kept their stash here for Death Mansion and I knew that Mr. Addison had a key. I assume that's where you got it."

She stopped and looked back at me. "I hope nobody else figures it out."

We got to where the maze would turn on itself and head back to the exit, but she pointed the flashlight toward a flap of burlap and disappeared behind it.

I followed.

We found ourselves outside the faux walls, in the Community Center, right in front of the ladies' room. She went in, the light came on, and I followed her.

This must have been the room where she'd applied the prosthetics. On the floor in front of a sink with a mirror, was a small leather suitcase filled with bottles, jars, brushes, sponges, pads, and color palettes.

Standing in front of the sink, gazing into the mirror, she started stripping off the fake scars, dropping them into the trash can.

I unzipped my jacket. "Who are you hiding from, honey?"

She knelt down and picked up a container of coconut oil from the suitcase, placed it in the sink and turned on the hot water. A solid in room temperature, she had to melt it to use it.

Bobbi glanced at me and answered. "Peter and Angela and David."

A sudden spark of terror snapped in my chest.

That's who Caroline is with.

"Why?"

She bit at her lower lip, concentrating on melting the coconut oil while the hot water ran over the glass container. "On Saturday night…"

Her voice trailed away.

"You can tell me, Bobbi. What happened Saturday night?"

She took a deep breath. "We were in the Playhouse, just the two of us. He made me do it."

"What? Who?"

"Have sex, there on the stage. He made a video." Bobbi spat out her words. She stopped talking and opened the jar, taking some white gunk out and rubbing it into her face.

"Who?"

"Fucking Peter Cambridge," she shouted, starting to sob.

"The video the cops found in Jake's apartment? That was you and Peter Cambridge?"

She turned her face toward me, her eyes wide with horror. "The cops have a sex tape of me? Have you seen it? Couldn't you tell that it was Peter?"

I held up my hand. "The cops aren't showing it to anyone, even me. They told me that the man in the video had been digitally obscured. No one knows that's Peter Cambridge. Tell me what happened."

Her mood changed to anger. She rubbed the oil into her face with renewed vigor. "All the while we rehearsed, he was oh-so-charming. Telling me how special I am, how talented I am. But we were always with other people, until Saturday night."

She took a washcloth and got it wet, working away some of the makeup and oil. "Angela was working from their house in Westport, so it was just Mona and Peter and me. Around eight o'clock, Mona said she had a migraine and left the Playhouse. Then it was just me and Peter."

She rinsed out the washcloth, her face still smeared with

oil and makeup. "Peter got up close to me and told me that he wanted to make me a woman, that he was attracted to me, that his wife wasn't having sex with him anymore."

"What did you do?"

She reached down and picked up a tube of acne cream to break up the oil on her face. "He said he wanted to make love to me. I told him no."

She stopped and glared at me defiantly. She repeated her words with emphasis. "I told him no."

Bobbi went back to rubbing the cream into her face. "He told me that if I wanted to stay with the production, I was going to have to make him happy. That's part of the deal. All the women he worked with had to have sex with him. He said I'd get fired if I didn't."

"I'm so sorry, Bobbi."

Her voice cracked. "And then he set up a video camera."

I held a hand up to my mouth. This was the same Peter Cambridge I'd been with?

This was too much like my uncle coming into my bedroom when I was Bobbi's age.

"When he was done with me, we were putting our clothes back on and I started to cry. He asked me what was wrong. He asked me if I didn't enjoy it."

She continued to rub cream on her face but glanced at me in the mirror. "When I first started rehearsing, I thought about being with Peter. Fantasized about it a little. But when it actually happened? It was disgusting. He was like some kind of animal. And he said that he'd make sure we'd have plenty of opportunities to have sex…any time he wanted. The way he said it scared me, Genie. Really scared me."

"What did you say?"

"I told him that I didn't think I could stay in the production." She turned and looked at me, her eyes wide. "He said that I *would* stay with the production and that if I told anyone, David would do to me what they did to Tracey."

I blinked. "The understudy?"

She nodded. "Peter said that she'd threatened to tell the newspapers that she was being forced to have sex to stay with the play." Her voice got very low. "Peter said that David gave her a drug overdose and killed her."

Oh, my dear God, Caroline is with those people.

"Did you tell anyone?" I could hear the nerves fraying my voice.

"I told my grandmother when I got home that night. Do you know what she said to me?"

"What?"

"To grow up." Her voice was bitter. "That's how girls like me get ahead in show business." Bobbi shook her head as she remembered, pounding her fists against her temples. "I told her that I didn't want to be in the production. I told her that I felt dirty."

She stopped for a moment, dropped her hands, and jutted out her jaw in defiance. "She told me that I would continue working in the production. I had no choice in the matter. She made me go to rehearsal on Sunday. While I was at the Playhouse, I had to run to the bathroom to throw up twice. It was awful, working around him. Acting like nothing had happened."

"What did you do then?"

She ran some more water and started to soap up her face. "I called Jake and told him. Then he called my grandmother. She still wouldn't take me out of the production."

"So, he kidnapped you."

"He was protecting me. On Monday morning, Jake drove me to my dad's studio. I stayed there in the backroom with him on Monday night. But then something spooked Dad. He tried to call Jake, and when he didn't answer, he got so rattled he took me to the Inlet Motel. Told me not to open the door for anyone."

I recalled that Mike had told me that the room had been

paid for with stolen credit card information. "How have you been paying for things, Bobbi?" I motioned to the plastic bag holding the sandwich, sitting on top of the paper towel dispenser.

She pulled a sheet of paper, folded multiple times into a tiny package, out of her jacket pocket. "Almost all of Dad's customers pay with credit cards. He kept the numbers just in case he got really desperate and needed to use them. Dad gave them to me."

"What happened at the motel?"

She ran the water into the sink again. "Angela and David showed up in the middle of the night with a sledgehammer. The same night they killed my dad." She leaned over and cupping her hands under the faucet, brought up enough water to moisten her face.

Fear gripped me again, my stomach roiled.

Caroline is with them.

"Angela and David killed your father?" I glanced at the doorway. I had the nearly uncontrollable urge to race out and drive to the theater.

As long as Mona is there, they wouldn't dare hurt Caroline. Unless Mona is in on this as well?

She shrugged. "All I know is they showed up, trying to break into my room on the same night Dad was murdered."

"But you got away."

She smiled slightly. "I snuck out the bathroom window. Good thing I'm not very big 'cause that damned window is freaking tiny. I snuck a peek around the corner once I was outside. They were both dressed in hoodies, and David was kicking the crap out of some poor man in the parking lot. I didn't stick around. I came here."

"Where's your stuff?"

She dried her face and took off the knit cap, shaking out her hair. Then she stood up straight and looked at me. She was pretty Bobbi Jarvis again. "Upstairs. There're a dozen rooms nobody's using. I have a blowup mattress, some camping stuff, and my laptop. That's all I need."

"How do you buy things?"

"I order ahead of time on my laptop. Use the credit card information Dad gave me. Take an Uber car if I have to go anywhere. I don't use the same credit card info more than once."

"You don't use your phone at all."

She frowned. "It has a tracking app on it."

"Yeah, I know." Holding up my own phone. "Your grandmother gave me access to it."

"Yeah? Don't feel too special. She also gave Angela access to it."

"So, you kept it powered down. Why did you use it at the diner?"

She stepped closer to me. Her voice was low. "Caroline got my part?"

I hesitated for a moment. "Yeah."

"While I waited for my sandwich, I had my laptop out. I saw Caroline post online that she was rehearsing at the theater for *Darkness Lane*. I tried to message her on my computer, but I didn't get any answer. I needed to warn her about being alone with Peter. I loaded the battery back into my phone and called her. She didn't answer so I left a message."

Then we both stared at each other. We'd both heard it.

Glass breaking.

There was terror in her voice. "They're here. We have to hide!"

Chapter Thirty-seven

"Who's here?" My voice was a nervous whisper.

She rushed to the small bathroom window. "Angela and David. They're here to kill me."

"Are you sure it's them?"

I came up behind her. We were looking out over the parking lot, which gleamed with a thin layer of ice. My car was there, but it wasn't alone. A dark-green Range Rover was parked next to my Sebring. The same Range Rover that David LaSalle drove.

Angela must have seen Bobbi's tracking app and gone to the diner just as I had.

And then they followed me here.

Bobbi answered. "Yeah, I'm sure. It sounds like they broke into the French doors in the back of the building."

My first instinct was to slide out the bathroom window and run. I tried lifting the window. It didn't budge.

Goddamned thing must be painted shut.

We killed the lights. I slid out of the ladies' room first and stood in the space between the real wall and faux wall of the spook house.

Bobbi stood next to me, fear plainly etched on her young face.

"Do you have any kind of weapon?" I whispered.

Her eyes were wide and her face was pale. "I have pepper spray and a baseball bat upstairs where I've been sleeping."

Jake's pepper spray. And a baseball bat. It wasn't much.

"Go hide."

"I can call 911."

"I'll call 911. Keep your phone turned off."

"Be careful," she whispered. Then she crept into the shadows and disappeared.

I stepped back into the ladies' room, closed the door, leaving the lights off, and punched in Mike's phone number.

He answered. "Genie, I'm a little busy here. What's up?"

"I've found Bobbi Jarvis," My voice was slightly higher than a whisper. "We're in Hawke's Manor. I think the people who killed her father and Jake Addison just broke into the building."

"What?" It was more of a shout than question.

"Angela Owens, Peter Cambridge's wife, and her brother, David LaSalle, they killed Adam Jarvis and Jake Addison." I could hear myself getting more hysterical.

"Are you in danger?"

"Yes, we are. They want to kill us too."

"Hide, Genie. The roads are a mess and power's out on the south side. All my guys are out doing accident reports or directing traffic. I'll find someone to get to you. Sit tight, I'm on my way but it's going to take a few minutes."

"Okay, stay safe."

"Hide."

I figured, sooner or later, Angela and David would find the ladies' room. Mike had given me good advice. Find a place to hide and then hunker down until the cavalry came.

"Geneva Chase, where are you? It's me, Angela Owens."

I held my breath.

How far away was she?

I can't tell.

I opened the bathroom door and stepped into the space between the wall and the burlap barrier. I pulled a corner of the fabric aside and peeked inside the Death Mansion hospital room set. My eyes had adjusted to the darkness and I could see an operating table, complete with leather straps meant to incapacitate a living victim, a table and tray holding brightly polished cutting tools—scalpels, bone saw, butcher knife, meat cleaver. Blood droplets were pre-splattered on the walls.

Weapons? Are any of those things real?

When this room was manned by the Drama Club members, a screaming, believable volunteer would be strapped to the table and an insane surgeon would go through the motions of evisceration.

I disliked Death Mansion and I hated this particular room.

Stepping inside, closing the burlap flap, I wanted to see if any of the cutting tools on that tray were real.

I need a weapon.

His voice was right beside me. "Hello, Geneva."

My blood turned to ice water as I turned and was blinded by the piercing shaft of light from David LaSalle's phone.

"Angie," he shouted. "She's over here."

"Where?"

"The operating room. Keep coming."

He'd been waiting for me, just inside the burlap doorway, like a predatory cat.

The beam of her handheld flashlight preceded her. It scoured the floor, moving assuredly forward, until she stepped into the room. The light moved from the floor to my face.

I instinctively held my hand up to shield my eyes.

"Geneva," she said. "I'm afraid we don't have much time. Where's Bobbi?"

"Bobbi?" I feigned ignorance.

"We both saw her tracking app pop up when she switched on her phone at the diner. And we both got there too late." Angela still had the light shining in my eyes.

I pointed to the flashlight. "Do you mind?"

She dropped the beam to my chest instead. "How did you figure out where she was?"

"I didn't." I lied. "She's not here. I thought she was, but she's not."

David suddenly grabbed my wrist and twisted my arm around behind my back with one hand and, using his other hand, gripped the back of my neck.

My shoulder exploded in pain. I heard myself cry out.

Same shoulder that hit the wall at the pimp's house.

My vision blurred, hot tears streamed down my cheeks.

"Where's Bobbi?" David growled.

"I don't know where she is." I gritted my teeth and directed my attention to Angela. "Why did you kill Jake Addison? He was trying to protect Bobbi from your husband."

Angela grinned and her eyelids tightened. "If he'd done that, we wouldn't be here. Jake took Bobbi and dropped her off at her father's studio. Then he had the balls to come to our house and ask for hush money. That little son of a bitch tried to blackmail us."

The fire in my shoulder flared when David tightened his grip.

I cried out again. Closing my eyes against the tears, I groaned. "So, you shot him in the back of the head."

Keep them talking. Let Bobbi find a place to hide. Need time for Mike to get here.

Angela answered. "One problem solved. We digitally altered the video of Peter and Bobbi and planted it at Jake's apartment. We took his computer and left a few clues to make the police think that Jake and Bobbi had run off together. Then we drove his car to the train station and bought two tickets to New York. All we needed to do was find Bobbi before the cops did. Tie up a loose end. Everyone would think they disappeared down a rabbit hole."

"What about Bobbi's father? What did he do to you?" My breathing was ragged. Tendons and muscle tissue on fire.

His grip tightened again.

I moaned.

How much more before I pass out?

"He was the one Jake was trying to get the money for. Adam Jarvis was in debt up to his ass with bookies. Jake said they were going to start breaking his bones if he didn't get some cash for his boyfriend." Angela's voice was snide. "He got his bones broken, but by David."

He whispered into my ear. "Before I shot him, Jake told me he'd taken Bobbi to her dad's place. But by the time we got there, she was gone. When we asked where, the father wouldn't tell us."

Angela interjected. "Not at first."

Her phone pinged. She took it out of her coat pocket and glanced at the screen. "You have another reason to act quickly, Geneva."

"What?" Fear mingled with burning agony.

"Mona Fountain just left. Her driver got antsy because of the ice storm. She texted me to let me know. That just leaves Peter and your daughter…alone."

"What do you mean?"

Dear God, don't let Peter hurt Caroline.

Angela's grin turned into an evil smirk. "Peter has a problem."

David chuckled. "He can't keep it in his pants."

Angela gave her brother a sharp look. "Peter is a sociopathic narcissist. He thinks he can take or do anything he wants, simply because he's Peter Cambridge. Like you, Geneva."

"What about me?"

"The night you slept with my husband." She put her phone back in her coat pocket. She pulled out a handgun, pointing directly at my face. "He never had any doubt he'd fuck you."

My stomach dropped.

Her voice was guttural. "Did you know he videotaped the whole thing?"

That's why that motherfucker left the lights on!

David was in my ear again. "You have a beautiful body, Geneva."

He ratcheted up the pressure on my shoulder and arm.

I clenched my teeth to keep from howling.

"I'm his security guy. I have access to all his computer passwords. He has a hell of a video collection. Peter's kept a record of all the women he's slept with. I especially enjoyed watching yours."

Angela explained. "It took me a few years to realize what a monster I'd married. The lawsuits from women he'd forced to sleep with him kept coming. That's what bankrupted us. This play, *Darkness Lane*, is our last chance." She took a step closer and pointed the flashlight back into my eyes. "Peter should never be left alone with someone like your daughter."

But he's alone with Caroline now. And these two killed Jake and Adam. They're all monsters.

David purred. "Tell us where Bobbi is and we'll go protect Caroline."

"We just want to talk with her. That's all." Angela kept the gun leveled at my forehead.

How dumb do they think I am?

Suddenly, David took my arm and twirled me around so that I was facing him. He let go of me.

Run?

I stepped back, staring into his glittering, blue eyes.

How far would I get?

His nostrils flared when he said, "Give me your hand."

No.

I involuntarily let both hands drift behind my back.

"I said hold out your hand."

I glanced back at Angela.

No help there.

She put the gun against the side of my head. "Hold out your hand."

I was surprised at how badly my hands were shaking.

He grabbed me by the wrist with one hand and took hold of my index finger with the other. "This is a game we played with Bobbi's dad. I started with his fingers, breaking them one by one. Then his arms, one after another."

"He talked," Angela whispered. "They always talk, sooner or later. Why put yourself through this?"

Good God, he's going to break my fingers.

David's voice was low. "He told us where Bobbi was after I broke his left arm. But I was having such a good time, that I went on breaking his bones. He was crying like a baby before I crushed his skull with the tire iron."

I saw the movement in the darkness, just a dull reflection from the flashlight Angela held. Behind David.

Then I heard it. A thud.

David's head rocked forward, his eyes rolled into their sockets and he twisted in place, dropping in a heap to the floor.

Behind him stood Bobbi Jarvis, fierce, eyes blazing, her bat cocked over her shoulder, ready to use again. She spat her words, "Fuck you, David, fuck you." She reared back and kicked him.

Angela called to her brother, collapsed, not moving. The flashlight was on him, the muzzle of the gun in her hand now aimed at the floor.

I leaped on her, pushing hard, legs tangling. The flashlight flew out of her hand.

We fell together. The air whooshed out of my lungs.

My hand scrabbled, grabbing, clawing. Finding her gun hand, I locked on tight, keeping it pointed away from us.

Our free hands punched, slapped, and scratched at each other, fingers searching for eyes.

I felt her gun hand straining for position against my own. Her dominant right worked against my weaker left. Struggling, the two of us twisting on the floor, she was muscling the weapon, aiming it for my midsection.

I didn't have enough strength to stop her.

Bobbi was suddenly there.

Her hand was between our two faces. She unloaded the pepper spray into Angela's face.

The woman stopped struggling. She screamed, hand blocking her eyes.

My own eyes filled with tears from the fumes.

Bobbi was standing now, her foot on Angela's gun hand.

I reached over, snapped the pistol away from her.

"Freeze." The man's voice came from behind me.

I recognized Mike's authoritative voice, loving him right at that moment. "Give me the gun, Genie. Carefully." In one hand he held a flashlight, the other held out to take the weapon.

I gave it to him. As I did, another officer handcuffed Angela's hands behind her back. Tears streamed down her cheeks, her face was bright red.

She sobbed. "No…no."

Mike moved quickly to where David was lying. Not taking any chances, Mike took the man's wrists, pulled them one at a time behind his back and cuffed him.

David moved slightly, a soft moan escaped his lips.

Caroline.

Glancing at Mike and moving at the same time. "The Playhouse…Caroline's alone with Peter Cambridge. He's the one in the sex tape."

I grabbed Angela's flashlight off the floor and took off at a dead run. I hit the front door of the mansion, shoving it hard, flying down the steps. I slipped and slid across the parking lot toward my car.

I eyed the trail, marked by the police tape.

Faster to go through the woods.

I trotted across the parking lot. My legs flew out from under me. My ass bounced on the hard surface and I sat there stunned. Tiny, hard pellets of sleet stung as they struck my face and hands.

Caroline.

I stood and, more carefully, shuffled toward the trail. Once I reached the path, I sprinted flat out.

Over dead leaves, fallen branches, tree roots, I ran.

All around me, I heard what sounded like gunshots. They were tree limbs, still heavy with October leaves, made heavier still with ice. They were snapping, falling dangerously to the ground.

Something else to watch out for.

I ran.

Past the trapezoid of yellow tape where Jake's body had been buried.

Air, in and out, like fire in my lungs.

Sleet, biting into my face, stinging my eyes.

Keep running.

Something behind me snapped like a cannon shot and fell thrashing to the ground. I glanced back at a tree limb, the size of a railroad tie under the weight of foliage frozen in a coating of ice.

Was someone behind me?

No time to look.

Legs pumping.

I reached the end of the trail, coming out into the parking lot of the Playhouse.

Careful on the slippery asphalt.

Up the stairs, through the front doors, across the darkened lobby.

I burst through the door to the theater.

On the stage, immersed in a spotlight, was Peter Cambridge, adjusting a camera on a tripod.

On the bed my Caroline sat, her shirt and bra off, her arms crossed protectively across her chest.

She was sobbing.

"You miserable rat bastard, get away from my daughter!"

I still had enough fuel in the tank to flat-out run down the aisle, taking the steps two at a time, and sprint across the stage to throw myself at the actor.

Peter and I slammed in a heap to the floor.

I straddled his chest and beat my fists into his face.

I felt Mike's hands pulling at my shoulders from behind me.

He said, "We got this, Genie."

I rolled off Peter and hunched on the floor while Mike twisted on the handcuffs. I struggled for breath, the nonstop marathon across Vet's Park taking its toll.

Mike was doing the same thing, gasping for air.

He must have been right behind me the whole way.

Out of the corner of my eye, I saw Caroline get up off the bed and lean down to snatch up her shirt, leaving the bra on the stage floor. She slid into it and sat back down again, still crying.

I got to my feet, the muscles in my calves and thighs shrieking in pain. My shoulder, banged where I'd been thrown into the wall by the pimp, shouted from the exertion of wrestling with Angela. I staggered to the bed and sat down next to Caroline.

"Did he hurt you?"

She sobbed. "He told me if I wanted to be in the production, I have to have sex with him."

I put my arm around her. "I know, sweetie. He did the same thing to Bobbi."

Caroline turned her face and stared at me. "Bobbi's alive. She left me a message on my phone, warning me about Peter."

I held her close. "I know, baby."

Mike stood the actor up on his feet. I'd managed to bloody his nose and smack one eye shut with swelling.

Seeing him for what he really was made me ashamed. I'd acted like a star-struck teenager. Not only had he bedded me, but he'd filmed it.

Then tried to do the same thing with Caroline.

I wanted to go over and kick the shit out of him again.

Caroline dropped her head on my shoulder. "Can we go home now?"

Chapter Thirty-eight

The headline on the six o'clock news that night was the ice storm. It hit much harder and faster than the meteorologists had predicted. Roads were clogged with dozens of accidents and spin-outs. Falling trees had cut roofs and houses in half. Huge branches, heavy with wet leaves and ice, brought down power lines and transformers, knocking out power for more than five thousand homes.

Indeed, the drive home had been treacherous and I had white knuckles the entire way. Twice, we had to find an alternate route to drive around live wires in the roadway.

Before parting company, Mike told me that he'd embargo the news about the arrests of Peter Cambridge, Angela Owens, and her brother, David LaSalle, until I wrote the story and posted it online. But he couldn't sit on it for long.

I'm going to have to find a way to win that man back again.

I knew it would be a big story, maybe the biggest in my career.

Enough to get me hired on another newspaper?

Was I ready for that? After the Connor's Landing story broke, I'd had a chance to move but decided to stay in Sheffield to raise Caroline.

Now Ben was selling us out. Things were going to be changing at the *Sheffield Post*. This might be my golden opportunity to choose my own fate.

Caroline and I picked up Mexican and took it home for dinner. But we sat in silence, the food in the middle of the table, our plates empty, the food untouched in its cartons. Neither of us felt hungry.

Looking down at my hands, I was surprised to see that they were still shaking.

God, I want a drink.

Caroline said something in a tiny voice that broke my heart. "I'm never going to get a chance like that again, am I?"

I frowned. "They were scary people, sweetie. It was never real to begin with."

She picked up Tucker and let him sit on her lap. "Poor Bobbi."

"I know."

"She thought it was her big chance, too."

"I know."

"She lost her dad, too." She scratched the dog behind the ears.

"Yes, she did."

"Peter told me he'd videotaped Bobbi and him together."

Where are you going, sweetie?

She looked up at me. "Have you seen it?"

I slowly shook my head. "The cops have a copy. They're not sharing it with anyone."

"If it ever got online…" Her voice trailed off.

I knew what she was talking about. Bobbi's life would be forever altered.

That night, Caroline turned in early. I brought my laptop down to the kitchen and wrote the story about finding Bobbi Jarvis and the arrest of two of the most famous people in the world.

Then I called Ben at home.

"Genie?" He answered. "We were just sitting down to dinner."

"Let it get cold. I just sent you your lead story for Sunday."

"Hang on, let me take a look."

I waited, checking my e-mail.

When he finally came back on the line, he said, "Holy shit, Genie."

"I know, right?"

"Are you okay? It sounds like you could have been killed."

"I'm fine. Is that tomorrow's headline?"

"Are you kidding? Biggest story we've ever broken."

I rapped my knuckles against the tabletop. "Still want to sell the paper?"

He was quiet for a heartbeat. Then he answered. "My back's against the wall, Genie. I don't have a choice."

"Well, you're going out with a bang."

Officially, Sunday was my day off.

I got up anyway, had breakfast with Caroline, and headed to work. I was glad to see that the road crews had gotten out with sand trucks. By the time I drove into the office, the thermometer had risen to nearly forty degrees.

I stopped along the way and bought a latte at Starbucks. I'd killed the rest of my vodka last night before passing out in bed and, that morning, I was struggling with a nasty hangover and a blanket of guilt.

When was I going to stop doing this?

Caffeine was just what the doctor ordered.

Getting back into my car, my phone twittered. It was Mike Dillon.

"Mike?"

"Hey, Genie. I've got the paper in front of me. Hell of a story. I've been fielding calls from every major news outlet in the country."

"Yeah," I bragged. "We scooped 'em."

"Something you should know, though."

"What?" I put my latte into the cup holder and turned on the engine.

"We got hacked, sometime last night."

"Oh?"

"I've got our tech guys on it. It looks like someone was nosing around the Bobbi Jarvis files."

I pulled out into traffic. "Do you think one it's one of the news outlets?"

"We don't know. But my guys tell me that whoever got in, had access to everything, including Peter's library of sex videos."

"Like the one with Bobbi in it?"

"Yeah."

And mine?

"Shit." The last thing in the world Bobbi needed was that going viral.

Fear suddenly clutched my chest.

Has Mike seen the one with Peter and me?

"Okay, fingers crossed it's nothing."

Sunday mornings at the office are lonely affairs. Most everyone was off, so the company parking lot was empty and the newsroom was dark when I got there. I left the lights off and, when I got to my cubicle, I turned on my brass desk light.

Using my cellphone, I called Theresa Pittman. I knew that every news outlet in the country would be trying to reach her. I hoped that she'd recognize my number.

"Geneva Chase?"

"Theresa, I wanted to see how Bobbi was doing?"

"She's in her room."

"I see. Is Nina still there?"

"Yes."

I decided to go for broke. "Bobbi told me something troubling at the Community Center yesterday. Did you know that Peter Cambridge raped your granddaughter?"

There was an icy silence.

"Did Bobbi tell you what Peter Cambridge did to her? That he videotaped her sexual assault?"

Her answer was hissed. "It was consensual."

"She's underage, Theresa. In the eyes of the law, Peter Cambridge raped her."

"This conversation is over."

The line went dead.

I spent the next half hour researching Morgan Stiles, the producer, looking for a way to reach him. I finally found a phone number and punched it in.

"Yes?" A man's voice.

"I'm looking for Mr. Stiles?"

"Who's this?"

"It's Geneva Chase, we've met." I took a sip of my latte.

"I remember. You're Caroline's mom."

"Yes, sir. I'm also a reporter."

"I remember," he repeated.

"What are your plans for the production?"

"*Darkness Lane?* It's dead."

The connection went cold. He'd ended the conversation.

I glanced at my watch. It was only eleven in the morning.

There really wasn't any reason for me to be in the office, other than I felt comfortable there. It was where I was in control

But the whole day was ahead of me.

I really should be at home with Caroline.

I turned off the light, put on my jacket, and walked to the back exit, heading for the parking lot.

What I saw almost stopped my heart.

Bogdan Tolbonov was standing next to the black pickup, holding an iPad. "Miss Chase." His voice was incredibly deep, like listening to a man at the bottom of a well. His apish face split into an ugly grin.

"What?" I stood on the concrete deck.

He waved at me with hands so big they could have been the paws of a bear. He wanted me to come closer.

I took a deep breath and edged down the steps until I got to the bottom. Muscles clenched, I stayed there, still twenty feet from the big man. "What?"

He turned the iPad so that I could see the screen. "Do you know what this is?"

It was a video, full screen, of Bobbi Jarvis and Peter Cambridge. It was the unadulterated video that the actor had in his collection. Not the one that had been hidden at Jake's apartment.

It was clearly Peter Cambridge and Bobbi Jarvis.

The sound was turned high. I easily heard the actor grunting.

"Yes, I know what that is."

He nodded. "Good." Bogdan turned the iPad around so that it was facing him again and he made a production of pushing one of the keys on the screen. "This is our only warning, Miss Chase. Stay out of our business."

"What did you do?"

Without another word, he got into his truck. The engine awoke with a throaty growl, and he slowly pulled out of the parking lot.

What was that about?

When I got home, Caroline was nearly hysterical. "It's awful, Genie. Awful."

"What?"

"Somebody posted Bobbi's sex video online. The kids are already slut shaming her. Not just from school, from all over the world."

Chapter Thirty-nine

Bobbi Jarvis went to live with her mother in New York City and changed her name to Taylor Pittman. She altered her hairstyle, the color of her contacts, affected a New York accent, became a new girl.

Caroline stays in touch with Bobbi and tells me she's doing the best she can to be anonymous. According to Caroline, Bobbi cut off all communication with her grandmother.

For good reason.

As for Angela Owens, Peter Cambridge, and David LaSalle, bail was denied and they were incarcerated at the Garner State Correctional Facility in Newtown, awaiting trial. Angela on two counts of murder, David for three, and Peter on a growing list of charges including endangering the welfare of a child, rape, producing child pornography, and being an accessory to murder, both before and after the fact.

According to my sources, Angela ratted her own brother out, looking for a plea deal. She told authorities that not only did they kill Adam Jarvis and Jake Addison, David LaSalle administered the lethal dose of Fentanyl to Tracey Fine, *Darkness Lane's* understudy.

It turns out there's a video of Peter Cambridge having sex with her as well.

Betsy Caviness, who torched her abusive husband, pled guilty to voluntary manslaughter. She's also in Garner awaiting sentencing. She could get as many as ten years in prison, but most likely would be sentenced to less than four. It was the best deal she could have hoped for.

Caroline and I declared an uneasy truce while I work on myself.

As long as she doesn't come home from school to find me passed out on the kitchen floor, she's cutting me some slack.

And for my part, I'm thinking about going back to AA.

No, I haven't done it yet. But I'm thinking about it.

As far as the Tolbonov brothers go, Mike Dillon gave me another stern warning to keep my distance. He knows how pissed off I am about what they did with Bobbi's video.

They hacked into the SPD computer network, took the video, then posted it online, not because they had a vendetta against Bobbi Jarvis. They never met Bobbi Jarvis.

They did it because Bobbi was someone I cared about, and those bastards wanted to hurt me for what Shana, John, and I did in Bridgeport. We freed four girls from a life of sexual slavery. We intruded on their business.

They wanted to hurt *me*.

For Valentin Tolbonov, the worst thing he could do was to damage someone I love.

Caroline.

Mike's advice was to leave it alone. Let the police and federal investigators do their job.

Something else about Mike? He never brought up the video that Peter Cambridge had taken of him and me in the hotel that night.

Mike's too much of a gentleman.

I did my best to put the Tolbonov brothers out of my mind, until I got a package in the mail about two days after the arrests at Vet's Park. It came in a plain, brown wrapper, hand-addressed to me. I opened it and found a handwritten letter. It read:

Geneva Chase—you can never let anyone know that you have this. You'll know what to do with it.

It wasn't signed.

It didn't have to be. I knew who it was from.

It was Jim Caviness' notebook.

To see more Poisoned Pen Press titles:

Visit our website:
poisonedpenpress.com
Request a digital catalog:
info@poisonedpenpress.com